Regatta

Fiction by Douglass Wallop

Regatta
Mixed Singles
Howard's Bag
Stone
The Good Life
The Mermaid in the Swimming Pool
So This Is What Happened to Charlie Moe
Ocean Front
What Has Four Wheels and Flies?
The Sunken Garden
The Year the Yankees Lost the Pennant
Night Light

Nonfiction

Baseball: An Informal History

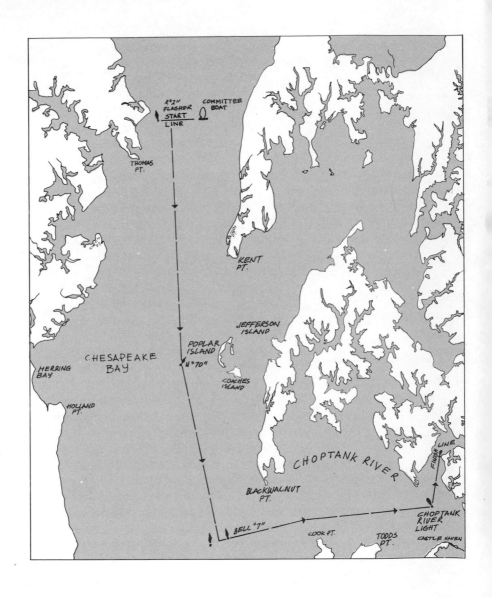

Regatta

Douglass Wallop

W · W · NORTON & COMPANY

NEW YORK · LONDON

First Edition

Library of Congress Cataloging in Publication Data
Wallop, Douglass, 1920–
Regatta.
I. Title
PZ4.W215Re   1981   [PS3573.A44]   813'.54   80–15077

ISBN 0-393-01364-2

W · W · Norton & Company, Inc. 500 Fifth Avenue, New York, N.Y. 10110
W · W · Norton & Company Ltd. 25 New Street Square, London EC4A3NT

1 2 3 4 5 6 7 8 9 0

Part I

One

VENETIAN IN ORIGIN, regattas go back to the days of the Doges, when gondola races were held on the Grand Canal. Then as now, regattas were social and sporting events. As they have evolved on many U.S. waterways they are social and sporting events of a special sort. Intoxicants are consumed. People raft up and boat hop. They get drunk and fall overboard. Vendettas are waged. Feats of copulation are performed. Marriages are strained and snap. There are fist fights and broken bones. Intended as occasions of pleasant social intercourse, regattas, like so many occasions of pleasure, can bring stress and turmoil, physical pain, insurance claims, and even lawsuits. They can also be spectacles of great beauty.

Oxford, Maryland, ten miles east of the Chesapeake, is a village of fewer than a thousand souls. A thriving port of entry long before the Revolutionary War, it is one of the older towns in the United States, a colonial heirloom. The village is spread upon a cape of choice land, rich in greenery and filled with deep shade. Green-shuttered white houses line its streets. The Tred Avon River winds about its shores like a blue bracelet.

For many, the high point of Oxford's year comes during the second weekend in August, when the resident yacht club, the Tred Avon, sponsors what has come to be known as the Oxford Regatta. Of all the many regattas held on the waters of Chesapeake Bay and its tributaries, the Oxford Regatta is probably the most popular. Its highlight is a thirty-one-mile race which begins near Annapolis and ends in Oxford, with the finish line at a red flasher buoy just offshore from the yacht club. Closer to home there are races for other craft ranging in size from small catboats to the majestic and extraordinarily photogenic Chesapeake Bay log canoes—slim workboats, lightning-fast and top-heavy with sail. Threading its way through the regatta traffic is a small white ferryboat. The weather is usually fair and hot. Blue river and white sails glitter under the high August sky.

Regattas have been held annually at Oxford since the nineteen-thirties, always staged by the Tred Avon Yacht Club until, in 1979, permission to sponsor a regatta at Oxford was granted to a newly sanctioned group calling itself the Sandy Cove Sailing Association. The weekend selected was in mid-July, leaving the traditional second weekend in August available as usual to the TAYC.

To oversee its inaugural regatta, the Sandy Cove group chose a fifty-six-year-old widow named Roberta Lodge, a Bryn Mawr graduate and a woman of intelligence and poise. Running a regatta was by custom a man's job but Roberta tackled it with assurance. She felt she was every bit as smart as any man and a lot smarter than most. With her smoothly tanned face and white hair, Roberta was a strik-ing-looking woman and men found her appealing. She liked men and enjoyed their company but she had no desire to get married again and knew she never would. That summer the man she saw most frequently was a newcomer from upstate New York, a widower named Tony Korbut. Although he didn't realize that Roberta knew about it, Tony Korbut within the past three years had served a prison sentence at Lewisburg, for income tax fraud.

Since the death of her husband, Roberta had lived alone on the town's deeply shaded main street in a fine old white house which once had belonged to her father. The rear lawn ran all the way down to the river and here, at a cocktail party on Sunday afternoon, the successful skippers would receive their trophies.

On the back of Roberta's house, overlooking the lawn and the river, was an enclosed room, a so-called Florida Room, with glass jalousies and bright summer colors. In this room on the eve of the regatta, Roberta sat at the telephone, talking to first one committee member and then another about final arrangements for the next day's event.

In the world of yachting, the occasion would be of no particular significance. It was not big-time racing. It was not a trans-Atlantic race, not Fastnet, not Newport to Bermuda, not even Annapolis to Newport. The crews for the most part were not blue-ribbon crews and when the regatta was over it would rate no more than a couple of paragraphs in the local sports pages.

But to many people it was an affair of great moment. One of these was Roberta Lodge and that evening she was on the phone almost without letup, taking care of last-minute details.

Although the race would end in Oxford, the focus for now was at the other end of the course, in Annapolis, where the cruising-boat contestants had already converged for the next morning's start. That evening the yacht club at Annapolis began to fill up early and by six o'clock there were no tables to be had in the cocktail lounge. At the long bar, people stood four deep and in the dining room there was an hour's wait for seating. Yet the mood was festive. Conversation in the lounge was a steady roar, rising to happy barks and squeals. Shinbones and cheekbones gleamed with fresh sunburn. Dress was a mixture. Many wore shorts and dungarees, but some of the older women wore flowered dresses and some of the older men sported expensive jackets and trousers of every conceivable hue and combination—sartorial holdouts against the pervasion of denim. These older men in particular seemed to be enjoying themselves hugely, and in some cases mysteriously. Meeting, they bent double with laughter, as if the sight of one another had brought instant recall of a past race, a past indiscretion, a past caper with someone else's wife or perhaps merely with a bottle. A burst of laughter marked the memory and served as greeting.

"Gonna tear 'em up tomorrow?"

"Gonna tear 'em up!"

They passed along.

One guessed that many of those present wanted to be nowhere else, happy in the thought that at midsummer of 1979, with inflation rampant and with the Middle East torn by crisis that would only get worse, there was no more comforting place to be than their yacht club.

Observing the crowd, one might also have sensed an attitude of expectancy. Here and there the happy-hour pleasantries were broken by quick glances toward the entranceways, glances which seemed to indicate more than casual curiosity as to who might be arriving. Most knew that a celebrity was in town, a prominent international yachtsman, owner and skipper of the elegant fifty-eight-foot sloop *Iceman*. That he also happened to be a prominent Broadway producer was of far less interest. In this setting he was known primarily as a yachtsman. The man's name was Mel Fontaine. The yacht club newsletter had been mailed out three days earlier. "The *Iceman* Cometh!" its headline exulted. Ordinarily Fontaine would not have trifled with such a small-time event. His boat was cruising the Chesapeake that summer with a skeleton crew when he learned of the race and decided on a whim to enter. Using his ship-to-shore telephone, he rounded up the members of his regular racing crew, his "gorillas," and mailed in an entry blank.

Mel Fontaine had not entered the world of big-time yachting until he was thirty-eight. Within ten years he had come as close to conquering it as any one man can be said to conquer it. He learned sailing with small boats known as Finns and Solings; surrounded himself with the cream of instructors and crewmen. Soon, in the swift, able *Iceman,* he was following the ocean racing circuit from the British Isles to Australia, from Newport to Nassau, competing successfully with the likes of *Running Tide, Tenacious, Carina, Scaramouche, Kialoa, Charisma,* and other blue-ribbon craft of the seventies, establishing a reputation not only among his wealthy racing peers but among those who raced at the local yacht club level—weekend sailors who read of the big boys' exploits in yachting magazines. Although he had never skippered an America's Cup contender he was, by now, as he approached forty-eight, every bit as well known in the yachting world as Ted Turner, Bus Mosbacher, Bob Bavier and Bill Ficker, to name a few who had.

In a country where many public figures are envied and few admired, Fontaine was to some of those present a figure of admiration—almost solely, it was safe to say, for his nautical prowess. Respected for his sailing skills and distinguished racing record, he was perhaps both envied and scorned for a way of life that was described by some as modern and realistic, by others as brazen. His name was often in gossip columns, usually linked with that of Elaine Fowler, the young woman who was his almost constant companion, his "Ice-Lady," as one magazine had put it. In magazine articles, although he hardly looked the part, he was sometimes portrayed as a swashbuckling amoral desperado and the girl as a sort of Southern Sex Express. At good colleges across the land were two of his three children, and in a glass house overlooking Puget Sound an alcoholic wife. The third child was a daughter two years older than his mistress.

Keeping abreast of his Broadway and sailing careers would not have been possible except in the jet age. Most top-notch ocean skippers depended upon commercial air schedules. Fontaine used his own plane, a twelve-passenger jet with its own pilot. Thus, taking a taxi from mid-Manhattan to Newark Airport, trotting to the waiting plane, he could be in Fort Lauderdale in two hours and in another fifteen minutes could be hopping into the cockpit of his gorgeous sloop, his racing machine, which lay in its slip, ready to go, filled with provisions and sailbags and its full ship's complement, which over the years had included a crew of strong young men, among whom there was always a heavy turnover, and a succession of beautiful young women, most recently Elaine Fowler.

In the cocktail lounge heads continued to turn. It was now past seven and it was known (because somebody had been interested enough to ask the headwaiter) that Fontaine had made a dinner reservation for six–forty-five.

Not until seven-fifteen did he appear. What people then saw was a man dressed casually in a pale-blue shirt and suntan trousers bleached nearly white. A blue and white sports belt encircled a slim waist. Slung loosely about his neck was a red bandanna and over one arm he carried a blue denim jacket. With his wavy grey hair, heavy-lidded, deep-set eyes, his mouthful of strong even teeth, his facial appearance might have suggested less a swashbuckling desperado than perhaps an off-duty vicar.

At his elbow was his young woman, hollow-cheeked and aloof, and looking, as the magazine had said, "the part of a sheik's consort with her mass of dark hair, her dusky skin and remarkable slanted grey eyes that might well have been peering out from above the hem of a veil." With a soft white knit shirt she wore faded blue jeans. Her shoes had very high spike heels. The jeans hugged her hips, indenting her waist. Elaine Fowler had been discovered working in a diner in a small town on the coastal plain of North Carolina and there recruited, just as others in small towns all over America are recruited to take their places in the ranks of bunnies and models, split-ends and flanker-backs, actresses, mistresses, left-handed pitchers, whores, courtesans, point-guards—an army with ranks in constant need of replenishing. Discovered before she was sixteen, she had now served seven years, including most recently a two-year stint with Mellon Fontaine.

The waters parted as the couple walked through the room. It was a walk that seemed to possess a quality of stateliness. Although it took much less than sixty seconds for them to pass through, it seemed much longer, perhaps because of the deliberate pace and because of the way heads were turned, at first a few, then more, then virtually every head in the room, as word was passed along the bar and from one table to the next. Here and there a hand was raised in greeting, a forelock touched, but with few exceptions the crowd seemed diffident, reluctant to do more than look on.

"Yo, skipper! Mr. Fontaine. Mel?" One of the exceptions pushed forward as the couple approached the dining-room entrance. He was a stocky, swarthy man in a red and white horizontally striped shirt and about him there was a look of avidity. He looked avid for recognition. "Mr. Fontaine . . . remember me? Pete Moran. Edgartown. Seventy-two." His head dipped and for a moment there were two chins where there had been but one. " . . . just like to say— welcome aboard!" Pete Moran thrust out his hand. Fontaine grasped it loosely and dropped it. "I sure like the way you been showing your tail to *Charisma* lately," Pete Moran said. "See ya out there tomorrow."

With a steady smile, Fontaine bore on.

Like a sideswiped crab pot, Moran drifted astern.

Peering forth from the dining room, the headwaiter was already holding a chair for the girl. "Good evening," he said to her and then, "Good evening, Mr. Fontaine." The girl sat. Across from her, Fontaine glanced about the room with a nod, the same steady smile of greeting, of acknowledgment, and then as he took his seat there was, perhaps incredibly, a scattering of applause. As it went rippling through the room, he nodded and smiled again.

The girl's eyes showed disinterest. White makeup had been smoothly applied to her lips. The two top buttons of her shirt were open. On her plate was a handsome menu, tasseled blue and white, embossed with a cut of a sloop in full sail—blue and white to match the decor of the room, the blue walls and white ceiling, and the blue and white ceiling fans, the white tablecloths and blue tumblers. She opened the menu and began to study the ornate blue script lettering. Lifting a tendril of hair into place above her temple, she looked about the room and then down at the menu again.

As she continued to sit with her head bent over the list

of entrees, Fontaine could be seen eyeing the whitened lips, the dusky smoothness of her face. Most of the men in the room, from their respective vantage points, were doing the same, and in the minds of those with knowledge of her background there might have been a question: with a willing coterie of would-be actresses to select from, why had Fontaine chosen as his mistress a barely educated girl from rural North Carolina? For some the girl's particular brand of beauty might have been answer enough. Elaine Fowler had been widely publicized as a femme fatale, nationally portrayed as a sex object, but in the sad light in her eyes, the planes of her face there was a melancholy that gave her a special allure—an allure that had nothing to do with pinup sex, with explicit sex, nothing to do with the lank moist acrobatics of a pornographic film.

"What will you have?" Fontaine asked.

She closed the menu. "Maybe just a drink, I'm not very hungry," she said.

Fontaine looked up at the waiter. "Chivas? For the lady? And a chef's salad—also for the lady."

While Fontaine gave his own order the girl's eyes never left his face. When he was finished and the waiter was gone, he closed the menu. Smiling into her eyes, he covered her hand with his own. She looked down at his hand and then off into the distance.

Fontaine looked toward the bar where the waiter had gone for their drinks. Soon the waiter returned and placed the drinks before them. At the next table sat a clean-shaven man in a black turtleneck shirt and tan linen jacket. He was having coffee, the last of a large party to leave the table. He had been watching Fontaine and the girl. Now Fontaine noticed him. Their eyes met. Fontaine seemed about to speak. The other nodded solemnly. "Mr. Fontaine," he said. Fontaine smiled and nodded, then frowned, as if trying to remember something and not succeeding. "Don't I know you?" he asked. "Anthony Korbut," the man said. "We met a couple of years ago at the New York Yacht Club."

"Sure," Fontaine said without conviction. "Sure. How've you been?"

"You were having lunch with a sailmaker," Korbut said. "He was cutting a new spinnaker for you."

Fontaine nodded. "Sure. I remember now." He raised his glass and tipped it to Korbut, who raised his coffee cup in return. "Miss Fowler," Fontaine said. Again Korbut nodded solemnly. The girl smiled.

Fontaine was civil but clearly disinterested. "Sailing tomorrow?" he asked.

"No," Korbut said. "I'm on the committee boat." He raised his hand, indicating the vacated seats at his table. "The rest of the committee just left."

Nodding, Fontaine sipped his drink and they began to talk. The girl took a book from her lap and opened it on the table. The book dealt with sociological phenomena and she was reading about child abuse in the United States.

"I saw a picture of your spinnaker in *Yachting* a couple of months ago," Korbut said. "Was that the one he cut for you? White on black?"

"White on black," Fontaine affirmed. He paused. "White icepick on black."

"Ah," Korbut said with a nod.

The girl looked up. Very huge and very black, she thought. And between the shoulders, right at the bulge, the long white icepick. Stiletto. Slanting at a forty-five–degree angle. Pointing downward.

She kept reading but found it difficult to concentrate. Finally she put the book back in her lap again and sat alone with her thoughts. When her salad and Fontaine's roast beef arrived she ate very quickly, with quick jabs of her fork, trying her best to tune out the conversation, not always succeeding. Here a sycophant, there a sycophant; in ones and twos they approached the table. How many crew members did he carry? What size jib winches? Where would he anchor at Oxford? Which shore would he favor going down the bay? At one point she counted ten men clustered about the table. While Fontaine answered their questions their eyes were on her. Dinner over, they drifted from the dining room into the cocktail lounge where, with Fontaine and the girl seated at a large round table, the audience grew larger.

Chatter, and then attentive listening, the sound of a single sonorous voice, Fontaine's, making a point, telling an anecdote. Laughter. Chatter, and then again the respectful attentive quiet as his voice once again was heard, measured, controlled, and then the smile, the fastidious flick of an ash. The girl was seated on a low sofa, grasping the knees of her jeans. She looked down impassively as Fontaine talked, seldom changing expression. Somebody asked if he was responsible for the highly successful theatrical production *Oh, Calcutta!*. He said no. "That's funny—I thought it was yours." Again Fontaine said no. There were looks of impatience. Among those present the preferred topics were sailing and the next day's race. The persistent questioner was a gaunt young man in a pale-blue headband. "Tell me, Mr. Fontaine, did you once work for Mark Dandridge, the old-time movie mogul?" Fontaine returned the steady smile, the look of great reasonableness, the dip of the cigar ash. "I wasn't aware that this was an interview," he said with a laugh that showed his splendid teeth. "Yes, young man," an older woman said. "Let's stick to boats." The young man ignored her. "I'm Jim Nicholson, Mr. Fontaine," he said. "I get out the club newsletter." Fontaine nodded. "The answer is yes, I did at one time . . . work for Mr. Dandridge." "Is it true what they say about him?" Fontaine spread his hands. "What do they say about him?" "*You* know. What an old bastard he was and everything." "This is for your—club newsletter?" Fontaine asked, still with his reasonable smile. "No, this is personal curiosity," the young man said. "Leave it, Jimmy, leave it," somebody said. "What I'd like very much to know, Mr. Fontaine—" another speaker began. "Mel—please," Fontaine said. "Well—okay, Mel—what I'd like to know is how you ever managed to catch *Charisma* in the Nassau race last winter after you got such a lousy start . . . "

Through it all the girl sat without expression, looking at her hands, occasionally at Fontaine's face, and then at her hands again.

"This plane you use—whose plane is it, Mr. Fontaine?" The questioner was the same gaunt young man in the blue headband. "Is it the company plane?"

Fontaine's smile was patient. "I have no company," he said. "I'm an independent producer. The plane belongs to me personally. It gives us wonderful mobility. I can see my kids when I want to, or we can take side trips whenever we feel like it. All I have to do is pick up the ship-to-shore phone, call the pilot, put into the nearest port, rent a car and drive to the nearest airstrip and the pilot picks us up, right there at the airstrip."

"Gosh, you make it all sound so easy," the young man said. There was an edge of sarcasm in his voice. Fontaine's smile flickered. Carefully he stubbed out his cigar. His hand left it. He was ready to go. "Everybody is flattered that you're racing with us," somebody said. "But some are a little resentful."

"Why would that be?" Fontaine asked.

"I guess because they know you'll walk off with the race."

"I wish I thought so," was the reply. "I'm not much for local knowledge. I've done the Annapolis-Newport race a couple of times but that's about it for the Chesapeake. But we'll sure be trying."

Elaine looked at her hands and every few moments she looked about the room. Her attention had long since wandered. She was thinking about a man named Harry Crowder, expecting that any minute he might walk in.

Rising, Fontaine held out a hand and pulled Elaine to her feet. "Good luck to one and all," he said, "and now if you'll excuse us . . . "

Two

A MAN WHO ASKS the cost of a yacht is a man who can't afford to own one. So spoke J. P. Morgan, yacht owner and financier of note, who made the remark perhaps as a warning to the unwary potential boat buyer or perhaps merely as a self-assured commentary upon his own considerable financial resources. It was a remark that somehow caught the fancy of those who stockpile quotations and it became imbedded in the national folklore, but by the nineteen-seventies its validity was gone.

On the eve of the race down to Oxford, at a boat slip on the Severn River, Harry Crowder was putting a few final touches on his sloop *Sundance*. As a man who ran a boat yard, Harry knew firsthand that boating no longer belonged solely to the rich. Just as decades earlier it became a nation of automobile owners, America had now become a nation of boat owners. More and more thousands each year were fleeing the land at every opportunity—for a month, a week, a day, an afternoon, whatever they could manage. They did so for a variety of reasons, including the need to get away from the very automotive society which once had brought pleasure to so many.

If the national boating boom could be ascribed to any single factor, that factor might well have been a chemical substance known as fiberglass. Unknown before 1950, fiberglass permitted assembly line production of stock models from a master mold. Fiberglass hulls were not only economical to build, they were also easy and inexpensive to maintain and repair. A few purists continued to hold out for the custom-built boat of wood but the new breed of yachtsman was generally no purist. He was a man who found the idea of owning his own cruising and racing yacht enormously appealing and (largely because of fiberglass) well within reach. In speaking of a yacht, J. P. Morgan was speaking of something of great size and expense—something he and Commodore Cornelius Vanderbilt might cruise in, something Sir Thomas Lipton might race. But a yacht, no matter its size, is a yacht. It is by definition a vessel used for pleasure. Within the space of thirty feet and often considerably less, Americans sailing on both coasts and upon the Great Lakes and the Gulf of Mexico could have on a smaller scale much of what was the exclusive province of yesterday's millionaires—a cruising-racing yacht complete with inboard motor; bunk space for four or more; a galley with icebox, stove, and running water; a dining area; toilet, navigation instruments, sail inventory and racing gear and even a ship-to-shore telephone.

All this, of course, was not to say that the boating scene lacked for millionaires. Although much of Harry's work was done for men of relatively moderate means he also did work for the wealthy—for the owners of large expensive yachts who confined their racing to the Chesapeake; and even occasionally for those elite mariners who engaged in trans-ocean racing, men whose hobby could cost them as much as a hundred thousand dollars a year. Harry knew about men such as these. He had sailed with them, crewed for them, and it was from one of their number that he had been lucky enough to acquire his boat. *Sundance* was thirty-two feet long, pale yellow, with a gracefully tapered transom. Campaigning six months earlier in southern waters, she had been badly damaged in a collision during a race from Miami to Montego Bay, Jamaica, and her owner, a man as superstitious as he was wealthy, felt she was jinxed forevermore. He had no wish to have her repaired and Harry was able to buy the boat for a small fraction of its value. After solo sailing it from Jamaica to the Chesapeake, he had put it back into shape and raced it with success.

Harry ran his boat yard for a living. He raced for the pleasure of it and because it was something he did truly well. It also helped fill huge gaps in his life. For eight years now he had been living alone, ever since the day in 1971 when his wife walked out on him. He had the unpleasant sensation of knowing that in the eyes of his wife he was not much good and possibly even contemptible. On the day their marriage ended she had most certainly looked at him with contempt. In her eyes, she had made a very big mistake. The fruit of that mistake was a son, a year and a half old on the day they parted and now nine.

Born and raised on the Eastern Shore, Harry had gone to college in New England, where he met Marcia and married her. When he brought her home, the marriage went quickly sour. They had met on common ground but once he had taken her back to his ground, his land, she quickly disliked it, and almost as quickly disliked him. In college she had been attracted by his rugged good looks and perhaps nothing more. If she had loved him in New England she did not love him on the Eastern Shore, and maybe the answer was that she simply had never loved him at all.

His was a land where in the world of the seventies the men still spoke of their wives as the old lady and the old bitch. It was one of the last places on earth where feminist notions would ever penetrate. Marcia hated his friends, his old buddies, their red-cheeked, Hogarthian appearance, their Rabelaisan love of eating oysters and drinking bourbon, their love of the pleasures of the flesh, although the latter, she ascertained, were almost invariably more culinary than carnal, more outdoorsman than libertine. She mimicked them: "Sooner shoot me a goose than screw me a woman—*any day!*"

Most of all Marcia hated their attitude toward women, toward their wives. "They're like a bunch of schoolboys, seeing how much they can get away with, trying to put something over on their mothers, so proud of how drunk they got the night before, always talking about the hell they're going to catch when they get home. They hate their wives, yet at the same time they acknowledge their power, acknowledge them as *authority* figures. I mean—

Harry—what the *hell!*"

The marriage blew up after a year and the occasion was Thanksgiving dinner on Tilghman Island, with the thirty-seven different foods and all his relatives and their views, loudly and unabashedly racist, loudly and unabashedly patriotic, fiercely and stubbornly proud of their heritage and of themselves. Marcia was a real bitch all afternoon, eyes veiled, lips compressed, barely concealing her disgust; and his relatives, women and men alike, barely concealing their desire to kill her right there and then; she in her white pants suit, in the old white clapboard house with the oystershell roads and the 1955 Ford convertible up on blocks in the front yard and inside the house the biggest color television set money could buy. She fixed on the food. She called the food revolting and said that people so gluttonous were peasants. They had left the kid with a sitter and when they got home she looked at the kid with great pity, as if to say, Oh, you poor kid, you poor baby, what's to become of you; what's in store for you? She was feeling genuine horror that her child might be raised here among people she hated. What was in store for the kid was Philip. She called Philip that very afternoon. It had been going on all the time behind Harry's back, even while she was pregnant, yet always by telephone. Philip was in New England and she didn't see him, only talked to him on the telephone. All this Harry learned later—and also learned that her mother had been all for it. If Marcia had any misgivings about leaving, she didn't show them. She knew where her best interests lay. She knew where and how she would live her life, how best to salvage the years that remained. She had made a mistake, had married Harry Crowder, and now she had to do the best she could. Marcia would do very well. She would marry Philip, a man who appreciated her, a man whose own Brahmin background went well with her cool, slim, angular beauty.

That afternoon when she told him she was leaving him, Harry defended his relatives, his people, his land. He got drunk and threw things around in a rage. She watched him, cool, unafraid, the light shining on the high cheekbones, disdain and perhaps even a trace of pity in the clear eyes. He had always been impressed by her lack of fear.

When she was gone he was left with the empty feeling that comes with knowing one has done nothing wrong but still has lost. His only failure was that he was deemed not good enough. It left a man very little room to stand. To fight legally—but there was nothing to fight. To hate with a pure fierce hatred—to hate her would have made it easier but he had never been able to. She had asked him to demean his own people and his own land and this he would never do, but he could not hate her because he could never see her as totally wrong.

While they were married Harry had a job with the state and talked of going on to law school. After Marcia left him he quit his job and went to work in his father's boat yard. The years had gone swiftly, with little to punctuate them except the one month a year he had with his son. In the early years Harry roistered, drank a great deal, sailed a great deal, had women now and then (usually when he was drunk; seldom when he was sober). The decade passed. A bad decade. The country seemed to be collapsing. His own world had already collapsed. He bought a sports car and set out to lead the life of a swinger, and to some he might have appeared to be a tough guy, hard drinker, big blade, but inside he was in mourning. His drinking increased until, toward the end of 1977, he found that he was on the verge of becoming an alcoholic. He licked it and since then had limited himself to beer, supplemented by cigars. Occasionally he felt himself tempted to slip back but so far he had not. For six years he worked with his father and then, hoping that a change of scenery might change his luck, he had left his father's boat yard on the Eastern Shore, moved to Annapolis, and taken over a yard of his own. In May his father died of a heart attack in a log canoe race.

Now, on this evening in July, with an hour or so of

daylight remaining, Harry stood in the cockpit of his boat, wearing sneakers and a pair of navy-blue swim trunks. At thirty-seven, he was strong and agile. In the years when he was drinking heavily he had run to flesh but now his body was trim and hard-muscled. His dark hair was long and shaggy, not cultivatedly and fashionably long—simply shaggy, like the hair of a man who has gone for many weeks without getting a haircut.

The job he now faced was to jump overboard and scrub the bottom of *Sundance*'s hull. In a race a clean hull was vital. *Sundance* had been painted only a month earlier but even a bottom newly painted, with the very best of bottom paint, was quick to collect marine growth, and the faintest patina of mucous could affect a boat's speed.

A large green sponge lay on the cockpit seat. He picked it up, stepped to the rail and then, thinking better of it, went below and put on a ragged blue sweat suit. The sweat suit was for protection against the jellyfish which filled the river in summer. He hooked a boarding ladder over the rail and then, sponge in hand, jumped overboard. Clawing and kicking in water over his head, he began to wield the sponge. He worked first up under the bow and then worked his way slowly aft, clearing away the faint slime that had formed along the waterline of the hull, and at the leading and trailing edges of the keel and rudder. Ordinarily the scrubbing operation would have been done at his boat yard, but his doctor had asked to borrow his boat a couple of days earlier and Harry, because he was casual about such things, had let him have it. The slip (and the expensive house on the terraced slope beyond) belonged to his doctor and it was from here that *Sundance* would be leaving next morning for the start of the race. Harry by now had reached the stern. Still in the water, clasping the after-edge of the rudder between his knees to free both hands, he checked for growth on the rudder's top edge where the anti-fouling paint had not reached, then ran the sponge down both sides of the rudder, scrubbing it smooth. When it was all done to his satisfaction he climbed aboard once more. In the cockpit he peeled off the sopping sweat clothes, stripping down to his swim trunks again and tossing the sweat pants and sweat shirt, now heavy with water, in a sodden clump on top of the cabin.

It was by now seven o'clock. The Severn River flowed past the foot of steep, heavily wooded bluffs. Beyond his plastered hair, houses were perched among the greenery, spotted high above the water, and above the greenery a pale-blue sky, its color draining as the light faded.

Going below now, he checked about the cabin to see that all was in order. He wound his stopwatch, clicked it on, let it run for a few seconds, clicked it off, put it back into the drawer beneath the alcohol stove and continued with his mental checklist. On the counter next to the small sink lay a sheet of paper on which he had computed the next day's tides, along with the predicted rates of current at each tidal stage. He thumbtacked this to the bulkhead just to the right of the companionway ladder. The table which normally stood in the small dining area had long since been removed so there would be more room for sailbags. He looked about. First aid kit. Fire extinguishers. Jib sheets, spinnaker sheets. Life preservers. Everything seemed to be in good shape.

Stripping off the wet trunks, he picked up a pair of khaki trousers, dried himself with one trouser leg, and then put them on, along with a khaki shirt. Locking the cabin, he made his way along the finger pier toward shore. On the way home he would continue with his preparations. There was ice to be bought, and beer and soft drinks, and food for sandwiches. Harry was very intense about a race. It was a take-out from his real life and he gave it all he had. The feeling of intensity would continue until the race was over. During the evening he would think about the race and the course to be covered. At some point he would check the weather reports, and would do so again at seven in the morning, when the official National Weather Service forecast was issued from the Baltimore-Washington International Airport, once known as Friendship.

After his purchases were made and the car was unloaded, he would probably go over to the yacht club. While he was at lunch there had been a telephone call from Elaine Fowler. She had left a message saying she was in town. She would be at the yacht club that evening and wanted him to come over if he could.

Three

HARRY HAD MET Elaine Fowler the previous January in Jamaica after a race from Miami to Montego Bay. He was crewing on a sixty-five–foot yawl for an Annapolis hardware tycoon named Blake, and the boats in the Miami-Montego race always laid over in Jamaica for a week or so before heading off again. It was during this same week that Harry bought the damaged sloop that became *Sundance.*

In Montego Bay, Blake's big white yawl was berthed three slips away from Fontaine's *Iceman,* and Harry noticed the girl the very first evening they were in port. She was hard not to notice. She was sitting in the cockpit in a yellow dress that showed her shoulders, and her hair was sort of folded on top of her head. Harry was sitting with some of the other guys in the cockpit of Blake's boat, all ogling her, analyzing her anatomy, muttering and laughing. It was obvious that she knew she was being looked at but she didn't turn her head, just sat there with her hands in her lap, showing her profile beneath the rich dark mass of hair. Soon Fontaine came up from below, looking suave in a fancy yellow plaid jacket, and they went off together. From the onlookers there were a couple of low whistles but Fontaine and the girl didn't turn, they just kept walking. Beautiful people in the mellow light of evening in Jamaica.

While Fontaine was around she seemed like nothing much more than a sexual ornament, all dressed up, clinging to his arm; sometimes draped over the foredeck in a pale-blue bikini, or sunning herself in the cockpit, like a courtesan on call, ready whenever Fontaine should give the word.

But then Fontaine's pilot arrived and Fontaine flew back to the mainland for a few days. Elaine was left with the gorillas on *Iceman*. Some of the guys on Harry's boat played touch football on the beach with some of the *Iceman* gorillas and she played too. She wasn't bad at all, running for passes, slim tanned legs flashing, hair tumbling as she struggled through the soft coral sand. Harry played for a while and then, lighting a cigar, watched from the end of the pier.

Among the wealthy owners there were a lot of elaborate parties that week at the Casa Montega and the other plush hotels, but with the younger crowd, the crew members, there was mainly a lot of boat-hopping and horsing around on the beach. Elaine stuck with the younger crowd.

At first Harry kept pretty much to himself. He rented a snorkeling outfit and lay face down in the turquoise water, studying coral formations, watching small purple fish flit past the coral. The fish cast swift darting shadows over the sunlit sand. Harry lay there face down and imagined that his son was lying face down next to him, wondering what his son would think of it all. Often when he was doing something new or something that seemed interesting, he imagined that his son was with him and sometimes he found himself talking aloud, saying, "How do you like that, old buddy? What do you think of *that*?"

Elaine spoke to him the morning after Fontaine flew back to the mainland. Popping his head up through the forward hatch, he saw her sunning herself a short distance down the beach, sprawled on a maroon sleeping bag in a one-piece white bathing suit. Harry yawned, got something to eat, and put on his trunks. When he went ashore she was still there. Her head was pillowed on her arm and she seemed to be asleep but as he walked by she called, "Hi."

He turned. "How are you?" she asked.

"Okay," Harry replied. "How are you?"

She was up on one elbow, smiling. The white bathing suit was cut very very low. When summer came, bathing suits like that would be the fashion. "I'm Elaine Fowler," she said.

He nodded. "I'm Harry Crowder."

She touched the sleeping bag. "Come sit down. You're with Blake, aren't you?"

Harry sat beside her. They talked about the weather and the race and about Jamaica for a while and then she asked him if he would walk up the beach with her.

"Wait right here," she said. "I'll be right back."

She went aboard *Iceman* and a few minutes later reappeared in a man's white shirt with the tails knotted over a blue bikini. Harry wondered what was wrong with the first bathing suit. Maybe she thought it didn't show enough. She needn't have worried.

They walked up the beach. She had very high arches and her feet made delicate prints in the wet sand. It was a beautiful afternoon, warm but not hot, just the way it would be all week. By day the trade winds blew in from the sea. In the evening they died and then during the night the breeze came down from the mountains.

When they were far up the beach she took off the shirt and went into the water. A tiny sailboat with a tattered sail ran fast toward shore. Three tiny naked brown bodies were perched on the rail. She waved, then jumped from the water and waved again; jumped high out of the water and kept waving. Finally the kids waved back, grinning.

Afterward she sat on a seawall, drying off in the warm sun. Harry sat beside her and she told him that Fontaine had flown to Miami and thence to New York. His private plane was kept at Miami airport and the pilot had an apartment on Biscayne Bay. The pilot brought the mail once a week to wherever they happened to be and hung around if Fontaine wanted him to hang around, otherwise went on back to Miami and waited until Fontaine called him on the ship-to-shore telephone.

The seawall where they sat was just down the road from the airport. A plane warmed its engines with a vast roar which quickly died. She was looking at him, cocking her head. Her eyes were bold. Now she was looking at his cigar.

He dragged on the cigar, following the tattered sail with his eyes. "Do you—inhale that thing?" she asked.

"Sometimes."

She was frowning a little now. "When I was little—I can remember this very well . . . my father smoked cigars. He used to say, 'Would you like to see the smoke come out of my nose?' And I'd say yes and he'd blow smoke out of his nose. Then he'd say, 'Would you like to see it come out of my ears?' and I'd say yes again and he'd say, 'Okay, put your hand against my chest,' and I'd put my hand against his chest and he'd draw in the smoke and as he blew it out he touched the lighted end of the cigar to the back of my hand and I cried."

She took a deep breath. "Here," she said, placing her hand against his chest. "Do it."

"No."

"Come on, I want to see if it hurts."

He shook his head.

"Come on."

He flipped the cigar into the sea.

"Big macho," she said.

"Who?"

"You."

"Why?"

"Sitting around smoking cigars while everybody else plays football."

"That's macho?"

"Something about you that's trying to be macho."

"The hell there is."

"Sort of an attitude about things. Like you don't give a damn."

He didn't reply.

"What do you give a damn about, Harry?"

He shrugged. "Sailing . . . "

"That's all? Sailing? That bores me."

"If you're bored, why are we here?"

She smiled. "Good question. Why did I pick you up?"

"Why did you?"

"Another good question." She was still smiling. "I guess because I liked your looks. Because you were the best-looking guy on the beach."

She was up from the seawall, taking his hand. "Come on. Let's walk."

That evening at supper the guys on his boat started making jokes about the risk he was taking, the danger that lay in messing around with Mel Fontaine's girl. When Fontaine got back he would hire a couple of Jamaican thugs to haul Harry out beyond the reef and dump him overboard, turn him over to the sharks.

In Montego Bay the money was on the rim. The wealth stopped at the beaches. Away from the beaches, inland, up in the mountains, there was incredible poverty.

Harry and a couple of the other guys rented a car and drove up into the mountains. The people carried things on their heads. Their hovels, Harry thought, resembled nothing so much as chicken coops.

When he told Elaine about them she was not particularly impressed. She told him she had been very poor as a child. "Our whole family was poor." She was lying face down on the sleeping bag and he was stretched beside her. "We lived in a trailer on the road to Ahoskie. Our trailer was really shabby. My best friend lived across the road in a really beautiful trailer. Man, *what a trailer*! It didn't just sit there on top of the ground, it was planted, like a house. It had a foundation and her father even planted shrubbery around it. God, it seemed like a palace. I was really jealous."

The next morning she came aboard the boat early to get

him. In his blue swim trunks he walked with her to the end of the pier, still half asleep, feeling grumpy. She laughed at him. "Come on, Harry," she said. "Let's go do something."

He sat on the edge of the pier, yawned and scratched his ribs.

She was wearing her one-piece white bathing suit and her hair was tied in pigtails. "What's wrong?" Standing above him, she placed her bare foot on his leg.

"Why don't you go do something by yourself?" Harry said.

"Why?"

"Why not?"

"Why should I?" she demanded.

"Go play touch football," he said. "Go fishing. Go take limbo lessons." Harry was scratching his ribs again. He yawned. "When the hell is Fontaine coming back, anyway?"

"Friday. Hmmm. Are you afraid of Fontaine, is that it?"

He wasn't sure if she was taunting him or if she was serious. "Should I be?" he demanded.

"Just answer. *Are* you?"

"Hell no."

"Are you afraid of anything?"

"Everybody's afraid of something," he said. "Aren't you?"

"Not as much as I used to be." She kicked his leg. "Come on, you bastard, just walk with me a little. Can't you just *walk* with me a little?"

While they walked along the beach he told her something about his marriage and his son. She listened intently and when he was done she told him something about herself. She had been nothing, she said, until she met Fontaine. He had changed her life. She had had no education, couldn't even speak the language very well. He had sent her to modeling school, made her take lessons to get rid of her red-clay southern accent, bought clothes for her, gave her books to read.

"It was so amazing," she said. "I mean, here's this man, this biiiiiig maaaaaaaan. He can create stars, he can have any girl he wants—and he picks me. Wow!"

"Wow," Harry said.

"He takes me to the most wonderful restaurants. Concerts. Broadway shows. Sometimes we fly to Paris for the weekend."

"Wow."

She smiled. "Listen, I want to go up into the mountains, okay?"

He nodded. "Maybe you could fly up for the weekend."

"I want you to take me. Please."

Harry wondered if the reason he was spending so much time with her had something to do with the fact that she was Fontaine's girl. She was gorgeous, God knows, but there was also something challenging, something pleasantly dangerous about it, and maybe this was part of the attraction. He wasn't sure.

That afternoon he hired a taxi and they rode high into the mountains, deeper and deeper into upland jungle. The taxi driver was a woman who, each time they passed bananas, explained that bananas grew upside down. The miserable houses lined the road. Elaine looked at them without saying anything.

Deep in the mountains they came upon a broad clearing, a plaza baking in the sun and filled with dogs. The dogs were mongrels but unfamiliar even as mongrels—crosses, Harry thought, between jackals and greyhounds, lean and yellow, and the plaza was filled with them and filled with people. The taxi slowed and they were surrounded by the people and the dogs, and the sun glittered on the black faces and white clothing of the people and on the yellow hides of the dogs, and on a thin trickle of water that arched feebly in an ancient stone drinking fountain.

Elaine wanted to get out. The taxi driver said it would be okay and they got out. Elaine linked her arm through

Harry's and walked rapidly with long, loose, head-tossing strides, through the people and the dogs, once around the plaza.

Then they got back into the taxi and started back. So far that week any bodily contact between them had been incidental,—a hand at an elbow, a hand brushing a leg, hip brushing hip, but now in the taxi her leg was pressed tight against his. She made no attempt to move it. She was wearing a wraparound navy denim skirt and it lay half open. All the way down the mountain Harry sat with his hand on the inside of her leg. Near the foot of the mountain the taxi driver paused to show them a view and they sat there for a few moments in silence. The Jamaican sun baked the fields of sugar cane. In the distance the sea was blue and white, green and white. Harry's hand was still on the inside of her leg and it felt scalding.

That night on the beach he made love to her on the maroon sleeping bag, his shaggy body against the perfection of her own, and he had an impression of a woman practiced and consummate just as he might have expected, but then toward the end she was gasping and clutching at the sand.

As he almost always did, he felt sadness; the release, the spurt of pleasure, and then so soon the deep sadness.

When it was over he rolled away and lay on his back, looking up at the stars. She reached for his hand. "A bottle of V.O.," she murmured. "It's been a long long time."

"What?"

"I got off," she said.

"Good."

He lay there in the darkness, looking straight up.

"Are you okay?" she asked.

"Yes," he said.

Another long silence.

"I hope you're not lying there worrying about Fontaine," she said.

He hadn't been thinking about Fontaine.

"There's nothing to be worried about," she said.

"How about the sleeping bag? The guys on your boat . . . "

"Who cares? I told you. There's nothing to be afraid of."

"I'm not thinking about myself."

"Well, don't be afraid for me. You don't understand." She was up on one elbow. "He wouldn't even care. As long as I'm around when he wants me he doesn't care what I do. I have carte blanche. Not that I use it."

After a moment she asked, "What's funny? What's funny, goddamn it . . ."

Harry was smiling in the darkness. "What was that expression you just used?"

"Carte blanche?"

"I guess you were serious . . . "

"About what?"

"About being educated."

"I've barely gotten started," she said. "I read a lot on the boat—when I'm not screwing Fontaine. When I'm not screwing, I'm reading, you might say."

Picking up her dress from the sand, she slung it over her shoulder, then sat with her arms on her knees. "Oh, shit," she said. "Ineffable, unspeakable, unmitigated shit."

He smiled. "You really *are* educated."

Next morning again they lay side by side on the sleeping bag, this time in the warm sunlight, not far from the boat slips. Several times already that morning he had felt she was about to tell him something, and he thought it again now. There was a towel over her head and he thought she was asleep when he heard her voice, sounding dreamy and faraway. "I can see the road," she said. "I'm playing in the dirt out front. My mother is with me, or maybe it's my older sister. I'm bouncing a ball but the ground is uneven. I have on a blue denim pinafore with a white collar and I have on black stockings and high black shoes and I'm about two feet tall. I have a lot of hair. My mother is shelling peas, or maybe it's my sister. I can hear the peas dropping into the pan, rolling in the pan. I used to love the sound of peas being shelled . . . " Her voice drifted off.

Toward noon Harry said he wanted a beer and they left the beach and went to one of the hotels. She ordered a daiquiri and he sat looking at her, acknowledging to himself that she was a very beautiful girl. The mass of thick brown hair, tumbling forward as if of its own weight, strands and tendrils escaping, the whites of her eyes very clear, her cheeks flushed from the sun. He kept looking about the darkened room and then back to her. She got up and left for the ladies' room and he watched her go. She looked slender and fragile and he could put his hand at the small of her back and lift her with one hand above his head if he wanted to. But she wasn't for him. God knew she wasn't for him, even if he had wanted her. No woman was for him.

When she returned she sipped her drink and started talking of her childhood again. "After my mother died, we moved back into town. My father got married again and I lived with him and my stepmother. My sister went off and lived by herself. She was much older. That must have been around 1963 or 1964, I guess, because I'm twenty-three now."

She paused. "When I was almost fifteen . . . "

Again she paused, shook her head, then got a fresh start. "The night before my fifteenth birthday my father tried to rape me . . . "

For a few seconds she sat in silence, covering the top of her glass with her hand, looking down at the table. Finally she took her hand away. "And he did," she said. "Actually *did*. The sonofabitch *actually did!*"

Harry took a deep breath. What she had just told him he found hard to handle. All around him voices hummed, glasses clinked, and he sat there trying to take it in.

In telling him, she had tried to sound sophisticated and even offhand but for a few seconds her southern accent had been very strong.

She told him that for a very long time she had felt she

was totally alone. She had been afraid to tell anybody and for years she had kept it a secret.

"My sister knew," she said. "And eventually I told Fontaine. Now I'm telling you."

"God," Harry said. "My God." He didn't know what else to say. He knew that in some of the rural Eastern Shore counties, back in the remote areas, there was supposed to be plenty of it going on but there didn't seem much point in saying so. Questions ran through his head. How would a girl react? A child? Hate men for the rest of her life—or crave them? Crave only younger men—or only older men? Hate all men? Or only older? Run from older men—or toward them?"

That evening, although she asked him to, he found that he did not want to make love to her and he was not quite sure why. He thought it might have something to do with what she had told him about her father, something to do with striking her where she had been injured. Not quite that, but something like that.

Now and then that week she practiced walking as the Jamaican women walked, trying to walk from the hips, trying to make the weight of each step disappear before her foot reached the ground.

At one end of the beach, the end near the airport, stood an old stained yellow stucco hotel with many arches. In the long twilight he sat across the road from the hotel, on the low stone wall that separated the road from the beach. Elaine had eaten aboard *Iceman* with the gorillas. Now she was coming up the road to meet him, carrying a small bongo drum and trying to walk as the Jamaicans did. Drawing near, she placed the drum on her head but after a few steps it slid off and she caught it as it fell.

Sitting next to him on the wall, she took off her dark glasses and narrowed her eyes against the falling sun. They watched the evening plane come in, a blue and silver bullet growing large against the still-blue sky.

She kissed him and then drew away. Her eyes were

clouded. "Hey, Harry . . . " She tapped the drum, then dug her long nails into the hide of the drumhead, looking at the nicks her nails had left. For a few moments she sat gazing out over the sea, then murmured, "I don't turn you on any more, *do* I?"

"Why should it matter?" he asked.

"What's happened?"

For a while Harry sat looking at the sea, then he tried to explain to her what he had felt after she told him about her father raping her.

She listened intently and when he had finished she said, "It turns Fontaine *on*, not off. At least whenever I happen to mention it he gets all hot."

Harry looked at the sky with disgust. He hurled his cigar stub into the sea. "Christ!" he said.

Next day they walked, as they had already done several times that week, to look at the damaged boat. That afternoon Harry made an offer, a ridiculously low offer, which the owner accepted.

"Now how will you get it back?" she asked as they walked away.

"Sail it," he said.

"By yourself?"

"Yes."

"God! Do you know the way?"

He shrugged. "Just go back the same way we came," he said.

"Don't be funny. I mean do you know about navigation and the stars and all that stuff?"

"I can navigate."

"I don't like it," she said. "How about hurricanes?"

"This isn't the season for hurricanes. No hurricanes in January."

"You might get eaten by sharks."

"So . . . I get eaten by sharks."

"My God, Harry!" Her face was twisted, her eyes angry.

"Don't you care about *anything?*"

"I'll get there," Harry said. He looked off down the beach. "There's Blake. I guess I'd better tell him I won't be sailing back."

Blake was a small, wizened, unnautical-appearing man with a face of pickled pine, pale tan with liver spots. He had a gleaming black hairpiece and black eyes. In the evening when he headed off for dinner with his friends at the Casa Montega, his white dinner jacket was very long, making his legs look short, which in fact they were. He spoke avidly of Cannes, Deauville, the Greek Isles, as if for a successful man the world had not enough destinations. One evening instead of going for dinner at the Casa Montega, he had eaten on the boat with the members of the crew, entertaining them with anecdotes. His favorite race was the biennial race from Newport, Rhode Island, to Bermuda. "The wives and girls all fly over and wait for the boats to come in . . . " His black eyes gleamed. "You can imagine what it's like, particularly after a very tough crossing, thirty-foot waves one year, not knowing whether you're going to live or die and suddenly life is very sweet and there on the quay is something beautiful in a bikini or in a white dress with a parasol, waiting in the sunlight. You can imagine what it's like. The tension and the release. The sex is incredible. For three days everybody up to the kneecaps in semen. You can just imagine." "How is that word spelled?" one of the guys muttered. "What—semen?" Blake looked puzzled. The guys on the boat didn't think Blake was very bright. Rich but not bright and not a very good sailor. They hadn't done very well coming over from Miami and Harry wouldn't mind missing the race back.

Blake was a friend of Fontaine's, or perhaps more accurately a toady of Fontaine's. Like Fontaine he had a private plane at his disposal. Now in flowered swim trunks and matching flowered shirt he stood on the beach and watched as Harry and Elaine approached. Harry told him that because of the boat he would not be racing back to Miami.

Blake seemed unconcerned. His eyes were upon Elaine. He asked her if she would like to fly over to Port au Prince for the evening, "just for the hell of it."

Elaine said no.

Blake said he was organizing a scavenger hunt and maybe she'd like to be in on it. "Just a few of us with private planes," he explained.

"Gee," she said. "An *aerial scavenger hunt!*"

"How about that!" Blake said.

"Wow!" she said and Harry could see now that she was putting him on. "What are some of the treasure things going to be?"

"Got any suggestions?"

"Mmmmm—a hooker . . . from Haiti?"

"That might be impractical," Blake said.

"You could give it a try."

Blake chuckled.

"A douche bag from any Miami drugstore."

Blake looked at her uncertainly. He now transferred his attention to Harry. "Remind me to talk to you back on the boat," he said.

Harry assumed he would be asked to change his mind and race with them to Miami but it wasn't about racing. After supper Blake got him aside up on the foredeck and said, "Listen, Harry, not that it's any of my business, but do you think it's really a good idea for you to be seeing that girl so much? You may be playing with dynamite."

"I'm not worried about it," Harry said, looking him in the eye.

"But that's just my point, maybe you *should* be, my friend. I know a little something about Mel Fontaine. He's a very powerful man and that's private property you're fooling around with in case you don't know it. Listen, man, you've got a nice boat yard. People like it, and they like you, but—things could change."

Harry turned. In the fading light he peered up at the rigging. "That mast doesn't look quite straight," he said. "It could use a little tuning."

"Maybe you'll tune it for me before we leave."

Harry said he would.

"Listen," Blake said, "I've noticed that she's the one who's doing the chasing, not the other way around, but maybe that's not the way Mel Fontaine will see it."

"Screw it," Harry said. "It's not your problem. Besides, the week's about over."

This was Wednesday night. The race back to Miami would begin on Saturday. Fontaine was scheduled to return on Friday and Elaine had asked Harry if he would take her out to dinner on Thursday evening as a rite of farewell.

Harry spent Thursday on his new boat. In late afternoon he returned to Blake's big white yawl, put on a clean shirt and was walking back down the pier when he saw Fontaine sitting in the cockpit of *Iceman*. He looked up as Harry passed. "Good evening," he said.

"Good evening," Harry said and walked on, dropping from the pier to the beach, walking a short distance and then turning when he heard his name called.

Elaine was running after him, wearing the same yellow dress she had worn the first night when she and Fontaine had gone off into the twilight. Her feet were bare.

Drawing near, she said, "He's back. He came back early."

Harry nodded. "I can see that." Fontaine was watching them from the cockpit.

"God*damn* him!" she said.

"Is that the way you talk about the man you love?"

"I'm worried that I'll never see you again, you bastard."

"Thanks."

She was looking into the falling sun. "I'd like to see you again, Harry."

"Maybe on a race someday," he said. "If you're still racing."

"Seriously. I want to *see* you."

"Why?"

"Because I *do*."

"What would come of it?"

"Maybe something."

He looked out over the water, not replying, then looked back toward the boat. Fontaine was on his feet; now he was disappearing below.

"Harry . . . "

"So long, Elaine. Good luck. No kidding. Good luck. Take care of yourself."

"Harry!"

"So long." Patting her shoulder, he started off. When he turned he saw her walking slowly back toward *Iceman*.

On Saturday Harry watched the big boats sail out beyond the reef, where they got a starting gun and headed for Miami.

For three more days he worked on his boat, and then, with stopgap repairs and jerry-rigging, he set out for Florida, hoping he wouldn't get any of the thirty-foot waves described by Blake, but in southern waters it was the time of the year for calm weather. The winds were good and the days were fair and he made it to Miami in ten days. Entering the Inland Waterway at the first opportunity, he headed north and after another two weeks he turned into the Chesapeake and a couple of days later into the Choptank River. Near the head of a remote creek lay his father's boat yard, a small simple yard the most prominent feature of which was an old faded aluminum diner which had been towed in and set in place. His father used one end of it as an office and the other end as a shop where he could work in bad weather.

Jonathan Crowder was past forty when Harry was born. He was the same age as the century—seventy-nine—when he died. He was a gentle man—tough as leather but gentle and humble and shy—and the best sailor Harry had ever known. From his father he had learned all he knew about boats and sailing.

Regatta

His father was a waterman. Much of his life he earned his living oystering and crabbing. Like many watermen he left the water upon occasion. At various times in his life he had been an automobile mechanic, a painter and a carpenter, but he always went back to the water or some place very near it. To help send Harry to college he had worked on the water by day and as a security guard at night.

On the day Harry reached the creek in his damaged boat he had been in Annapolis almost two years, but in this job he wanted his father's know-how. He wanted to rebuild the boat under his father's eye.

Harry loved the creek. It was a place where in spring and summer, heron glided along the wooded banks and mud turtles popped their heads from the water. This was early February but the worst of the winter was gone. In unseasonably warm weather he and his father had set to work, gouging out the damaged material, laying bare a gaping hole above the waterline on the port quarter, then building up layers of fiberglass, thickness upon thickness, gradually filling the hole, sanding, shaping, molding and gel-coating until the new work was a smooth blend with the hull, and when the hull work was done, replacing the rigging and rebuilding the bow pulpit which had been sheared off in the collision. Finally, they had painted the boat yellow and, at his father's suggestion, named it *Sundance*. There on the creek, working on the boat that February, had been the last happy time Harry had ever spent with his father.

In March had come the heart attack. For two months his father had sat, impatiently recuperating, while Harry had driven down from Annapolis twice a week to visit him in his rooming house. Then, in May, against his doctor's orders and without Harry's knowledge, his father had raced a log canoe and dropped dead at the tiller.

Four

HARRY'S BOAT YARD was in southeast Annapolis in a section known as Eastport. Like the rest of the town, Eastport was changing fast. In recent years the shoreline and skyline were being increasingly dominated by high-rise condominiums and it was just a question of time before the rest of the waterfront was gobbled up by developers, but in certain sections the streets were still lined with shade trees and modest old row houses, and there was still room for boat yards and sail lofts.

In the deal for his yard Harry had also gotten himself a place to live—right on the grounds. The house was there first and years later the boat yard had been built around it. Little about the house was orthodox. From a distance it had the appearance of a bygone America, a vertical frame shaft resembling perhaps a railroad blockhouse, tall and forlorn, its grey siding shabby in the dim orange lighting of the boat-yard parking lot. The house's best feature was its view. On the creek side there was a cement patio from which a flight of crude stone steps descended directly into the water. At low tide as many as six steps were exposed; at high tide perhaps two. From the patio there was an unbroken view across the waters of Annapolis harbor.

Inside the gates of the yard stood a low frame building where Harry had his office, and off to the left a much larger building which he rented out as a sail loft. Strewn about the grounds were empty cradles. These in winter held boats which had been hauled out for storage. In spring and summer boats were placed upon them while their bottoms were being scraped and painted. At dockside were two large cranes used to lift boats from the water onto the cradles.

Friday was a heavy shopping night and it took Harry

much longer to make his purchases than he had planned. By the time he turned from the street and passed through the gates it was eight-thirty and nearly dark. Pulling into the small parking strip behind the house, he went first into his office, an unimpressive cubicle with ill-fitted plasterboard walls and dominated by a massive, diagonally set desk fashioned from an old door. On this desk were a telephone, piles of literature from boating supply companies, and a sheaf of telephone messages. In the light of gooseneck lamp he looked through them. One was from Elaine: "Elaine Fowler called again—same message, come to yacht club." Another was from a customer complaining about the amount of a bill for bottom-painting. In some Annapolis yards by summer of 1979 labor charges were as high as twenty dollars an hour. Harry's yard was comparatively small. He employed only three men, his operation was reasonably simple and so far he had been able to hold labor charges to sixteen. His paint jobs ran less than those of the large yards but even so there were plenty of complaints. Somebody else was complaining about a through-hull fitting. Harry knew about this one. One of his workmen, a hotshot sailor named Gus Whitney, had done a sloppy job on it; and although firing a man was not something that came easy to him, Harry had already fired him for it.

Another message had been left on his desk by Sam Hooper, his good right arm. It said, "Call me tonight. If I'm not home I'll be at Marmaduke's." Sam was Harry's yard foreman, and in sailing races his spinnaker man and top crewman. Marmaduke's was a local tavern.

Finally there was a message from a man named Walters Hackett and Harry sat briefly frowning over it. "Mr. Hackett called," it said, "and wants to tell you he's sailing in the race tomorrow. He says good luck."

Harry folded the message slip and cleaned his thumbnail with it. Walters Hackett was the one who would need good luck. Hackett was a retired plumbing fixtures executive who had moved to Oxford from New Jersey and

thereupon bought himself a twenty-seven–foot sailboat
without knowing the first thing about sailing. Before his
heart attack, Harry's father had done a lot of work for
Hackett, changing some of his rigging, adding a stern pulpit, installing an electric bilge pump, mounting a compass
and a knot-meter and answering innumerable questions.
That spring, on the days when he drove down to Oxford to
visit his father, Harry had taken time to give Hackett and
his wife a few sailing lessons on the Tred Avon. He was
doing it mainly for his father, because they had spent so
much money with his father and been such good customers.
But he also felt sorry for the Hacketts. Their need was
acute. Hackett was in his mid-sixties with his wife about the
same age, and in spite of what Harry had tried to teach them
they still didn't know much. Hackett had mentioned entering the race but the last Harry heard he hadn't been able to
get himself a crew. Hackett, at his age and with his limited
experience, had no business taking on the challenge of a
thirty-one–mile race down to Oxford but he was a bull-
headed old bastard and was obviously going to take his
chances.

Harry looked again at the message from Elaine. In the
six months since Montego Bay he had thought about her
very little even though he had been flattered by her attention and even though he could acknowledge that she was a
beautiful girl. On the occasions when he did think about her
he would think about her beautiful face and body and then
invariably he would remember what she had told him about
her father, and he would feel all over again the disgust and
the sadness and the pity.

Turning off the gooseneck lamp, Harry closed the office,
walked across the graveled lot to his car and began unload-
ing his provisions. Once they had been deposited in the
kitchen he passed into the living room and turned on a
lamp. The house, like his office, was sparely furnished. In
the living room there was a television set and a couple of
easy chairs, a low table covered with boating magazines.

The stark white walls rose to a high ceiling. He had once done a little photography and the walls were hung with photographs which he himself had taken. There was a close-up of his father at the helm of a boat, an old man in a faded blue shirt buttoned at the neck, his face grizzled, his white hair still thick, lifting a little in the breeze. There was a huge enlargement of a snapshot he had taken of a Chesapeake Bay log canoe in full sail. A heron standing slim as a stick, immobile at the edge of a creek. The photographs showed where his heart lay. His heart was still on the Eastern Shore.

Slowly he climbed the creaking stairway to his bedroom, where the furnishings were no more elaborate than elsewhere. It was a small room. There was a large daybed without a headboard, and next to the bed a table and lamp. On the wall above his dresser hung a picture of his son, an enlargement of a color snapshot he had taken, framed without a matte so that from a distance it looked somewhat like an oil painting. It was a good picture, one of the first he had ever taken, and he had captured the kid at a special age, just as he was moving out of babyhood. He was smiling an angelic smile, the light fell over his already darkening blond hair, there was space between his two upper front teeth, baby teeth. In the picture his head and torso were erect and he was squatting on his haunches like a little frog, and on his feet were his very first shoes, a pair of blue sneakers piped in white.

It was the age when his son had just begun walking, the age when all he could say was tick-tock and kitty-cat, and all day he went staggering around in yellow corduroy overalls, with his hands up in the air—for what? Balance . . . fear . . . apprehension . . . to ward off all the evil that might come to somebody sixteen months old; to ward off the evil that would come from falling; or whatever other evil. But even with his hands aloft he kept grinning and laughing. To Harry it was dumfounding. To him it was a miracle that from a swollen stomach could come this thing that went staggering around on chubby legs with the blue tennis shoes, saying tick-tock and kitty-cat. Now sometimes when he thought about it, he felt something that was love and ecstasy but which was also very close to agony.

When Marcia walked out, the tennis shoes were left behind. Roger was on his second pair by then. The first pair was already too small and had worn spots. After Marcia and his son were gone Harry found one of the shoes under the bed—he never found the other one. Picking up the one shoe, he looked at it for a long time and presently he got a folding ruler and measured it. It was exactly five inches long and two inches wide and the length surprised him because while five inches was small, on his son's foot it had looked even smaller, particularly with the white cotton socks, not folded over but standing up straight like a man's sweat socks, and above the socks the chubby legs disappearing into the yellow corduroy overalls.

Now he was almost nine and each summer, always in August, he came down to be with Harry. So much of their time together had been spent in a boat, sometimes just he and the boy but more often the three of them, himself and his son and his father, and the three generations in the boat gave him a good feeling. Sometimes in the boat he found himself looking at the boy very closely, wondering what they had told the kid about him. Whatever it was, the kid wasn't showing it. He was cool, like Marcia. He bore their mark, Philip's and Marcia's mark, and Harry recognized this. It was as if he were their child, Philip's child, not his, that he was being made in Philip's mold with Philip's ideas of right and wrong, and he knew he should be grateful because it could have been much worse.

When the kid came down from Boston it was usually Philip who came along to make the switch. Philip, slender, grey at the temples, tortoise-shell glasses, a quick smile quickly fading, scholarly, confident, and to Harry's disappointment not at all soft; beneath the exterior there was a lot of iron. He could pick no holes in Philip and their relationship was very civil.

Only once had Marcia come. At the Baltimore airport they had a drink between planes, she arriving with the kid on one plane and taking the very next one back to Boston, the kid sitting there with them at the table, looking a lot like Marcia, reserved, polite, grinning when spoken to, looking up from the magazine he was poring over so intently. Marcia was impersonal. It was amazing how impersonal she was.

This year, or next year at the latest, the boy would be flying down alone and then in a few more years the day would come when the visits, the arranged visits, would end because the kid would be old enough to be independent, free to arrange his own time and his vacations and his own visits. And then what? Now Harry was being given his parental rights but when the boy grew older the test would come. Then Harry would have to make it on his own. Would the kid like him, would he admire him, would he be his friend? He couldn't be sure and he didn't like to think about it. In the days when he was still drinking, when he thought about it very much he sometimes went out and got drunk.

Harry went down to the kitchen and put away his provisions. When the telephone rang he thought it would be Sam, but it was Marcia, calling from Boston.

"Harry . . . " Her voice was tentative, and because she never called him except about travel arrangements for the boy; and because it was still too early to be talking about travel arrangements, and because Marcia was never tentative, always crisp, he had a strong feeling that something was wrong.

"Is Roger okay?" he asked.

"Yes, he's fine," she said. "Just fine . . . How are you, Harry?"

"Okay," he said. "Working hard. Thanks for your note, it was very nice." His father was the one member of his clan that she had genuinely liked and she had written a note when he died.

"I was so terribly sorry," she said, and he could tell that she meant it.

"Thanks," he said.

Then she plunged straight in. Philip was going to Switzerland to a place on the shores of Lake Lucerne to be an adviser to somebody or other about something or other and she was going with him and they were thinking how wonderful it would be to take the boy, and the only trouble was that it would be smack in the middle of August. "It just came up yesterday," she said.

The previous owner had had the telephone company install a long walkaround telephone cord and Harry paced from the kitchen all the way into the living room. Through the one window, sparkling off to the left, were the lights of Annapolis. To the right lay the outer harbor, with its patterns of fixed and flashing red, white, and green lights, spreading out toward the bay.

"Harry . . . "

"I heard you," he said.

"Maybe I shouldn't even ask," she said. "I'll simply forget it if you've made your plans, and I know you have."

He had made no particular plans. It would, of course, be different this year because his father wouldn't be around and they wouldn't be in Oxford. Whatever boating they did would be out in the bay near Annapolis, but he had thought he might take the boy to Washington to do some sightseeing and to Baltimore to see a baseball game, and he had bought a rollaway cot.

He took a deep breath.

"I can tell I shouldn't have called," she said. "Listen, Harry, it's very simple. It's your time. It's your time with him and I won't do anything—not anything to interfere with it. It's all yours. Why don't you just forget I called."

"Where's Roger?"

"Right here."

"Listening?"

"Well . . . he's right here beside me, yes."

"He wants to go?"

"He wants to do what you . . . want him to do. That comes first."

"Okay. Tell him it's okay."

"Are you *sure*?"

"You say it's a big opportunity and it sounds like it would be. I won't stand in the way. For God's sake go. Maybe he can come down for Thanksgiving."

From the other end there was deep silence.

"Listen, it's settled," he said. "Tell him I said it's okay. Perfectly okay. So let's say it's all settled. Have a good time and take care of yourself. Goodbye."

"Are you *sure*?"

"I'm sure. Goodbye."

"Okay, thanks, Harry. Goodbye."

He stood there with the receiver in his hand for a moment, looking out over the harbor, then walked it back to the kitchen and hung it up.

Three minutes later he picked it up again and dialed. Marcia answered.

"Listen," he said, "is he still there?"

"He's gone downstairs."

"Can I speak to him a second?"

"Certainly . . . I'll call him . . . "

A moment later he came on. "Dad? Hi."

There was a click indicating that Marcia had hung up the upstairs phone.

"How are you, old buddy?"

"Fine. Okay. How are *you*?" His voice was big and brave.

"I'm just fine, Rog. Listen, I wanted to talk to you about Switzerland. I just want you to know that it's okay. It's a great thing for you to do. It's a very interesting country and this is a wonderful chance so don't feel bad about it, okay? It wouldn't be quite the same this year without Pop, so let's just say we're giving ourselves a year to get over it, sort of.

And you can come down Thanksgiving instead. Thanksgiving can be really nice, still warm, and the rock may still be biting. We'll take the boat out and maybe drive down to Oxford and on down to the wildlife sanctuary below Cambridge. See a bald eagle. Okay?"

"Okay, Dad."

"Send me a postcard."

"Okay, Dad."

"Okay, son . . . " Harry's voice started to break. "You just concentrate on having a good time. And—well, like I say . . . send me a postcard."

"Okay, Dad, I will."

"Okay, Roger Dodger . . . Good night, buddy . . . "

"Good night, Dad."

Harry hung up the phone again. In the kitchen he stood in the dark with his eyes closed.

After a while he went upstairs, changed his clothes, came back down and called Sam to see what he wanted. When there was no answer he left for the yacht club but when he got there somebody told him that Mel Fontaine and his girl had just left, so Harry went back to his car and headed for Marmaduke's in search of Sam Hooper.

Five

ONCE THE IMPROMPTU QUESTIONING was over, Fontaine and Elaine left the yacht club as they had entered, moving in a stately promenade, Fontaine smiling left and right, favoring those present with little half-salutes of farewell. The girl's face was a smooth mask, betraying none of the irritation and disappointment she felt that Harry Crowder had not responded to her telephone message, but she had already determined that she would damn well not let the evening pass without seeing him. To see him was very important to her. Very very important.

To accommodate his boat while it was in Annapolis, Fontaine had slip space at a marina less than three blocks from the yacht club. He and Elaine started walking, hip close to hip, his hand hanging loosely over her shoulder, her stilt heels clicking on the sidewalk. After half a block or so, as they left the more brightly lighted area behind, his hand reached into her blouse, methodically unbuttoning the buttons until the blouse swung wide open. Then he removed his hand. They walked the rest of the way in silence, and even as they stood at the curb, waiting for a car to pass, bathed in its headlights, she made no attempt to close the blouse or even to turn aside. It was a sequence that turned him on, and she was complying without giving it much thought.

Iceman was berthed in the favored slip, the one nearest shore, and for almost anyone it would have been hard not to be impressed by the boat's size, the height of its mast, the sleek beauty of its lines. In the light of a half-moon, ripples lapped gently against the hull. Shadows fell over the deck from the spars and rigging. Elaine did not notice. For her, its beauty was so familiar that it was beauty no longer.

As they neared the slip they were hailed by the marina owner—himself a crack yachtsman and a man long known to Fontaine. He sauntered down over the lawn from a brick cottage in which a dim light burned. "Your boys have all gone ashore," he called.

"Yeah," Fontaine replied. "I told them they could. Sailing tomorrow, Paul?"

Elaine buttoned one button. Reaching down to grasp the stern line, she pulled the boat closer to the dock, stepped into the cockpit and disappeared below. In a few minutes she returned with two glasses. Fontaine exchanged a few more words with the marina owner and stepped aboard. She handed one of the glasses to him and they sat in the cockpit, one across from the other. The cockpit contained a dazzling array of navigation instruments. Their dials were mounted with symmetry and balance in the bulkhead, where they could easily be read by a man at the wheel.

Elaine let her head fall back, looking up at the clouds which now veiled the moon. There was a faint breeze from the east, showing up in the tips of the trees over the brick cottage where Paul, the marina owner, lived.

Fontaine was sprawled on the cockpit seat with his feet elevated, resting his heels on the spokes of the large chrome wheel used by the helmsman, his left arm hooked back around one of the huge chrome winches, his drink on the seat beside him.

"I'll be going back to the yacht club for a while," he said.

She knew why he was going. Very much against his will, his daughter Mary Ann was a neophyte television actress. She was appearing that night and he was going to the yacht club to watch her. Elaine knew that he would not ask her to go with him and under the circumstances she was glad of it. Under almost any circumstances she would have been glad of it. His daughter hated her—and hated Fontaine.

Withdrawing his arm from the winch, he began lighting a pipe, slowly, deliberately, his face thoughtful in the flare of the match. Smoke billowed about his face and drifted off with the breeze.

Sipping his drink, he set down the glass and looked back over his shoulder. The marina owner had gone back into his house for a moment but now he stood in the open doorway, silhouetted in dim orange light. Soon he stepped out and walked slowly about the lawn, pausing now and then to look up at the sky, checking the weather.

Fontaine was looking at the girl. "Anything wrong?" he asked quietly.

"No," she said. "Why?"

He drew steadily on the pipe, not replying.

Presently Elaine asked, "Won't you miss her?"

"I have plenty of time . . . " He tilted his watch to the

faint light coming up through the open hatch.

"Well . . . " She looked over her shoulder and then got slowly to her feet. "I'm going down."

"Go right ahead."

"I hope it's okay," she said.

"Thanks." He extended his hand. She touched it and then turned away. "I'll be back as soon as it's over," he said.

In *Iceman*'s aftercabin a single light burned. More private and slightly larger than *Iceman*'s other accommodations, the cabin was far from spacious, and its furnishings were spare as they would be on any yacht engaged in trying to win sailing races, even one as large as *Iceman*. There was a double bunk and two hanging lockers, both with doors ajar. In one hung Elaine's blouses. Visible in the other were a couple of sports jackets, one of yellow plaid and one of deep red. Over one of the doors hung a white bathing suit.

Elaine still carried the book she had been reading at dinner. Tossing it onto the bunk, she turned off the lamp and crossed to the porthole. Its window was open. She heard Fontaine clear his throat and she could smell the smoke from his pipe. A few moments longer she stood there and then lay on the bunk, her eyes closed, waiting, wondering if it was true that she was finally going to do something about the whore's life she had been living now for almost eight years.

When Elaine was a child in North Carolina, her older sister read her lovely fairy tales about beautiful girls and handsome princes but when she was nine her mother died and her sister moved away. It was after this that her father began to beat her. When she was still young she had thought he was beating her for misdeeds but now, in the light of some of the things she had read and of what had happened later, she suspected that he had beaten her because he was yearning for her body. If she was right, her father could be given credit for at first resisting what he felt —even though his only effective resistance was to beat her.

In any event she no longer believed that beating her represented the stark cruelty that she had once thought it to be. By now her reading had led her to believe or strongly suspect that in beating her he was punishing her—for stirring him to feel what he was feeling. He was trying to beat the allure out of her. Not knowing what was happening to him, he had struck her in panic. Not knowing what was happening to him, he cared enough to beat her for it—even though he knew she was of course innocent of any misdoing, except what might be considered the crime of arousing him to unseemly passions. Back then, at ten, eleven, twelve, there had seemed nothing complex about his behavior. He had simply been a man of great and coarse cruelty, his face bronzed and fleshy, the thick grey hair curling out from under his John Deere farm cap.

The night before she was fifteen, his resistance disappeared. By then he was remarried and his wife, Elaine's stepmother, was in the hospital in Rocky Mount with an appendectomy. He had by then already stopped caring for his new wife and had taken to abusing her instead of abusing Elaine. He had just lost a job and was drinking heavily. At fifteen, Elaine was extraordinarily beautiful and had been since she was eleven. After school, in the afternoon and early evening, she worked at a diner. On the second night of her stepmother's hospitalization, she returned from the diner to find her father drinking beer and watching television, just as he usually did. That night when she was asleep he came into her room and covered her body with his own, sobbing and saying, "My baby, my baby, oh my beautiful baby, my beautiful baby . . . " over and over again, on and on, never stopping. She struggled at first and then could struggle no longer.

The next morning she fled to her sister, moved in with her, and her father did not come looking for her. After three days she told her sister about it and for a short while her sister talked of going to the police and then to an aunt, but they went to no one. Her sister was not a strong person and she was every bit as afraid of the father as Elaine was. Her sister became resigned and tried to comfort her by turning philosophical. "Shoot, honey," she said, "back up there in the hills, way back up in the country, there's so doggone much going on, fathers and daughters and brothers and sisters and first cousins and I don't know what-all. A girl I knew in high school, she told me once when she was twelve years old her stepfather did it to her and made her own mother sit right there on the edge of the bed and watch. Her mother just sitting there and crying while he was doing it. Both of them scared to death of him."

Those were days of misery. She shared her secret with no one else. Even though her sister loved her, sharing it with her sister had not really helped. Sometimes at night she woke up trembling. She had always been considered bright but now in high school she was failing her subjects. Years later she would read a pretentious article which asked: "Is a daughter ever totally innocent? Ever totally unaware? Father and daughter stand facing each other across the snakepit." The article posed a question which at fifteen she had dimly sensed. It was a time when books and movies were filled with stories of devil-children, of devil-in-the-flesh explanations of evil. She began to wonder about the evil within her. It was as if in her mind his sin had become hers. Every day she lived in dread that he would come to take her back but he never did. He didn't come near the diner and didn't come near her sister's apartment. One afternoon at the diner she met a man named Marioso and that night went off with him in a silver Alfa Romeo. Nobody came looking for her.

In her fifteen-year-old mind, Marioso planted fatuous theories about the nature of slavery. In a master-slave relationship, he told her, the slave had all the better of it. Upon the master fell the burden of responsibility. To be a slave was to be free; to be an owner was to be a slave. A love-slave lived in a dark velvet nest.

To Elaine, so desperately in need, it had seemed a comforting theory and to embrace it helped her to live with herself. It also helped to think that the life she was living was highly sophisticated. Hardly more than a nymphet, she already looked old for her age. Marioso clothed her in short dresses and anklets and bracelets and he painted her eyes with makeup. He took her to Las Vegas and to casinos in the Bahamas. She began to feel that she had a sort of worldly identity, a sophisticated image that linked her with the most illustrious of courtesans. She was living in a world apart, a long way from the diner, a long way from high school in a small North Carolina town, and a long long way from the dizzying, suffocating minutes with her father in the bedroom, and the months of misery that followed.

Now, listening intently, she raised herself on an elbow but there was no sound from Fontaine. Water softly lapped the hull and from the street nearby there was the sound of passing cars. She got up and went to the cabin window again and looked out at the boats in the other slips. Lights burned in some of the cabins and from the afterdeck of one there came the sound of plaintive music. A woman's soft laughter floated over the water. There were ten slips, each one filled with an expensive chunk of sailing machinery. The aggregate cost of the ten had to be more than three million dollars. The world of yachting was expensive. It was a world she knew well by now. For after the gambler Marioso and others much worse she had gone on to yachtsmen and as she moved from one to the next and finally to Fontaine she continued to accept the benefits conferred by master upon slave—the creature comforts, the good food and drink; sun and spray and the long indolent afternoons on the boat; the fun of flitting about the Caribbean; the company of the men who inhabited the yachting world. Some were coarse and vapid, as heavily stupid as her father, but many were accomplished and highly intelligent, and although a few might pretend indifference they were almost to a man deeply taken by her dark beauty.

Fontaine was not only glamorous, he was also considerate and kind, and she accepted him as a prize. Barely twenty-one, with little responsibility save to sleep with him, she let the days drift by. Lounging on the foredeck as the long beautiful hull slid through the waves, she could believe that her legs would always be slim and firm and tanned. It was as if she had escaped unscarred. Seeing the blue and white water stretching to the horizon, she could believe that youth and beauty were all that mattered and that they would never end. And when Fontaine began to take an interest in her mind, began to help her and educate her, she could almost believe that she was living in one of the fairy tales her sister had read to her long ago.

The fairy tales had not come true for her sister. Almost twenty-seven when Elaine was born, her sister was the only person in the family she had ever cared about and just eight months earlier, on a warm and humid November day in North Carolina, she had gone to her funeral. Her sister had lived in a yellow brick apartment house resembling a barracks. She had a corner apartment with a view of the Shoney's Big Boy where she took many of her meals. In the other direction was a view of the diner, now abandoned, where Elaine at fifteen had met Frank Marioso and gone off with him in his silver Alfa Romeo. Her sister had died of uterine cancer from the estrogen she was taking to keep vibrant for her job at the small-loan office; to keep free of wrinkles, to keep menstruating; kept alive to die in the yellow brick building, rarely missing Thursday-night choir practice at the Bethel Baptist church, or midday Sunday dinner at the Ramada Inn on the outskirts of town.

When word came from the marine operator, Elaine decided that she must go, even though she could hardly bear the thought of encountering her father, whom she still had not seen in all the years since the rape. By now he was married a third time. He and his wife spent a good part of each day surf-fishing, seated on the beach in folding canvas chairs, drinking beer and watching the rods they had stuck into the sand, waiting for the tips to bend against the sky.

There were twin half-brothers, twin farmers, still in their teens, whom she hardly knew. Her father had procreated early and late.

She would take the chance. If she came close to her father she would look through him. She would pretend he did not exist.

Fontaine made available the pilot and the plane. He would have gone with her if she had asked but she didn't want him there to see and be seen by her father and the new wife and the half-brothers and by the shuffling relatives in their ill-fitting suits and white shirts that were too large for their tanned, wrinkled necks.

Wearing a black dress, her face cleansed of makeup, she sat in the last pew with the pilot beside her, and in their rental car they drove afterward to the cemetery, where her sister was buried next to her mother. Her father, red, beefy and coarse in a shiny black suit, stood on the far side of the open grave. As the minister began to speak she saw him leering and smirking. He had been drinking. Even before the body was lowered he began circling and cut her off on the way to the car. "Hey-o there, Eelaine . . . " He had always mispronounced her name. So had her sister and all the rest of the family. Only her mother had pronounced it correctly. "Hey-o there, Eelaine, it's your daddy. Don't you recognize your daddy?"

She tried staring through him, as she had vowed to do, but she felt faint; wanted to pour out her hatred but the words wouldn't come. She felt something horrifying. Complex and horrifying. She ran to the car. "Start it up, start it up, let's go," she sobbed. "The fucking sonofabitch fucking sonofabitch fucking sonofabitch . . . " The pilot got the car in motion. Her father stood there faintly grinning as they drove off down the graveled lane of the cemetery.

Her sister's funeral was a turning point. It was after the funeral that she began to read about incest. At the same time she let herself begin to think about what had happened to her as a child, when for so many years she had blocked it from her mind. Incest as a serious problem was barely explored. Surprisingly little had been written but from what she read she was at first able to take comfort. It helped to know about all the many others who had experienced what she had experienced. It helped to have the problem stated in a detached, analytical, even statistical way. So much of it seemed related to her own experience. Studies showed that an incestuous father, for example, was likely to be a heavy drinker, a man who changed jobs frequently, a man who dominated his family. Often there were crowded living conditions. Often the mother worked the night shift. Often the father had little schooling.

Yet it was a mistake to assume, as her sister had seemed to assume, that it went on only back up in the "hill country" or in the ghetto. Incest was a taboo, and taboos were not wasted upon desires that did not exist. Incest was not confined to the poor. It was everywhere, in all sections of the country and in all classes of society. In her own case it had been once and never again, but often it developed into a marriagelike state with the father or stepfather taking the role of husband and the daughter the role of wife. Almost all cases had one thing in common: secrecy. Secret shame.

She was listening intently. Overhead a foot scraped. The cockpit was directly above her cabin and now she heard the rattle of ice cubes in his glass. He was taking his time, doubtless putting it off as long as possible, not really wanting to go, yet unable to stay away. She felt sorry for him, which was a good sign, she thought, because it meant she no longer idolized him as she once had done. She felt great affection for him as well as enormous gratitude, but she did not like what he had made of her and she knew it was time to leave him, yet she knew that for many reasons it would not be easy. It would not be easy even to tell him, but once the race was over she would do it.

Sitting on the edge of the bed, she felt the movement of the boat, a slight gentle rocking which indicated that Fontaine had pulled it close to the dock. Now she heard him step off.

Waiting a moment or two longer, she kicked off the spike heels, padded into the main cabin and started then up the companionway ladder. She could hear his voice and now she could see him, talking to the man named Paul. They were standing near a white picket fence that lined the sidewalk, talking in low tones.

Climbing the final two steps, she stood waiting. The moon slipped out from the veil of clouds and its pale light touched her face.

Fontaine opened a gate and closed it behind him. Paul went back into his house and Fontaine started walking in the direction of the yacht club.

Elaine went back down to her cabin, put on a pair of sandals and left, buttoning her blouse as she went.

Six

FIVE MINUTES after leaving the marina where his boat was berthed, Fontaine was opening the front door of the yacht club. Refrigerated air rushed to meet him. Ahead lay the stairway to the lounge and as he was going up a young man in white jeans and a pink shirt was coming down. The young man's head jerked around. "Mr. Fontaine?" From three steps above, Fontaine turned.

"Mr. Fontaine," the young man said, "my name is Gus Whitney. Could I talk to you a second, please?"

Gus Whitney was tall and husky, with the beginnings of a beard matching the shade of his thick blond hair. "What's on your mind?" Fontaine asked.

"I'm just wondering, sir, if by any chance you're in the market for any new crew members. I don't mean for tomorrow's race. I mean for your permanent crew."

Fontaine looked down at him without replying. "I've been sailing Cal-25s," the boy went on, "and doing pretty well so far."

"Are you racing down to Oxford tomorrow?" Fontaine asked.

"Yes sir, I'm racing my -25."

"Gus—*Whitney?*"

"Yes sir."

"What do you do for a living, Gus?"

"Mostly I've been working in boat yards."

"Are you working now?"

"No. No, I'm not."

Fontaine nodded. "Find me in Oxford tomorrow night, Gus. Maybe we can work something out." Fontaine took another step and turned. "Are you married?"

"Separated."

"Okay, find me in Oxford and we'll talk about it." Fontaine took another step and turned again. "What would you do with your boat? We're pulling out from Oxford Sunday."

"I can get my wife to sail it back. She's racing down with me tomorrow."

"I thought you said you were separated."

"Yes sir, I am—but she still crews for me."

Fontaine nodded. He stood there looking down at Gus Whitney, studying him closely. "I think we should be able to work something out. Bring along your gear and see me in Oxford."

"Thank you sir. Thank you *very* much."

Fontaine went on up the stairway and into the lounge. By now the lounge was empty and so too was the bar. On the eve of the race everybody had left early. Fontaine approached the bar and took a seat on one of the stools. He was recognized by the bartender, who greeted him with deference. "Mr. Fontaine . . . what can I do for you, sir?"

A large color television set hung from the wall behind the bar. At his request the bartender switched it on and then tuned it to the proper channel. As the picture faded in, Fontaine looked over his shoulder. He had the place to himself.

That evening a young actress known as Jeanne Roselle was being seen coast-to-coast, playing a small part in a very long-running private-eye show. Her history as a television actress was brief. Following a small part in a daytime soap serial she had landed a spot in a beer commercial and the response had been warm enough to lead to her present assignment. From the beer commercial her face was already familiar all across the country. At the William Morris agency they were very high on her. She had a slim body, dark eyes, thick dark hair cut short and a nicely shaped mouth.

Jeanne Roselle was Fontaine's daughter Mary Ann.

Sipping ginger ale, Fontaine watched the screen. It was an hour program and he had already missed almost fifteen minutes, but he knew from an advance copy of the script that she had not yet been on. Filling the screen now was the face of an aging movie actress, very much down on her luck, who had been given a spot as special guest star. The picture faded into a couple of thirty-second commercials and when these were done he sat waiting for a glimpse of Jeanne Roselle.

He waited with impatience. Fontaine had contempt for what he watched. Indeed, he had contempt for most television, as well as for television audiences. He was amazed by those who watched the trash that was offered. Who *were* these people, these people whose ancestors had founded this country? Easily pleased, people, sitting in studios and laughing on cue at inanities; sitting in the darkness across the land, ogling whores and hoods and making it fabulously profitable for those who purveyed the fare they so willingly lapped up. He never failed to find them a source of amazement.

Fontaine's parents were second-generation French who grew grapes in Napa Valley, California. His upbringing was modest. After high school he was sent to business school to master shorthand and typing, for his father had a theory about how a young man in America might best advance himself. An intelligent and highly proficient male secretary would be greatly in demand, the father reasoned, and there could be no quicker pathway to the confidence of a powerful executive. On that night in 1979, Fontaine could still type a hundred words a minute and was still skilled in shorthand even though he no longer had occasion to use it. As a young man he had taken his skills down to Hollywood where at twenty-four he became private secretary to Mark Dandridge, one of the legendary film moguls, a man of great power, extraordinary cynicism, and some cruelty. Fontaine was there in time to witness the last few years of Hollywood's golden age and the last high-energy years of his boss, a crustaceous monster who devoured beautiful young women.

At age twenty-seven, Fontaine had been married more than a year to what, in 1979, would be known as a world class beauty, a failed starlet who was by then the mother of "Jeanne Roselle." The dragon asked for his wife. It would only be for short periods and when he was finished with her Fontaine could have her back, little the worse for wear. Fontaine was horrified. He refused. Years later, when the kids were half-grown and Dandridge was long since dead, he learned that although he had been unwilling to yield up his wife to Dandridge she had been quite willing to yield up herself and had done so behind his back for almost two years. Now, an alcoholic hag, she sat in the glass house on Puget Sound.

In Hollywood, Fontaine was a boy genius, a *wunderkind*, although not of the sort usually written about. He was never an actor, never a director. His was the unglamorous end of the business. As secretary to Dandridge and then his assistant, and finally as an associate producer, he had been primarily a business man. He dealt with financing, with banks and budgets, but he had developed a fine eye for what was profitable, and soon after coming east he backed a show that ran two years, and then one that was still running after three. There was an occasional flop but the flops were far outnumbered by the hits. When he took up yachting he was thirty-eight and by then he had made all the money he would ever need.

In moving east, Fontaine had felt he was rising in the world. It had seemed a step upward to go into the theater, just as it had seemed a step upward to go into the elite world of racing yachtsmen. Fontaine had been an elitist from an early age. Through self-education, exposure and will-power he had become eclectic. He owned a Renoir, a Modigliani and a Paul Klee, not to mention the work of art represented by his boat, a 58-foot sloop built in Finland at a cost of $425,000, give or take a few finnmarks. He appreciated fine wines and fine foods and professed deep love of Vivaldi. In the Fontaine homes, first in California, later in Connecticut, watching television had been discouraged when the kids were growing up. Television was filled with cartoons and cowboys, sit-coms and game shows, cops and thugs.

At the moment he was looking at cops and thugs, in a program which included his flesh-and-blood daughter, a daughter he still very much loved and who, when she was younger, had loved him. After her mother cracked up she had turned against him, although her hatred had not become acute until he picked up with Elaine

What a piece of work is man, how noble in reason . . . in apprehension how like a god. In a scathing attack on television, a crusading young critic had scornfully offered the quotation from Shakespeare and Fontaine had gleefully seized upon it. He wondered if he would have felt so strongly about the medium if his daughter had not been intent upon making a career in it, and if at that very moment she had not been living in Encino with a man he detested, a middle-aged television executive named Armand. The mirror image, the couples in counterpart, did not escape him, yet he found the analogy easy to dismiss because he was so far superior to the man she was living with because he cared so deeply for her welfare, and primarily because he was her father.

Even without special reasons, his contempt for television was real enough. He had tried to explain his feelings to Mary Ann. Take hatred for example, he said. Even on an hour-long show there was simply not enough time to examine the texture of hatred and give it dignity, to integrate it with a real human being. There was merely time to do a sort of select-o-matic hatred. Man is cuckolded—man hates cuckolder. Son becomes addict—mother hates pusher. Legitimate hate situations, yet there was not enough time to know the people and to feel long, deep, and satisfyingly what they felt. The audience was not asked to identify with their emotion, not to experience it, nor to endure it, not to know their hatred well and feel it as one's own, but merely (select-o-matically) to identify it by type; a matter of multiple choice—love, revenge, fear, greed, choose one. In the legitimate theater there was a vast difference.

Two boozy young men with bloodshot eyes and baggy shorts had taken seats a few stools away. They went all but unnoticed by Fontaine, who was now watching the screen intently. His daughter at last was on. She was playing the part of a hooker—not the lead, not numero-uno hooker; just the secondary, little-sister hooker. Numero uno was the faded movie star, looking properly worn and bitter, although not nearly so much so as the wife who lived on Puget Sound. His daughter Mary Ann was trying with some success for a blend of the virginal and the wanton.

One of the men was talking to him, telling him something about the other side of the bay. Fontaine looked at him dispassionately for a second and then back at the screen, but Mary Ann was out of the scene now. She had two scenes. The first was gone and reasonably impressive. At the Morris agency it was felt she might make a very good offbeat Dolley Madison.

Armand, the man she was living with, was working on a pilot for a series on the Washington of the 1830's. If it worked it could spread to other eras, other decades of the nation's history. Humanize. Deglamorize. Change a nation's thinking about its heroes. Reduce them in stature. Make them not unlike the people who would watch in their living rooms. For those who could subsist only on unreal heroes, tough luck. Deglamorization of American heroes, American myths, was a project very close to Armand's heart. It would be a project in honesty. Project Honesty.

The men on their stools were talking in loud drunken voices about strategy for the next day's race, braying about tides and currents. Fontaine was not listening to them. He was contending with a conflict within himself about his daughter, feeling a certain amount of pride in her beauty and in the knowledge that she had landed the part on her own, yet feeling revulsion that his daughter was on national television playing the part of a whore, and sadness that she hated him for his way of life and for his string of young women, most particularly Elaine Fowler.

Now he was distracted by the men beside him as Jeanne Roselle appeared for her second scene. The men were chortling and pounding their knees and pounding on the bar. "Sump'n, ain't she, Cap'n?" A close-up and then another. On each close-up she parted her lips. She had a little girl's lips. Soft, petulant, slightly pouting, smoothly textured. "How'd you like a little of that, Cap'n? I'm talkin' to ya, Cap'n."

Steadfastly Fontaine kept his eyes fixed upon the screen. His daughter was gone. Now the TV street thug was pushing the revenge button. Revenge so swift and empty, revenge zipping from a silenced automatic. There could be little pleasure in swift extermination, in revenge so dispassionate. Revenge should be passionate. It cried out for complexity. The American Indians and myriad other cultures had made revenge a thing of intricacy. Revenge was punishment—for whose benefit? Modern thinking tried to remove the element of revenge from punishment. Modern thinking concentrated on the plight of the person punished. Was punishment good for the soul of the wrongdoer? Was it corrective? Would the wrongdoer become a recidivist? In early cultures it was the avenger, the person wronged, who was all-important. There was little concern for the person punished. Revenge was for the benefit of the avenger, it purged the soul, its aim was to ease the heart, to lift a weight that the avenger found all but unbearable.

" . . . name's Royce—and this here's my friend Clem Vale. Hey, Cap'n! We're talkin' to you . . . "

For a moment Fontaine sat with his eyes closed, hardly knowing where his thoughts about revenge and punishment sprang from; certainly not from his trivial irritation with the men next to him.

They were standing now. Their oversize khaki shorts hung well below their knees.

One of the two was staring at him angrily from his bloodshot eyes. "Look, friend," he said, "we're from the Eastern goddamn Shore of Maryland. I don't know how much you happen to know about the Eastern Goddamn Shore of Maryland but lemme—"

"Practically nothing," Fontaine said.

"Well now, goddamn it, maybe you should!" They were both weaving a little.

Fontaine smiled. "Allow me to buy you a drink." Tossing ten dollars on the bar, he slipped from his stool. "Gentlemen, good night." Gravely they shook hands all around.

Seven

IN THE EASTPORT SECTION, Marmaduke's tavern was a favorite hangout for the sailing crowd. Here gathered the young men who made sails and sold boats and worked on them for a living, trooping in after work to drink and talk about boats and sailing and women.

The tavern was a long low building, overhung from across a narrow street by the high brick wall of a two-block-long condominium. Leaving his car double-parked, Harry got out.

The interior was simple and unpretentious, with dark wood and bright lighting. On the left, in an enclosure off to itself, was the bar, jammed with young men with beards and jeans, shaggy hair, and deeply bronzed faces. With a quick glance, Harry saw that Sam was not among them.

Wooden tables filled a large room to the right. Friday nights were bargain nights and the place was usually jammed. Tonight there was a mob scene. Harry stood there scanning the noisy, exuberant, table-hopping crowd, a crowd which for the most part avoided the yacht club like a plague.

Sam was not to be seen. With a final glance, Harry turned away and drove home.

In the kitchen he opened a can of beer and sat with it on the patio, looking out over the harbor, sipping the beer, watching the lights, all of it a nightly ritual, except that tonight it was very different.

The difference was the telephone call.

Driving to the yacht club and then to Marmaduke's and on the way home, he had thought of nothing else. On the phone he had tried to be big about it, he had even tried to be calm about it, but now he was doing a double take. His head was pounding and the hand holding the beer can was unsteady. He felt rage and frustration.

Gazing out over the water, he tried to calm himself. He was sitting in the dark but the dark was filled with blurs and dots of light. Lights outlined the suspension span of the long bridge stretching across the bay. Crossing the bridge were the moving lights of cars, high above the water. The red eye of a tanker, moving northward; the vertical flashing red lights of the radio towers on the north shore of the Severn, the panels of light in the dormitories of the naval academy, these and all the others that already were so familiar to him. And out over the harbor, the blinking flasher buoys, some red, some green, some white, and by their colors and by the intervals between flashes he knew them all, knew all the flashers and from many nights of watching knew many of the stars.

Three generations in a boat.

He was looking at the lights and thinking of his son. His father in the spring and now the kid. He was being lopped off at both ends.

Philip: *How did he take it? Do you think you hurt his feelings?*

Marcia: *I think maybe at first but then he called back and talked to Roger and everything was fine.*

He was taking it very hard. He sat there telling himself that it was not all that important, that it would be okay, but he didn't believe it. Something had ended. He was sure of it. Something had ended and he was bothered by it. Feared it.

He looked at himself and saw a man not far from forty, a reformed near-alcoholic, rising each day at dawn, burying himself in the newspaper, working with the men in his boat yard, stripped to the waist in the broiling sun; and at night going out to Marmaduke's or someplace to drink beer and talk about boats and oil companies and boats and high prices and boats and the Baltimore Orioles; working and talking and waiting for the next sailboat race and waiting for August.

Philip: *We don't really need the money and I'm sure he doesn't make much to spare.*

Marcia: *It's a matter of pride. He's never missed a month and I'm sure he never will. He's already saving to send Roger to college.*

Harry was standing at the rail, gripping it with both fists.

Harry: *Smug bastards.*

He slumped back into his chair again.

From where he sat he could see a telephone booth, a shaft of light across the cove. There was something about an empty phone booth at night, when it was all lit up inside and nobody in it, the only bright thing in a whole block, or out on the highway the only bright thing in a country mile of darkness. The sight of one always made him feel very lonely.

Whenever he drove past a phone booth at night he wanted to pull over to the shoulder of the road and place a call to New England. Call her, or call her mother, call somebody, but it was all beyond his rage, immune and oblivious to his rage, her mother now in the grave, her mother now safely dead, so that all he could do was desecrate the grave, and he had never made the call.

His beer was gone. He went back to the kitchen for another can and had just returned to the patio and slumped once more into his chair when he heard the car. He turned. Headlights washed over the grounds of the boat yard. It was a taxi, moving hesitantly through the gates and then to the parking strip behind his house.

The door opened, slammed shut, and somebody was heading around the house toward the side steps of the patio. "Harry?" Her foot was on the bottom step. "Is that you, Harry?" She was climbing the steps. "Why didn't you come to the yacht club, you bastard? Didn't you get my message?"

He smiled. "Hello, Elaine."

"Is that all? 'Hello, Elaine'?" She held out her arms.

He kissed her, patted her head. "I got your message. I got both your messages, and I went to the yacht club but I was too late. They said you'd just left. I'm sorry."

"Are you glad to see me?"

"Yes."

"You don't act like it."

"Of course I'm glad to see you. How have you been? What are you doing in Annapolis?"

"God!"

"What?"

"You sound like a creep. Even worse than before."

"Thanks," he said. "All right—*here*. Sit down and shut up. Have a beer. And tell the cab driver to turn off the motor, for God's sake."

She laughed. "That's better." She patted his hand. "A *little* better. What's wrong, Harry. You're not really glad to see me, are you?"

"Of course I am."

"Something's bothering you," she said.

"It's not you. I've had a tough night. My wife's bugging me."

He had dropped into a chair and she sat on the rail, facing him. She wore jeans and a white shirt, and in the hazy moonlight her face and hair looked as beautiful as he'd remembered them. "That's one of the things I've decided about you," she said. "You've got a hangup about your wife."

"How about the driver? His motor's still running."

"I can't stay," she said. "I only came for a second." She looked over her shoulder at the lights in the harbor. "What a view!" She turned back and looked at the lighted window upstairs. "What a crazy house, Harry. Is this where you live?"

"This is where I live," he said.

"You've really changed since Montego."

"Maybe so have you."

"How?"

"I don't know. You seem older somehow."

"Maybe that figures," she said.

"Want a beer?"

"No thanks. I don't have time. At least you're alive." She looked over her shoulder again. "I kept thinking about you on that boat, all by yourself. While we were racing back to Miami, I kept going up on deck and looking back over the water. I kept thinking I might see you. And then after we got to Miami I read all the papers to see if you'd been drowned, or lost at sea or something."

"I made it," he said.

"I felt better after I read the papers," she said. "Hey, Harry . . . would you like to take me upstairs and make love to me? Think about it a minute before you answer."

"I thought you were in a hurry."

"I'll tell the driver to turn off the motor."

"No."

"You're so flattering, Harry."

"I told you—I've had a bad night."

"I'm leaving Fontaine." Still seated on the railing, she was looking at him intently.

"When?"

"This weekend."

"How's he taking it?"

"I haven't told him yet."

"How *will* he take it?"

"He's always said he'd let me go when the time came. Besides, he's got a waiting list a mile long."

"Why don't you marry him?"

"He'll never divorce his wife. Besides, I wouldn't want to anyway."

"Why not?"

"I don't know. He sort of eats me alive—my God! Don't say it!"

"I wasn't going to." Harry paused. "Why are you leaving?"

"Maybe I'm getting scared. Lately I've been reading these books about—excuse the expression—incest. One of them really scared me."

"Why? In what way?"

"It said the scars are so deep that you've hardly got any chance at all of leading any kind of a normal life. I mean, once you've been screwed by your father, kiddo, you've had it. That's all. Curtains. Give it up. What it was saying, this book was *saying*—was that because of five minutes on the night before my fifteenth birthday I was finished for life. Doomed. Holy shit! It really shook me."

"There's no reason to believe that," he said.

"No reason to believe that," she mimicked. "God, Harry, I'm not even sure I like you any more."

"I'm listening," he said.

"Almost like a curse," she said. "That lasts all your life. But I'm not giving in to it. It's not going to lick me."

"Good."

"I could spend the rest of my life being a love-slave," she said. "Or a lazy bitch who's hung up on luxury. But it's not going to be that way."

The telephone rang.

"Excuse me," Harry said. He walked through the house to the kitchen. The cab's motor was still running and now its lights were on. He answered the phone and carried it to the living room. It was Sam.

She came in from the patio and threw her arms about his neck. He was trying to listen to Sam. There was a problem about their crew for the race the next day.

"I'm coming to live with you," she murmured. "That's what I came to tell you."

Staring at her, he began to frown. "Gotta call you back," he said to Sam.

He carried the phone back to the kitchen and hung it up. She followed him. "I'm serious, Harry," she said. "I've gone as far as I can go with this life. I have to do something. I've been thinking about it and you're the one who can help me."

"Help you how?"

"I need a place to stay, a place to be, and I've decided I'd like to be with you while I'm finding a job and then if you and I don't work out I'll leave, okay?"

"I don't think I'm your man," he said.

"I think maybe you are. Listen! For God's sake! I need help. Will you help me or not?" She looked toward the cab. "I've got to go. Are you sailing in this race tomorrow?"

"Yes."

"The same one we're in?"

He shrugged. "I guess so. It's the only race in town."

"The one that ends up in Oxford? Isn't that where your father is?"

"Not anymore. He died this spring."

"I'm sorry, Harry. I'm sorry." She kissed his hand. "Harry . . . "

"What?"

"Will you see me down there tomorrow night after the race is over? At least buy me a drink or something, so we can talk?"

"I guess so."

"Is it a promise?"

He took a deep breath. "Yes."

"It's a real hardship, isn't it?" She was holding both his hands. She sighed.

Squeezing his hands, she stepped out to the patio and ran down the steps. He followed in time to see her get into the cab and then stood watching as it drove away. After a while he went back in and called Sam.

Eight

IN THE GREATER Annapolis area that evening, two other scheduled participants in the next day's race were moving along distinctly different pathways.

One was Clem Vale, the slightly more inebriated of the men in baggy khaki shorts who had confronted Mel Fontaine at the yacht-club bar.

Having arrived at the yacht club with a snootful, having accepted the drink Fontaine bought for them, and having had a few more at their own expense, Clem Vale and his friend Royce were on their way to Baltimore, drunk as lords. Clem could hardly have been happier.

Such was not the case with an unfortunate older woman named Margaret Hackett, who was spending a night which could only be described as miserable.

In the newly swarming world of boating, for every crack sailor there were at least a hundred novices, a new breed of seafaring landlubber who often felt that boating could be fun for the whole family. Family boating had produced an often unhappy individual known as the Boating Wife. Although she had come to boating at a considerably more advanced age than most, Margaret Hackett was one of these. She hoped she would not be one much longer.

That morning she and her husband Walters had boarded their new boat and motored up from Oxford. On the morrow, God help them, they would sail in their first-ever race.

On the way up the bay, while her husband manned the tiller, Margaret Hackett had intermittently puttered about down in the cabin, vaguely following her husband's mandate to coil the spinnaker sheets and get things shipshape.

At her age! Coiling spinnaker sheets and getting things shipshape! How could she have allowed it to happen?

This was a question which occurred to her often. It occurred to her toward twilight as they motored into Annapolis harbor and found a secluded cove for overnight anchorage. It occurred to her an hour later as she experienced the perplexities and irritations of cooking with alcohol and Sterno. Now it was long past midnight and the question was still offering itself as she lay on her back in the triangular space known as the foreberth—two triangular slabs of orange naugahyde fitted together to compose the larger triangle which was their bed. Over the naugahyde was spread a sleeping bag and in the sleeping bag were Mr. and Mrs. Hackett.

Now and then in the course of her lifetime, Mrs. Hackett had read newspaper feature articles about this and that husband and wife who lived aboard a small but doughty boat which they took all over the world, at home alike in Bangkok and Baltimore. The boat was usually described as sea-kindly. The wife was invariably called the First Mate and was depicted as both salty and yar, thoroughly at ease on the water.

Mrs. Hackett was finding such a woman incomprehensible. Not only was there the miserable experience of cooking, there was also the matter of sleeping in a triangle. With two people lying side by side, the feet of one tended to angle toward the feet of the other. At the opposite end, one's head tended to drift aft toward the adjacent cubicle of bathroom, which Mrs. Hackett steadfastly declined to call the head. Her pillow kept sliding off and dropping to the bathroom floor, leaving the back of her neck resting on the wooden ledge which bounded the base of the Great Triangle. Periodically she retrieved it, always with difficulty, for merely to move was an effort—and to move was to collide with the tightly wedged body of her husband. Each time she moved he stirred, once half-waking to protest that he needed his sleep, otherwise he would be unable to sail a decent race on the morrow.

Mrs. Hackett had doubts about his ability to sail a decent race no matter how much sleep he got, but she was an uncommonly loyal wife and would not have dreamed of hurting his feelings.

In the entire arrangement the only saving grace was that the front hatch was open, and directly above her head was a square patch of sky. This evening the sky was filled with a veil of high, wispy clouds. Looking straight up, she watched the clouds move and occasionally glimpsed a pale half-moon.

In spite of this attractive feature, however, she was far from happy. She lay there and lay there, worrying about the next day's race, unable to find repose. Several times she felt close to dozing but each time she was bumped by her husband. In the triangular berth, both bodies tended to move toward the midline, the line that ran from the apex of the triangle to bisect its base. It was precisely this point that her husband's head was occupying. Hers was shoved off the mark perhaps a foot to the right, and it was just here that her pillow kept dropping to the floor of the bathroom.

As the night drew on, Mrs. Hackett began to experience what she had come to know as a "spinnaker attack." It was close to three when she finally decided that she could stand it no longer.

Carefully she began the job of extrication. At her age it was not easy, nor would it have been at any age. Getting out of the sleeping bag was like withdrawing one's self from a scabbard, with nothing to help but one's elbows. Now, with one elbow on the toilet seat and her feet still in bed, she managed to slide the final distance until she was somehow standing in the tiny head. Here she carefully turned 180 degrees, made her way through the galley, and climbed the companionway ladder to the cockpit.

In the three-A.M. darkness, seated sadly in the cockpit, a quilted jacket covering her decorous nightgown, she asked herself once more how it could possibly have happened, this blight upon the golden years of her retirement.

The answer, she knew, was closely related to her husband's eccentricity, to the essential nature of the retirement process, or quite likely to both.

Back in New Jersey she had been reasonably certain that when her husband pictured himself in retirement he saw a placid old gentleman in a rowboat, dreamily fishing in a sunwashed cove, sifting the memories of a lifetime.

But with Walters Hackett, as it turned out, memories were quickly sifted.

All too soon it became evident that he did not want solitude, nor did he want too much peace and quiet. Perhaps above all he did not want to go unnoticed and unsung. In his own company he had been a very important man and when he moved to his new home he had expected the populace to note with pride and pleasure that the retired head of Hackett Plumbing Fixtures Corporation was now living in its midst.

During the weeks they spent looking for their house, their realtor did nothing to lessen Hackett's self-esteem. More than once he remarked upon the great asset he would be to the community and Hackett soon had an impression of a countryside filled with people all very much looking forward to his arrival, because his realtor had said so.

As his retirement home, Hackett had bought a sprawling single-level brick house complete with a modest strip of waterfront and a dock, paying an arm and a leg. He had also bought himself a Boston Whaler, a small fiberglass runabout powered by an outboard engine.

After the Hacketts had been in residence about a month, their realtor was still their principal acquaintance, followed in loose order by an electrician who had done some rewiring, a man who had dropped by several times to fix the oil burner, and one who made a good living pumping out septic tanks.

In those early days they were invited to a cocktail party at their realtor's house, where they were introduced to some of the people who had been dying to meet them. Hackett found these people vague and leathery, possessed of a hoarse self-assurance that seemed to speak of old money and showing no indication whatever of wanting to meet him.

As he listened to their chatter a world took shape. He heard a phrase he would remember— "going to weather." A mahogany-faced man with tufted white eyebrows had been going to weather in a boat which, in his opinion, went to weather better than any boat he had ever owned. A comely young woman slipped a smoothly tanned arm over the sleeve of his madras jacket. He didn't seem to notice. He kept on talking about going to weather. Others spoke of their own experiences in going to weather.

The young woman was most attractive. By now they were a semicircle. Her gaze went from one face to another, sliding each time swiftly past Hackett's, ignoring him for the nonsailor that he was. He asked: "When you speak of going to weather, what do you mean exactly?"

He saw the flicker of a smile but these were civilized people and the man with the tufted white eyebrows told him in a polite if mildly patronizing way that going to weather meant going into the wind.

He left the party feeling less important than when he arrived.

At the time, Hackett probably didn't even know it himself but Mrs. Hackett would realize later that a seed had been sown.

She for her part was making the transition to their new surroundings more smoothly than was her husband. She made friends easily and after a time they began to get a few dinner invitations. In the ringing voice he had used while presiding at board meetings, Hackett tried to interest his dinner companions in some of the problems involved in the manufacture and distribution of plumbing fixtures. He also spoke of his new house, of its many interesting features and of the linear footage of his waterfront.

"I don't know what to make of these people down here," he growled on the way home from a party one night in January. "They're not interested in a damned thing."

During the course of the evening, Mrs. Hackett had overheard him telling a rich widow with hennaed eyebrows that his outboard engine had a capacity of twenty-eight horsepower. He also talked to her about a valve his company had perfected for greater efficiency in oil burners. "Now you take your ordinary run-of-the-mill cutoff valve . . ." Mrs. Hackett heard him say.

A wife with a sympathetic heart, one who had always done her best to soothe wounded feelings, she now did her best to explain to him that he was not the only successful man who had retired to the area. There were many, many. Each had been a king in his own sphere and each, she felt sure, had found it tough going to realize that in retirement he was but one of many kings in exile, as it were. They could hardly expect the attention they had once known because here in retirement land there were no subjects, only other kings—each with not a courtier to his name save in some cases a wife.

Margaret Hackett drew the quilted jacket closer about her shoulders. It was getting chilly. She wondered how long before dawn. The cove was shaped like a horseshoe and houses stood on its banks. Two other boats were anchored nearby, each with its masthead light glittering. These, too, she supposed, would be in the race. On each undoubtedly there slept a man with dreams of glory. The area was like that. In the area of their retirement there was tremendous emphasis upon boating in general and upon sailing in particular and as the winter moved toward an end the seed planted at their realtor's cocktail party began to sprout. Hackett began to envision sailing not only as the cure for retirement boredom but as a likely pathway to local prestige. As Mrs. Hackett pointed out, he knew absolutely nothing about boating and for a while he hemmed and hawed, but then one night in bed, as she was drifting off to sleep, Mrs. Hackett felt a lurch. Hackett's feet swung to the floor. "By God, I'm going to do it!" he snarled. "Anybody who can build a company, anybody who can build an *industrial empire,* can sure as hell learn to sail a stupid sailboat!" He was standing at the bedroom window, barking into the night. A purchase quickly followed.

"Now then," he said in early April, "where would you say you were standing, Margaret? In relation to me, I mean?"

They were on the screened porch after supper. Long slim panels of light and shadow fell over the lawn.

Mrs. Hackett frowned. "I'm standing *behind* you," she replied.

"I don't mean that," he said with an indulgent smile. "I mean, what compass point?"

"What *compass* point?"

"Yes. What compass point? North? South? Where?"

Mrs. Hackett's eyes roved about the property. Compass directions were not her strong point.

"Where does the sun rise, Margaret?" he asked in a kindly tone.

She pointed in the direction of a huge willow. "Over there. Doesn't it? Of course it does."

"Okay, where are you standing then—in relation to me?"

She shrugged. "Sort of east? Sort of *north*east."

"More *nor*-nor'east," Hackett said. "Which means I'm standing roughly sou-sou'west of *you.* "

Mrs. Hackett saw no reason to reply.

"Now then," he said. "Knots. I think if we get our running bowline and our clove hitch and our sheepshank we should just about have it for the fundamentals. Just tie one whenever you happen to think of it. You could practice with the toaster cord."

For the golden years of retirement, Mrs. Hackett had had something quite different in mind from tying sheepshanks with the toaster cord, but her attitude had not yet hardened. In those early days she was every bit as proud of their new boat as he was. She was also delighted that he had something to absorb his energies. Often he was away for hours at a stretch, gone off to Easton, or even as far as Annapolis, to buy a new fitting; or off to one of the local boat yards to discuss his rigging, happily occupied. Once the boat was put into commission there were trial runs down the Tred Avon almost every afternoon. He was bringing to boating the same single-focus tenacity that he had brought to plumbing fixtures.

In those bright spring days there was still talk of the beauty of sailing, even the poetry of sailing. *Silver Heels,* for example, seemed a most poetic name for their glistening

grey boat. There was talk of leisurely cruises, of quiet con-
templative meandering through the waters of the Eastern
Shore, of dropping anchor in quiet coves and watching the
Great Blue Heron.

All this Mrs. Hackett found to the good. She loved the
place they had chosen for their retirement. She loved the
quiet dignity, the feeling of depth and tradition the village
gave her, and beyond the village she loved the land, which
in spring had endless shades of green and which, with its
lanes and cottages, resembled paintings of the English
countryside. If learning to tie a sheepshank would help, if
riding with him up and down the river and pulling a few
ropes made him happy, then she was game, so far.

In early May they went to a party where Hackett spoke
exuberantly of his new boat. In his exuberance there must
have been a hint that he already considered himself something of a seaman, one who loved the water and came in-
doors only to grace an occasional dinner party with his
leathery presence. Seasoned local sailors were present.
They were soured by his exuberance and tired of hearing
about his new boat. He was asked if he planned to race it.
Hackett replied that he hadn't given it much thought.
"Well, you can't really call yourself a sailor unless you
race," he was told. Late that night he lurched from the bed
and stood at the window. An announcement soon followed.

He was planning to race even before he had fairly
learned to sail.

Having for short weeks paid lip service to the grace and
beauty of sailing for its own sake, and having held out the
prospect of lazy cruises, he now sat at night frowning over
articles entitled, "How to Get the Most Out of Your Mainsail" and "How to Correct for Lee Helm" and "Going for
the Starting Line—Half the Battle!"

In beautiful May sunlight, Mrs. Hackett meandered on
foot through the village, past walled gardens, past veils of
weeping cherry and dripping daffodils. Hoarding her moments of privacy, she was having a love affair with the

spring, with a shower of forsythia, a tiny bird dipping seed from a feeder, the soft undulation of moist brick sidewalks.

Abruptly she was yanked away from all this and asked to spend her afternoons in an abomination known as spinnaker drill.

Poor old Mr. Crowder, who had done so much work on their boat, was recovering from a heart attack and his nice son Harry came down to see him a couple of times a week. Mr. Crowder got Harry to give them some lessons, and spinnaker drill was not so bad when Harry was in the boat. Harry was very considerate of her feelings. With Harry around, all was right with the world, but after his father died he wasn't around much, and she and Hackett were left alone with the spinnaker. Even though they went out only on mild days, spinnaker drill was an operation she had come to dread, partly, she knew, because it made Hackett so tense. His voice became higher in pitch, more strident, occasionally even hoarse.

Clearly he felt his spinnaker was a living, animate object that was out to get him. His apprehension was communicated to the central nervous system of Mrs. Hackett, where it was compounded, and this was the origin of her spinnaker attacks—frightening visual images in which the two of them were pulled by a savage sail over the brink of the earth.

Whatever his own fear of spinnakers, Hackett plunged ahead. Even Mrs. Hackett, who knew him so well, was amazed by his ardor, his acute need to master sailing and his myopic belief that he could somehow become a winning skipper. He remained unquenchable, obviously feeling that if he tried hard enough, read enough sailing books, took enough sailing lessons, he could succeed at sailing just as he had succeeded in business.

That spring, when Harry heard that Hackett was thinking about racing, he had tried to talk him out of it. "Wait another year," he said, "so you'll feel a little more at home in your boat." When he saw Hackett looking stubborn he delivered a warning on the subject of crew. "The two of you can't race that boat alone," he said. "You'll need at least one more in crew. At a *minimum.*"

Partly because it was a land of kings without courtiers, and partly because of Hackett's poor prospects in this or any race, a third crew member was hard to come by. He searched without success, calling all around the Oxford area, not overlooking their realtor, their electrician, and the man who had pumped out their septic tank.

Up against it, he had resorted to his younger—although not much younger—sister, Kitty, a supple divorcee from Connecticut, who would be picked up at the Annapolis public dock in the morning.

Mrs. Hackett was fond of Kitty but she could find little reassurance in the prospect of having her aboard. In fact, as she looked ahead to the next day, she could find little reassurance of any kind whatever.

The night moved on toward dawn. Margaret Hackett sat huddled in the cockpit, looking at the houses around the cove. Presently a light came on in one, and then in another. Families living ordinary lives. Families at peace. She sat there in the cold morning light, looking wistfully toward shore.

It was approaching six o'clock.

Just before six o'clock, Harry Crowder went down to the kitchen to stir himself up some breakfast. The water was boiling for his coffee when the telephone rang.

Frowning, he answered it.

"Skip?" A hoarse voice with a heavy Eastern Shore accent.

"Oh my God!" he groaned.

"My lands, Skip, I really am sorry, son. I don't know what came over me. First thing I know I'm here in Baltimore with this young lady—"

"Clem, you drunken son of a bitch!"

"Sonofabitch Royce's fault. He's a bad influence. My

lands, what a night!"

"Where are you, you dumb bastard?"

"Harry, so help me God I'd be on my way right this minute, feeling as bad as I do I'd get right out of this bed and start out, except I know I'd not be any good to you. I wouldn't be worth a good goddamn and nobody knows it better than I do."

"Where are you?" Harry asked again.

"I'm not rightly sure. It's a room. I'm not sure if it's where she lives or whether it's a room I hired for the time being or just what the hell it is. It sure is a terrible-looking place though. I'm really sorry, Skip. That sonofabitch Royce is a bad influence. Sonofabitch is an evil companion."

"Yeah, he stands there with a gun at your head . . . "

"I'm weak, Harry. I wouldn't blame you if you never let me sail with you again as long as I live, I swear to God."

Harry had known Clem Vale since they were in the fourth grade. He had always found it impossible to stay mad at him for very long.

"Did she roll you?" he asked.

"I don't think so."

"Sure you got everything that belongs to you . . . "

"Yeah, I think so. I think I have. Lemme look. I know it was here just a minute ago. Yeah, here it is—oh my God!"

"What?"

"She's coming back. I can hear her comin' up the steps."

The phone went dead.

Part II

Nine

Mare nostrum . . . our sea. So the Romans spoke of
the Mediterranean. Now on almost every spring, summer,
and autumn weekend the Chesapeake would appear to be
everybody's bay and one might guess that a good percent-
age of the population of its surrounding states have become
boating people. They cruise, they dawdle, they speed, they
fish, they race, they watch and are watched. Where once
there were stately square-riggers and later a vast fleet of
rugged workboats with their stained and yellowing sails,
we now see the water covered with pleasure craft; with
sleek sailing yachts, one-design racing sailboats, sailboats
large and small; fishing boats with and without cabins;
houseboats; tiny skiffs with light outboard motors; fear-
somely expensive flying-bridge power cruisers, four and
five tiers high; luxury runabouts with enormous horsepower and removable tops and upholstery and the fittings
of an expensive foreign convertible. These latter, the proud
possessions of some, were viewed with scorn by others,
namely the sailors and environmentalists.

Once the boating boom was well underway it had taken
hardly any time at all before there was a flourishing ven-
detta between sailors and powerboatsmen. Sailors saw
powerboating as pushbutton seamanship and powerboats
as stinkpots. They felt that operating a powerboat required
no knowledge of navigation and for that matter very little
knowledge of boats. With some justification they held that
powerboatsmen drove at excessive rates of speed and were
careless of their wakes. They contended that powerboatsmen embodied some aspects of Cadillac owners, tooling
their multi-tiered, flying-bridge monsters over the waterways much as they might drive a gas-guzzling luxury car

over a superhighway. Sailors saw themselves as something entirely different—as the favored of the gods, darlings of the ecologists and lovers of nature, who took a triangle of sail, offered it to the wind, and got beautiful motion. They prided themselves on their nautical lore, their prudence, and their enthusiasm for the environment.

Powerboatsmen for their part believed sailors to be smug and snobbish, that they tended to be elitist, and that because they had the right of way they tended to feel they owned the water. Perhaps mainly, however, they hated sailors because they knew sailors held them in contempt. Hated, they found it easy to hate back and they did so with great enthusiasm.

In both groups there were experts who were passionate about the water. Where once only commercial marine pilots knew the vast network of buoys and light towers, and only seasoned watermen knew the tricky tides, now they were the province of enthusiastic and often knowledgeable amateurs who had taken up boating as a hobby.

Nowhere over the entire bay was evidence of the boating boom greater than in the area of Annapolis.

On the Saturday morning of the race down to Oxford, boats began pouring out of Annapolis harbor at an early hour even though the weather was far from promising. Some headed out over the bay, bound for distant cruising and fishing destinations. Others were headed for an area south of the five-mile-long Chesapeake Bay Bridge, which links the Eastern and Western shores. The race would start at a point well out into the bay, about a mile south of the bridge. Here by eight-thirty the committee boat was already anchored and here the contestants were already gathering. The committee boat was a dark-blue sloop under bare spars and readily identifiable by the rows of pennants flying from its forestay and backstay, and for those who recognized such things it flew a special committee boat flag. The committee boat's job was to give the contestants a fair start,

Regatta

sending them across the starting line flight by flight, class by class, at five-minute intervals. The starting line was an imaginary line drawn between the committee boat, anchored to the east, and a red bell buoy roughly two hundred yards to the west.

On the foredeck of the committee boat stood a small black cannon perhaps two feet long overall and a foot high at the breech. This was known as the starting gun. Ten minutes before the start of the race it would begin firing blanks at five-minute intervals. The shots would be synchronized with the hoisting of "shapes," which looked very much like Japanese lanterns in solid colors, a white shape at ten minutes, blue shape at five minutes, and red for the start. These were run up from the foredeck on a light halyard and the cannon was fired as they reached the top.

Aboard the committee boat were the six members of the race committee appointed by Roberta Lodge, the regatta chairwoman, who was herself still in Oxford and would there remain throughout the day to see that all went well.

Those on the committee boat were themselves knowledgeable sailors. Among them was Roberta's friend Anthony Korbut, the man Mel Fontaine had spoken with at the yacht club. It would be his job to fire the cannon. Korbut at fifty-six was a man with a manner somehow both crisp and self-effacing. During the 1972 Olympics his surname was made into a household word by Olga Korbut, an accomplished Russian gymnast then in her teens. More recently, in a small town in upstate New York, his name had become notable on another account. As the owner of a successful restaurant, he had for years done his own bookkeeping and filed his own income tax returns. His return for calendar 1976 was duly filed in April 1977. It was scrutinized by a federal examiner, there were meetings at various levels, and ten months later the government prosecuted him for tax fraud. Korbut pleaded nolo contendere. He was fined $10,000 and sentenced to a year's imprisonment in the federal penitentiary at Lewisburg. While he was in prison his wife of thirty years had a stroke and died. Some people, Korbut among them, felt that her death had been brought on by the shock and shame of having her husband sent to jail, although of course he had no way of proving it.

Korbut was paroled after seven months. Out of prison, he sold his business; sold the boat which he had raced for years on Long Island Sound; sold the house he and his wife had owned in Florida. For sailors headed south for the winter, Oxford was a prime stop on the inland waterway. Korbut had stopped there once and liked it. Seeking a place to start a new life, he had chosen Oxford. Sailing had once been a good part of his life. Now he had totally given it up, but when Roberta Lodge asked him to serve on the race committee he said yes.

That morning he wore a visored black cap, a white turtle-neck, and sunglasses with large square panes. From a corner of his mouth jutted an unlit pipe. A discussion had begun among the other committee members about the possibility of raising the anchor and resetting the starting line. Ideally a starting line was set with the line perpendicular to the wind, or as nearly so as possible, so that a boat could start at either end of the line without undue advantage or disadvantage. In long distance races it seldom worked out that way. The course down the bay would be almost due south, and the wind early that morning had been oscillating from a few degrees east-of-north all the way down to south-east. The starting line was a compromise. It faced east-southeast.

The discussion continued. Korbut had never felt it made any great difference in a long race. If the wind was blowing steady from the northwest, from behind, that is, they would still have to start the race, wouldn't they? This is what he felt but he didn't care enough to say it. His job was to fire the cannon. While they talked and took sightings, he sat in the cockpit with a clipboard in his lap, studying the list of starters. The list showed a total of 153 entries spread over eleven classes. It included the name of each yacht, its class, the name of its skipper, his home port, his yacht club affiliation and—where it applied—his handicap rating.

It was decided to leave the starting line where it was, at least temporarily. Korbut poured himself some coffee in a white styrofoam cup and moved slowly up to the foredeck, his eyes on the boats milling around behind the starting line. It was eight-forty. The first start would be at nine o'clock and the first class to go would be the Alberg-30s, a class which always turned out in good numbers. Leaning against the mast, sipping the coffee, he watched them and whatever he may have felt was hidden by the sunglasses. At eight-fifty the white shape went up and he fired the ten-minute gun for the Albergs.

Ten

ALMOST AN HOUR EARLIER, just before eight o'clock, Harry Crowder had started the engine, backed *Sundance* from its slip and headed down the Severn River.

Harry wore a faded blue shirt and an old olive-green foul-weather jacket which had been his father's. His head was bare and his tanned, seamed face was damp from a drizzle which for the moment had stopped.

As he stood in the cockpit, his hand was light on the tiller and his movements were easy and casual but there was nothing easy and casual about the way he felt. He had sailed his first Annapolis-to-Oxford race at the age of fifteen and he had sailed many since. Normally Harry had a single-track approach to a race. Once in the boat he thought of nothing else and as the time for the starting gun approached he didn't even tolerate any talking. Intense concentration prevailed until the end of the race.

This morning was not the same. His mind was on the

race but it was just as often on Roger and on Marcia's telephone call.

Now and then it was on Clem Vale, for there was something else unusual about the race that day. He had a crew problem. Clem Vale had gotten drunk and shacked up in Baltimore, but Clem was only part of it. Harry had known he had a problem even before Clem called him at six o'clock in the morning. He had known he had a problem when Sam Hooper called him the night before.

On the foredeck now, just ahead of the mast, Sam stood munching a doughnut, taking it easy a while longer until there was work to be done. At his side stood Roy Welles, and the problem was not only Clem but Roy.

Before going to Viet Nam, Roy Welles was one of the best small-boat skippers in Annapolis. He had cracked up in Viet Nam, and for the first year after he got back to the United States he was in and out of VA hospitals. Roy had known the full horror of jungle fighting, the way it turned men into wary animals. Home from the hospital, he had set upon his brother one night with his fists and nearly killed him. The reason he gave was that his brother had come up behind him unexpectedly.

After that Roy was back in the hospital for a while but he had been out now for more than three years and was apparently back to normal. So it was thought. What Sam called to report was that two nights earlier Roy had hit his brother again and knocked him cold. The brother's wife called the cops and Roy was taken to police headquarters, where he stayed for two hours before his brother arrived to tell the cops to drop the charges.

These then were his regular crewmen—Sam, Clem, and Roy. Handling the boat with only two of them would present no great problem. Setting the spinnaker was the only possible trouble area but the boat was rigged so that all possible lines were led back to the cockpit for easy handling; and once the spinnaker pole was hooked to the mast the rest would be easy enough unless it blew hard and this, according to the weather forecast, was not likely. With himself and Sam and Roy they would get along just fine unless Roy started acting up. It was this risk that he and Sam had discussed and the decision had been to let Roy come along and to keep an eye on him.

Roy hardly looked menacing. His black hair was close-cropped; his eyebrows met over his nose. He was small and nimble and in a sailboat race he was very light on his feet. He was now about thirty-five—older than Sam, younger than Harry. He was wearing a grey sweat shirt with the sleeves cut off, Sam a navy-blue windbreaker. One on each side, they leaned against the mast as *Sundance* moved on down the river.

Sundance was running under power. No sails had been broken out and the boom and the furled mainsail were still smoothly bundled in a blue and white sail cover. The bright yellow hull glided swiftly downstream, trailing behind it a pencil line of foam in the dark-grey water. The sky was covered with a ragged overcast, broken here and there with blue slits and pools which promised better weather as the day wore on. The forecast was for partial clearing with winds light and variable, becoming mostly westerly eight to ten knots. The forecast told a story. For three days there had been a dry northeaster. Northeasters more often than not lasted three days and this one had about run its course. The dying easterly breeze would drop out and after a period of light or no air it would come in again from the west—if the forecast was correct.

Harry looked over his shoulder. The U.S. Route 50 bridge was behind him now, a band of orange anti-rust paint stretched from shore to shore high above the river. Ahead, still a good distance downstream, was the next bridge, an abandoned railway trestle which years earlier had carried the Baltimore interurban electric train to Annapolis. His course was set for its drawspan which swung open horizontally on a pivot and which had been locked in the open position ever since 1937, when the train stopped running.

On the right bank of the river the land had flattened out but on the left there were still cliffs, rimmed along the crest with houses and trees. The sun popped out and high on a bluff a patch of bright-green lawn lit up. Harry's eye traveled up to it and then down as he squinted ahead again, watching the water.

Sam took off his jacket, tossed it below, and leaned once more against the mast. He and Roy were talking but Harry couldn't hear what they were saying. Sam was blond and heavyset, strong and powerful, with pale-blue eyes and a cornsilk mustache. His forearms were huge. If Roy started giving them any trouble Sam could handle him but Harry didn't expect any trouble.

Clapping Roy on the shoulder, Sam moved aft to the stern and stood on the cockpit seat, one loose hand on the backstay. "Everything's cool," he said in a low voice. Harry nodded, his face expressionless. "Does he know we know about it?" he asked. "I don't think so," Sam said.

Harry had known Sam only since moving to Annapolis but he was already one of his best friends. On Saturday nights he had worked for years as bartender in a very tough section of Baltimore, and the next evening after the race Sam and Roy had a ride that would enable Sam to get back in time for his job. Harry would bring back the boat alone on Sunday. If Sam had been slightly larger it might have been fitting to describe him as a gentle giant. So far as Harry could tell he was afraid of nothing. He was a freak of nature, one of nature's excellent freaks. He was simpleminded and pureminded and neither term demeaned him. At thirty-three he was without guile, without artifice, knew that life was potentially a dagger, a straitjacket, a shock treatment, yet seemed to love it as simply and guilelessly as if he were a child. Harry still did not completely understand him. He knew all these things about him but was frank to admit that he could not add them up. He trusted him completely.

"Something wrong?" Sam was looking down at him

from the cockpit seat. "What is it? Clem?"

Harry shook his head. "No. I heard from Marcia last night." He told Sam about the phone call.

"That's a shame." Sam patted Harry's shoulder. "That's a lousy shame. I'm sorry, Harry."

"It'll be good for him," Harry said. "He'll learn a lot."

Just ahead now was the old railroad bridge. When he reached it, Harry took the boat through without reducing speed and then angled immediately off to the right, heading for the third and last bridge, this one resembling a Roman viaduct with squat stone piers and a series of low arches looping their way across the river. Heavy auto traffic could be seen speeding over it in both directions.

Once they had passed the railroad bridge, the bluffs on the left disappeared. The land dropped swiftly and soon flattened out into a long running silhouette against the sun, a strip of woodland screening from view the highway approach to the bridge. Here and there behind the curtain of silhouetted trees there was the glint of sunlight on moving automobiles. Although the cloud cover looked unbroken, the sun kept sliding out through the slits and each time it did the river was bathed for a few moments with a misty radiance before turning grey again.

Sam and Roy had gotten to work. They were up in the bow hanking on the jib to the headstay, Sam snapping on the shackles while Roy fed him the sail, which he was pulling fold by fold from its big red sailbag.

From the cockpit seat Harry picked up an air horn. Pointing it toward the bridge, he gave three blasts and then looked back over his shoulder. If there were boats behind, the operator would wait until they had caught up so he could let them through all at once, minimizing the inconvenience to motorists, most of whom found very little enchantment in being halted to let boats through a drawbridge. There were no other boats in sight; the river was clear all the way back to the railway trestle. Harry heard the warning bell and then the whir of the lift machinery. The cars had stopped and the spans were rising. At their maximum lift they would be straight up and down, and the opening would be very wide, but Harry didn't wait, didn't even reduce his speed. It was a game of sorts. When they were all younger they had played it as a nautical version of "chicken." To reduce speed and proceed warily was to chicken out. As he reached the bridge the spans had lifted barely enough to create a forty-five-degree angle, so that at the top there was only a narrow slit for the mast to pass through.

In the bow, Sam was looking upward, then back at Harry as if to ask him what the hell he was doing; then upward again, following the tip of the mast with his eye, coaxing it through. Roy knelt at the foot of the mast, his face expressionless. Not flinching, Harry split the middle. They had made it, and would have made it even if the gap had not continued to widen, which it was now doing as the spans continued to lift until they were perpendicular to the water. Sam looked over his shoulder, grinning and shaking his head. Harry shrugged. They were safely on the far side now. He waved thanks to the bridge tender who was looking from the window up in his little tower. The machinery was already grinding, ready to lower the spans again.

Sam turned his attention once more to the jib. It was now hanked on to his liking, and he began patting it down hard, compacting it so that its stiff dacron folds and bulges did not stick up over the bow pulpit and obscure Harry's view. While he did so, Roy led the sheets forward from the cockpit and tied neat, tight bowlines to the clew of the jib.

Holding the tiller between his legs, Harry took off his foul-weather jacket and tossed it through the open hatch. It landed in the sink. He checked his watch. It was eight-thirty. On the right bank, very close by now, were the buildings and grounds of the Naval Academy. Once the academy had seemed all of a piece architecturally but now there were new buildings to go with Dahlgren Hall and the others. The new buildings were modern in style with panels of black glass framed in white stone verticals. *Sundance* was running abreast of a seawall. Up ahead the seawall turned a corner to the right and the two long stretches of wall formed a right angle which enclosed bright-green practice fields used by the midshipmen. At the turn stood a beacon, a green flasher, to aid boats headed from the bay for the mouth of the Severn.

Before the bay bridge was completed in 1952, the only way to get across to the Eastern Shore was by ferryboat. In Harry's childhood the ferry still ran, leaving from Sandy Point just north of the bridge and crossing to Matapeake on the Eastern Shore. His father remembered an even earlier ferry, one which was boarded from a dock near the Naval Academy wall and ran from Annapolis over to Claiborne, a journey of an hour and a half. His father told of bountiful seafood suppers costing fifty cents apiece and served by waiters in white coats. A man content to stay put on the Eastern Shore, his father had left it only upon rare occasions. Another of his favorite memories was of standing on the top deck of the old ferryboat as it churned away from the Annapolis dock, standing at the rail, and looking back to see a Maryland-Navy lacrosse game in progress on the same green field that *Sundance* was now passing. He had told about it more than once until Harry had the feeling that he had witnessed the scene himself; the bright chilly afternoon in early spring, the bright-green field, the scurrying figures. He knew he could not have been there because he was not yet born, but by some hoax of memory he could sense his father's hand on his shoulder, could sense the two of them standing at the rail and watching the players grow small and finally disappear in the haze of spring.

With the Naval Academy seawall falling behind now, the view was unobstructed all the way out to the bay. Harry could see sails out in the area where the starting line should be and beyond these the misty silhouette of a tanker, and beyond the tanker the low blurred line of the Eastern Shore.

Up the bay to the left could be seen the long graceful sweep of the ferryboats' successor—the five-mile-long bridge carrying its usual sluggish Saturday morning load of traffic across to the playground that many deemed the Eastern Shore to be. Harry watched his course. Other boats were showing up now, most of them under power, some baremasted, others with mainsails hoisted and flapping as they motored along, a few under sail alone. The veiled sun cast a dull sheen over the water.

"Gun!" Sam sat on the starboard rail, looking intently out toward the starting line. Harry saw a puff of smoke far out over the water. On the white fiberglass bulkhead to the right of the open hatchway, Sam had taped a copy of the race circular showing the starting times for the various classes. He bent forward to look at the circular, then checked his watch. "Ten-minute gun for the Albergs," he said. "Fifty-five minutes to our start. We're in good shape." He took his perch on the rail again.

Harry nodded. "Catch the tide on this nun as we go by please, one of you guys."

Sam stood on the rail, one hand over the boom, looking down intently at the swirling grey water. The red nun buoy bobbed abeam and then passed quickly astern. "Still ebbing," Sam said.

"I think we can go up with the main in a few minutes," Harry said.

"Gun!" Sam said, looking off toward the puff of smoke. "Five minutes for the Albergs."

Roy was sitting on the port rail. "Maybe we can beat the bastard," he said.

"Who?" Sam asked.

"This guy Fontaine or whatever his name is."

"I wouldn't count on it," Harry said.

"Why not?" Roy demanded. "You feeling strong this morning, Sammie?"

"Strong enough." Sam paused. "How about you? How are *you* feeling?"

Roy nodded. "Fine," he said.

Sam was silent for a few moments, then turned to Harry. "See who's up ahead?"

"Yep." They had been steadily overtaking a light-blue Cal-25 under sail. The gold letters on the transom said *Pottagold*. There were two people in the cockpit. The helmsman was Gus Whitney, the guy Harry had fired. The young woman with red hair and faded blue sweat shirt was Gus's wife, Judy.

"Let's see if he says hello," Sam said.

"He won't," Harry said. "At least not to me."

From the cockpit of his blue boat, Gus looked back. Harry steered to port. As *Sundance* moved abeam, Gus looked straight ahead. Judy looked over and offered a weak smile.

"Gus-o," Roy called.

Gus turned. "Hey, Roy! Whaddya say, man?"

"Lookin' good," Roy called.

Harry bore away to starboard again and straightened his course. *Pottagold* fell behind. "They together again?" Sam asked. "I thought they were separated."

"They're practically divorced," Harry said. "But they still sail together."

"It's the only thing they've got in common," Roy said.

"They've got a kid in common," Sam said. "Don't they have a little girl?"

"Yes." Harry looked ahead. The breeze was still out of the east and as they moved out into the bay it seemed to be picking up a little. Water was beginning to slap the bow.

With the freshening breeze and the sound of the water and the boats all around them now, all traveling in the same direction, Harry always felt the adrenalin flow. He always felt mounting excitement as the starting line drew near but this morning some of the excitement was missing. He didn't feel the sharpness that he usually felt. The race didn't seem to matter as much.

Sam was ready with the mainsail, standing expectantly at the foot of the mast, the main halyard in his right fist. "Go up with it?" he called.

Harry nodded. "Take it on up!"

Sam and Roy hoisted the mainsail. Flapping a little, it slid smoothly up the mast. Cutting his engine speed, Harry pointed the bow directly into the breeze. This reduced the pressure of the wind upon the sail and made hoisting easier. "Up?" Sam called. Harry peered at the top of the mast. The sail was still a couple of inches short of the black line that signified maximum hoist. "A little more," he called. Sam horsed hard on the halyard and the tip of the sail inched higher. "Up!" Harry yelled. "Cleat it right there."

Stitched to the sail was his racing number, 31321, in large black numerals. With his free hand he reached back and drew in the mainsheet. The sail hardened; the numerals smoothed out and became taut. He picked up speed again, still under power, mainsail drawing and helping the speed. In the shifting clouds of sails around the starting line there was an opening and through it he caught a glimpse of the committee boat, then saw a puff of smoke and a second later heard the cannon. "Gun!" Sam shouted from the foredeck. Harry leaned forward and glanced at the race circular. "Delta two," he announced. "Twenty-five minutes for us."

"Good shape," Sam called.

They were drawing near now. Boats were maneuvering all along the starting line, some near the committee boat and others almost two hundred yards off to the right, near the red bell buoy which marked the line's westward end. A large white yawl was slanting across the line, taking a practice start to check the angle of the wind, then tacking quickly and circling out around the bell buoy to get behind the line again and join the other Deltas jockeying for position for the upcoming gun. A class now numerous enough for two divisions, Delta was primarily a repository for older boats, some of them stellar performers at one time—boats beautifully designed and beautifully built but which, in sailing parlance, had been out-designed. Encouraging the growth of Delta Class was a step on the part of governing bodies to have older and newer boats compete separately— and thereby de-emphasize the importance of money in racing. Older boats, no matter how successful their past performance, were at a distinct disadvantage because in the quest for the racing skipper's dollar, new designs—"rule-beaters"—were constantly coming off the drawing board onto the market, and newer usually meant faster. There were always wealthy men who felt that with a brand-new racing machine, one embodying all the latest designs and taking advantage of loopholes in the rules, they could clean up the fleet and so they bought and raced them and there was nothing illegal in any of it.

By edict, and by all the laws of ethical behavior and common sense, a skipper kept clear of the classes maneuvering for a start and Harry, slacking the mainsail, now dropped well behind the starting line. Even here traffic was heavy, with boats killing time until their respective starts, making final checks of their rigging, enjoying a final few minutes of relaxation, and watching the starts of the classes ahead. Back and forth they moved, keeping somehow out of each other's path, with an occasional cry of "Starboard!" as one or another claimed the right of way.

Slits of blue were appearing in the overcast again. Glancing through the pack of boats, Harry spotted a long black hull in the distance. Handing the tiller to Sam, he reached inside the cabin for his binoculars, held them to his eyes and focused. It was *Iceman.* With its class the very last to start, it had sailed off a quarter-mile to the southeast of the committee boat and was now tacking to run back.

"*Iceman.*" Harry pointed. "Way down there." Placing the binoculars on the cockpit seat, he took the tiller back from Sam. "Okay, Sammie, up with the jib in a minute." Sailing still deeper behind the line, he found clear water and then turned back into the wind as Sam raised the jib. A gun sounded. As a flight of starters crossed the line the sun came out, washing over the slanted sails for a brief second, then the sky went grey again. From the last boat across the line there was a cry of anguish. Starts were very important—less important in a distance race than in shorter races but important even so. In any long race over a broad body of water there might be only a few head-to-head moments. The finish could be one, although it might very well not be. There might be occasional tacking duels in open water and there could be huge jam-ups around a turning mark, but by and large the start was the one time and place where all boats could be counted upon to be together.

Sam stood on the top step of the ladder, peering forward over the cabin top. "Twenty minutes," he said. A loop of white twine encircled his thick bronzed neck and from it hung the stopwatch.

Harry killed the motor. Roy trimmed the jib. "Not too tight," Harry said. "We'll just drift along behind the line for a while, kill a little time, attaboy, Roy." They were sailing parallel to the starting line at least a hundred yards behind it, moving toward the committee boat end of the line. Far behind them were the spires of Annapolis, the steeple of St. Mary's Church, the green dome of the Naval Academy chapel. To the left was the bay bridge. Ahead was the Eastern Shore. "Anybody who wants any coffee or a Coke, this is the time to get it," Harry said.

"No thanks," Sam said.

"Looking for *Iceman*," Roy said. "Do you still see it?"

"Not now, I lost it." Harry was still looking. To the left and right of the committee boat, the sails looked like a forest of white tepees. "He's down there somewhere behind all those sails."

As Sam looked about, he was smiling faintly. "Awful lot of yachtsmen out today."

Harry nodded. "Yep." He knew what Sam was talking about. In Sam's eyes and in his own, yachtsmen were a special breed. They were smart rich men in beautiful boats. Not only were they smart—they were science-smart. Being science-smart enabled them to reduce the mystique of sailing to principles and truths of airflow and air pressure. They learned quickly about sail draft and helm balance and the reason why air flowed fastest about the convex side of a sail, why air was forced around the bulge of a jib, and why a boat sailing to windward was pulled by the wind, not pushed. In their big expensive boats with all the expensive equipment, all the wonderful instruments, they reduced sailing to a textbook operation—and money. Harry was not demeaning them. They gave him business; and furthermore he respected them. It took organizational ability and guts to sail a transatlantic race, yet he knew he could never be one of them. He was a seat-of-the-pants sailor. What he knew he had learned young and learned mostly from his father, and his father had been no yachtsman. He was a waterman.

"Seventeen minutes," Sam said. Roy now sat on the starboard rail, sipping Coke from a can, enjoying the scene. To people along for the ride, and for crew members not yet fully occupied, this was a special time of the race, the half-hour or so before their start. It was a time to see who had come out and how they and their boats were looking. It was a fashion show, a boat parade, a spectacle of humanity. Here was a skipper snarling at his crew, here one a picture of studied, purposeful composure, complete to corncob pipe; here a bearded giant who, jaw tilted, might have been posing for an ad for yellow foul-weather jackets; here a stocky man with a throaty voice who called out tensely, "Starboard, *Sundance*! Starboard!" although there was clearly no need for it. Harry spat overboard. "Hold your course," he droned, passing well astern. The stocky skipper was plowing on through. Somebody yelled at him, "Hey, starboard! *Hey watch it, you damned fool!*" The reply was a rueful laugh. "Where," asked the stocky man in a loud rhetorical voice, "are the courtesies of yesteryear? Where have all the Corinthians gone?" Most crew members by now had shucked off their foul-weather gear. On one boat the crew was dressed in matching outfits—T-shirts and shorts of the same lime green, looking like a basketball team perched on a windward rail. Through an opening Harry caught a glimpse of Walters Hackett—bareheaded, red in the face. Harry groaned at the sight of him. The opening quickly closed.

From Roy's throat there was a strange gurgling sound. Harry turned in alarm but Roy was only reacting to the sight of Blake. "Look what's coming," he said. "Look at the silly little son of a bitch—Morning, Mr. Blake, morning, sir." Blake saluted as he sailed by. It was a time for hailing other boats, for yelling good luck, for exchanging good-natured insults and, when traffic became heavy, for insults not so good-natured. There was at once a sense of pandemonium and yet also a grace and rhythm of movement and precision of timing, with boats running along the starting line, veering off from it, bow angling sharply across bow, hull at times all but grazing hull, repeated cries of "Starboard!" from skippers exercising vigilance and concentrating to avoid a collision; the steady purl of the water, the glide of graceful bows, the ringing sound of a spinning winch, the snap and crackle and rustle of a jib as a boat tacked. And then abruptly Harry saw *Iceman* emerging from the pack and sailing straight at them.

It was unmistakable with its long black hull and its tall slender mainsail and its huge genoa jib, the jib deeply overlapping the mainsail, drawn tight against the lifeline and reaching nearly to the afterend of the cockpit. The big boat had sailed up toward the bay bridge, far behind the line, and was now returning on a port tack. Harry, on starboard, fell off some to meet it. "Watch him under the jib, Sammie," he called. Sam looked out under the jib. The boats were approaching port to port. "Starboard," Harry called.

"Hold your course," came the relaxed reply. *Iceman* slid by, slicing the water, a black sliver, sleek and glistening. "Hold your course, Captain, hold your course," this time in a singsong, delivered as a pleasantry. "Morning, gentlemen, good morning." Fontaine was smiling, very affable, his hands easy on the wheel. He wore a white shirt looking as if it were made of sailcloth, with a blue and white horizontally striped dickey, all very Bretonesque. Not a lock of his grey hair was out of place.

They were passing hull to hull, separated by no more than six feet of water. As they passed, Elaine burst up through the rear hatch and jumped to the seat of the cockpit. She was wearing a white band about her hair and a light-blue zippered jacket. The jacket reached to her fingertips, making it appear that it was all she wore. Nothing else showed except her slim tanned legs. At the sight of her, Roy began to make gobbling noises.

"Hey, Harry!" she shouted. Harry looked quickly ahead to check traffic and then waved. She stood on the seat, smiling as the two boats, now stern to stern, kept going and the distance between them lengthened. "Gobble, gobble," Roy said.

Sam laughed at Roy and then followed the other boat with his eyes as it kept running along the line toward the red buoy.

"What in the name of God was *that?*" Roy demanded. He looked at Harry accusingly. "Skip, you've been holding out on us."

"I met her last winter in Jamaica," Harry said.

Roy shook his head with admiration. "Save some for me when you're finished," he said. "Maybe a couple of thighs."

Harry looked solemnly after *Iceman*. As he watched, Elaine disappeared below.

Eleven

BY NINE-FORTY-FIVE the Deltas and all the one-design classes were gone. At this point the breeze was holding relatively steady at five knots or so out of the southeast, and most of the boats were on a long port tack, slanting toward the western shore under skies that remained overcast.

One-design boats were boats of identical manufacture, all from the same mold. Cal-25s were a one-design class and so too were Alberg-30s, Tritons, Tartan-27s and Pearson-30s. For these boats the racing structure was simple enough. Within their respective classes they simply raced head to head without handicap allowances.

Still milling about behind the starting line, awaiting their guns, were the two divisions of the Midget Ocean Racing Club, known as MORC, pronounced Morsy; and boats racing under the so-called International Offshore Rule—the IOR fleet. This latter group included the fastest boats and the newest—the hot expensive boats and the rule beaters—and hence it was usually considered the most prestigious. It was broken down into Classes A, B, and C, with the largest boats in A, the smallest in C. Harry Crowder's *Sundance* was in Class C. *Iceman* was in Class A.

Boats in the IOR fleet, as well as in Delta and MORC, raced with handicap allowances intended to level out differences in size and equipment. Each boat was assigned a rating based upon a formula which took into account such components as its length, the size of its sails, the height of its mast, length of its boom, the distance from mast to stem, and a complicated series of hull measurements.

With the system of handicap allowances, Harry Crowder's boat at thirty-two feet long would be competing against other Class C boats but would also be competing for overall fleet honors against the fifty-eight-foot *Iceman* and other large blue-ribbon craft.

MORC was limited to boats less than thirty feet long and there were so many MORC boats that it was necessary to break the class into two sections.

At twenty-seven feet, the *Silver Heels* of Walters Hackett was in the midrange of the division containing the larger MORC boats. Fifteen minutes before his starting gun,

Hackett was weaving this way and that behind the line, trying to keep out of the way of other boats without giving the impression that he was running for cover, which under the circumstances, his wife felt, might have been the part of wisdom.

His commands had a sound of stern composure but Mrs. Hackett knew that behind this façade he felt poorly, and unsure of himself.

Although to her knowledge he had hardly wakened all night long, he complained of raw nerves from a poor night's sleep. He had also spoken of a "skittering" at the temples as well as a "light feeling" in his hands. Every now and then she was aware of his teeth clicking.

Mrs. Hackett, after her own nightlong ordeal, was finding some reassurance in what the weather told her about spinnaker runs. Generally speaking, spinnaker runs were made with the wind behind the boat. With the wind in the east—and sometimes even happily in the *south*east— she knew they could not set a spinnaker at the start and if she got lucky they might not have to set one *all day long!*

Thus comforted, she was able in these moments before the start to feel some sympathy for Hackett. As he went careering through the fleet, she could sense his wistful desire to be part of the scene, to establish a kinship with all the expert skippers in their big beautiful blue-ribbon boats with their fine tuning and slick bottoms and elite crews; to be as redoubtable, as self-assured as, say, the skipper at the tiller of the bright-red yawl they were passing, a sturdy figure in an olive foul-weather jacket, shoulders back, wearing a friendly grin, sliding so easily and casually about behind the line, tasting glory on a summer's morning, giving his orders in such an offhand way, tossing out a greeting here, a greeting there, "Sam . . . hi, Nat, how's the boy? . . . Milt . . . how'd you do last week?" A grin, a half-salute, breezy skipper, impossible dream.

For her husband's sake Mrs. Hackett for this one day would do her very best, knowing full well that the experience could hardly be anything less than a fiasco, quite possibly a humiliation, and that within a matter of days he would sell the boat and take up a new hobby, something with less potential for destruction—photography perhaps, or maybe a fruit and vegetable stand.

If she could survive the day, her marriage would survive boating. As best she could, she would overlook his intensity, his excitability, knowing full well that he was in the grip of something more powerful than himself.

What part his sister Kitty might play, she could not be sure. Kitty had not seen Hackett in his retirement. She had not seen him in his boating phase and most particularly she had not seen him in his racing phase. Mrs. Hackett was curious to see what might happen once Kitty caught a glimpse of her brother's new personality; his boating personality. Kitty might have detected some evidence of change that morning at the Annapolis public dock. After a great deal of shouting and uncertain maneuvering she was yanked aboard shortly before nine but whatever misgivings she may have felt were lost in the pleasure of seeing them.

Now as they maneuvered about behind the line, Kitty did not seem quite at ease. Kitty as a crew member was no bargain. In the very fact that Hackett had found it necessary to resort to her, there was something to be pitied. She had plenty of enthusiasm for sailing but very little know-how. On the other hand she was a good golfer and a good natural athlete, and Hackett's hopes were high. Such was the irrational degree of his enthusiasm that to hear him tell it anyone might have gained the impression that Kitty was a crack crew member, a hard-nosed spinnaker woman imported for the occasion all the way from the Nutmeg State.

The fact was that until quite recently the only time she had ever sailed in her life was at the age of eleven when she had been taken out for a spin on Barnegat Bay in a small boat known as a Jersey Sneak-Box.

Now as the moments of crisis drew ever closer, Hackett grew ever more tense. On the way out to the starting line he had delivered a garbled pep talk. Even though they had all come late to sailing, he said, they could make up for it with good communication, with concise thinking and precise unhurried movements, with "good attitudes and sea savvy"—neither of which he seemed to be displaying at the moment.

"How much time?" he demanded in a strained voice. "How much time, Mag?"

Mrs. Hackett was bad at compass points, at reading road maps, at distinguishing left from right, and at reading stopwatches. This last was a shortcoming she had not known about until just within the past few minutes.

The job of timing their start was hers. The watch was slung about her neck on a lanyard of braided yellow leather. She and Kitty wore turned-down white duck crew hats of the sort worn by Franklin Roosevelt at Campobello and elsewhere. To protect their hands the two ladies wore grey and navy striped gardening gloves with navy-blue palms.

Now as her husband waited impatiently for an answer, Mrs. Hackett held the watch in one gloved hand, raising it to chin level.

"Mag!"

A boat was approaching. "Starboard, six-seventeen," its skipper shouted and then, with the beginnings of panic: *"Starboard, six-seventeen!"*

"Hold your course," Hackett rasped.

Mrs. Hackett let out her breath. Bravely she concentrated on the speeding second hand and the tiny confusing intervals between the closely packed lines, distracted by the fear that at any moment they were going to bump into another boat—any one of several. Hackett was waiting impatiently for the time. "My God, Margaret!" he snapped.

Kitty gave him a curious look.

Focusing hard upon the stopwatch, Mrs. Hackett reminded herself yet again that he was a man in the grip of something stronger than himself.

Looking briefly about at other boats, at the faces of other

skippers, listening to the cries that rent the air, she realized there were others in much the same grip.

"Seven minutes," she called. When the second hand pointed straight up, it was much easier, in fact quite simple. "Seven minutes," she repeated with confidence.

"Okay, thanks, Mag. Thanks. Very good. Okay, let's steady down now."

Kitty seemed reassured.

Since becoming a boatsman, Hackett for whatever obscure reason had taken to using Vitalis when he seemed to feel it was called for and that morning he had used a great deal. Ashore, Vitalis seemed to work out well enough but on the water it could, Mrs. Hackett thought, be more of a minus than a plus, at least in his case. Instead of lifting and falling idly in the breeze, his hair, once it was blown erect, had stuck pretty much where it was. "Okay," he said now, "I'll tell you what I'm planning—so you'll know what I've got in mind."

"Suppose it storms, Walters," Kitty said.

"It's not going to storm," he said.

"But suppose it does."

"It's not going to. We'll face it when we come to it. How much time?" He paused, frowning. "I mean, what the hell," he went on with exasperation. "Suppose we have a tidal wave. Suppose we have an earthquake. Suppose this. Suppose that." Briefly the whites of his eyes were showing.

A gun sounded.

From beneath the turned-down brim of the white duck hat, Kitty was looking at him once more with concern.

"Okay, that was our five-minute gun," he said. "Now lemme tell you what we're going to do."

"That sounds like a good idea," Kitty said in a tight voice.

"How much time now?" he asked.

"Four and a half minutes on the dot," his wife said.

"Good. Good-o. Okay, Mag, at two minutes, sing out. Sing out at two and we tack immediately. Tack immediately at two minutes, got it? Then we sail back away from the line for one minute, right? One minute away from the line and then tack and head for the line again. Go right for the line and we should be crossing the line exactly as the gun goes off, because one minute plus one minute equals two minutes, do we understand each other?"

"Starboard, six-seventeen. Starrrrrrr-but. *Hey! Six-seventeen!!!*"

"Okay, hold your course, snakebrain," Hackett muttered. "Stupid reptilian bastard."

"Was that his fault or ours?" Kitty asked conversationally.

"Nobody's. Okay, lemme have a time check and let's make this a nice smooth tack, okay. Let's see if we can do our best work. How much time?"

"Almost," Margaret Hackett said, watch to her chin, focusing on the second hand.

"Almost what? I wanna hear numbers for God's sake. Not 'almost'!"

"Walters!" Kitty said.

"Ten seconds before two minutes," Mrs. Hackett said.

"Okay, sing out at two."

Mrs. Hackett focused intently. "Two!" she sang out.

"Okay, ready about!" he shouted. Mrs. Hackett reached for the winch handle. "Hard-a-lee! *Hard-a-lee,* for God's sake! Let the sheet go. *Let the sheet go!* Slack. Slack. Just remember we're not on the wind now, we're running back away from the line."

Hackett glanced at Kitty with a brief show of guilt. Kitty said nothing. Smoothly they glided off behind the line into uncluttered waters.

"At one minute we tack again and head back to the line for the gun . . . Margaret? Margaret?"

Again Mrs. Hackett had the stopwatch close to her chin.

"Lemme hear from you, Margaret, let's keep our lines of communication open. Talk to me, Margaret."

"One minute and a half," Mrs. Hackett said.

"Minute and a half, gotcha. I'll be fine once we get across the starting line. Okay, Mag, now lemme have it in five-second increments."

"What's that thing?" Kitty asked, peering over the side.

"Minute twenty-five," Mrs. Hackett sang out.

"Minute twenty-five—what thing?"

"That thing there in the water."

"*What* thing in the water?"

"Minute twenty."

"It's okay," Kitty said. "It was just a stick, never mind. It was just a stick in the water."

"For God's sake, Kitty!"

"For God's sake yourself, Walters!"

"Minute fifteen," Mrs. Hackett said.

"What did you ask me down here for?" Kitty demanded. "I thought it was supposed to be fun."

"There's no time for all that," Hackett said. "Belay all that. It *is* fun. What the hell do you think it is if it's not fun?"

"Minute ten . . . " Mrs. Hackett was staring intently at the watch now, mouth open, lips poised. "Minute five . . . "

"Okay," Hackett snapped. "Get ready. Get ready. We'll steady down in a minute and all be friends again. Ready about. Ready about? Ready about! *Ready about!* Okay, hard-a-lee. Hard-a-*lee!* Let the sheet go, Kitty. Okay, now get it in on the other side. Get it in! Help her, Kitty. *Help her!* Jib in a little more. Little more. Okay, jib right there. Right there for the jib. Okay, let's steady out. Going to weather now, headed for the line. Talk to me, Margaret. How much time, old girl?"

Mrs. Hackett raised the watch to her chin again. "Thirty seconds," she said. "Twenty-five . . . twenty . . . fifteen . . . ten . . . "

Hackett glowered. He went limp. "The hell with it," he said. "Forget it."

Letting the watch dangle, Mrs. Hackett placed her

gloved hands in her lap. In another moment the gun sounded.

"Hey!" Kitty said. "Look at all those boats! Why are they so far ahead of us? What are they doing away up there?"

"Crossing the starting line," Hackett said, barely moving his lips.

"Why aren't we?" Kitty asked. "What happened? Did you miscalculate, or what?"

Hackett didn't reply. His hair stuck up in spikes. He was glowering with self-reproach, the picture of misery, and Mrs. Hackett again found it in her heart to pity him. She knew what he had done. One minute away from the line and one minute back, true, but he had neglected to include the time needed in between; the rather considerable number of seconds needed to get the boat turned around, and by now the boats in their class were far far ahead.

"Okay, let's steady down now," he said as they at last crossed the starting line. "We've got a long way to go. Thirty miles. A lot can happen in thirty miles."

Mrs. Hackett was thinking much the same thing and wondering how in the world they would ever make it.

Under other circumstances and in other hands, a racing start could be a thing of precision, an exacting and sometimes gratifying challenge.

After Hackett's departure the next class to start was Class C, and on *Sundance* Sam was counting down.

"A minute thirty . . . one twenty-five . . . "

Harry Crowder would never know what it was like to be in the cockpit of an America's Cup contender but here on the bay, on any ordinary weekend, the start of a race gave him all he could handle. In any single class there could be as many as twenty starters, twenty moving boats, twenty hulls to avoid colliding with, twenty boats scrambling for space, vying for position.

The way a skipper approached a starting line told something about the skipper. Harry's approach was to expect no quarter and to give no more than he could get away with; to take what the rules allowed and no less. A man who showed timidity, who deferred to other boats, was at a great disadvantage. At the other end of the scale was the Captain Bligh type who tried to scare off other skippers with intimidating tactics and a loud mouth.

Harry was straining every nerve.

"One fifteen."

"Tacking at one minute," Harry said.

"Tacking at one minute," Sam repeated. Brow furrowed, facing aft, he was looking fixedly at the watch which he held in his palm, looking now and again over his shoulder at the set of the jib.

On the cockpit seat, Roy was squatting on his haunches, as agile and bouncy as a chimpanzee, winch handle in his fist.

In these critical moments before the gun, Harry's visual field was a mass of swarming movement. Concentrating on the set of his sails and looking for open water, he saw the rest as a blur of foam and clouds, a tilted mast, a head bent over a winch, walls of sails and bright-colored foul-weather gear.

From all through the fleet there were shouts, commands, some given in tones as calm as those employed by Harry, some delivered in tones of violence.

"Get that jib in, God damn you!"

It had the sound of savagery, so that even amid the excitement and tension one had time to wonder briefly about the owner of the voice, to wonder what real life was like back home or at the office, or in the nocturnal recesses of the soul; and to wonder too for a moment about the voice's poor cringing target, fumbling with jib sheet and winch handle.

"Hard-a-lee!" Harry called, and well behind the line they tacked swiftly and expertly.

Sam kept counting. "Forty-five seconds . . . forty . . ."

"Ease it in," Harry said.

"Easing in," Roy said, tightening the jib slightly.

"Fraction more."

Staring up intently at the interval between the jib and the spreader, Roy gave the crank a half-turn. The winch clicked once. Twice.

"Thirty-five seconds," Sam counted.

"Gimme thirty," Harry said.

"Thirty-three . . . thirty-two . . . "

"Shape down," Roy called, glancing at the committee boat. "Looking good, Harry."

"Thirty . . . twenty-nine . . . "

"Going for it," Harry said.

A good skipper was a bundle of conditioned reflexes. There was no time to think, merely to react. Ideally the thinking took place beforehand, when strategy and tactics were plotted.

No matter how carefully they were plotted, a skipper could find himself in tight quarters. Beginning his drive for the starting line, Harry found his boat sandwiched between two dark-blue hulls. He possessed the right of way over one and owed it to the other. All three parallel hulls were moving for the starting line at the same angle. Collision could mean hull damage as well as forfeiture. The offending skipper, the one breaching the rules of right-away, would be protested and for him the race would be over before it had begun.

"Twenty-five . . . twenty-four . . . twenty-three . . . "

The parallel courses continued, with the steady slap-slap of the water against bow, the steady movement toward the starting line, sails looming, hull closing upon hull until the rails nearly touched and the crews were face to face in their adjoining cockpits.

"Coming up, *Sundance!* Coming up!"

The breeze was down in the southeast and a port tack was the only possible start. The skipper to Harry's right, farthest from the wind, was asserting his right of way, meaning that Harry must angle off to the left and give him

room; yet to Harry's left, practically sitting on his rail, was
the third boat and this one, since it was closest to the wind,
owed right of way to both the others, yet he too was
blocked.

"Forcing me up, *Sea Song,* forcing me up," Harry called
to the skipper on his left.

"I got nowhere to go," came the strained reply.

"Eighteen . . . seventeen . . . "

Harry glanced quickly at the skipper on his right. *"Sea
Song* can't go up. He's boxed in."

"Keep clear, *Sundance,* " the skipper on his right warned.

Harry shrugged, then grinned.

After a moment the man on his right grinned back.
"Hell of a place to be on a Saturday morning . . . "

"Fourteen . . . thirteen . . . twelve . . . "

"Looking good," Roy said.

"Eleven . . . ten . . . "

"Let the jib go, Roy! Let it go, let it go!" The words
tumbled from Harry's lips. They were moving fast and he
was slacking the jib to cut their speed to make sure their
nose didn't stick over the line too early.

"Sea Song's going up a little," Roy said.

"Great," Harry said. "Okay, harden up and we'll go up
with him. Here we go . . . "

"Six . . . five . . . four . . . three . . . two . . . one . . . "

Pause.

"Gun!"

"In on the jib. Hold it. Hold it. Great!"

"Good start!" Roy said.

Harry's breath went out in a huge sigh and he was
feeling the release, the catharsis, and now this much was
over, done well enough, and they were moving smoothly
ahead, sails drawing, water slapping. Ahead there were
thirty whole miles of sailing, hours and hours of it. Ahead
lay their fate on this day in July. In sailing circles there was
general agreement that the winning skipper in any race was
the one making fewest mistakes and the one making fewest

mistakes was usually the most experienced. His father had said much the same thing in a different way. How good a skipper is a man? "All depends on how much time a man spends into his boat." Harry had spent a lot of time in his boat, this one and others. Today he wasn't sure how much good it would do him.

He looked over his shoulder. The Class B boats were swarming around, making ready for their start. *Iceman* was blocked from view.

Roy was sitting on the port rail, looking up at the sails. Sam had just put the stopwatch below. "Good work," Harry said. "Both you guys. Nice work."

By eleven-ten all the boats were gone, and aboard the committee boat there was an air of relaxation. There were congratulations back and forth on a job well done. No re-calls had been necessary and although the wind now showed signs of dropping out, it had held up long enough to get all the classes away in fair starts. So the committee members were able to relax. The first part of their job was done. At their leisure they would pull up anchor and motor down to Oxford and take up their vigil at the finish line, but they had all day to get there because if the weather forecast was correct it would not be a fast race.

Up on deck, Anthony Korbut was drinking his fourth beer of the morning. Hanging over the rail, he gazed down the bay at the fleet. Although he had only been in the area a relatively short time he knew some of the boats by hull and color and sail number. By reputation he knew the strengths and weaknesses of some of the top skippers, par-ticularly those in the larger boats. There were some excel-lent boats and excellent skippers in the Annapolis area as well as on the Eastern Shore but today the boat to beat of course had to be *Iceman.* Any local skipper worth his salt would be trying to take the measure of this refugee from the big time. Nobody would beat him boat for boat. In Korbut's opinion the one with the best chance of beating him on corrected time might be Oxford's onetime favorite son, Harry Crowder.

Sipping his beer, Korbut continued to gaze down the bay, following the fleet with his eyes. It was a beautiful sight, yet a sight that was even more beautiful when viewed from on high. There was a scene he would always remember—not from this bridge but from another. It was on the afternoon when he was on his way to prison and he was in the back seat handcuffed to a U.S. Marshal. As they crossed the bridge in the government car there was a race going on and he had seen the fleet spread out below in full panoply, a hundred or more boats headed in the same direction. The boats had been moving well that day, faster than these boats were moving now, yet on that day, viewed from above, they had seemed not to be moving at all. What he had seen looked congealed, a set piece, a frozen tableau, perhaps because their rates of speed were so nearly the same, preserving frozen intervals; this plus the identical set of the sails in boat after boat. If now he were riding across the lofty bay bridge and looking down he would see the same tableau. He would see a Coleridge fleet of painted boats with clean white sails, frozen on the grey water.

Twelve

THE COURSE OF THE RACE TO Oxford that day covered approximately twenty miles on the bay, almost eight on the Choptank River, and a little more than two on the Tred Avon.

The directions were south, then east, and finally a short distance north.

The course resembled a huge capital L, with the long vertical representing the distance southward down the bay;

the base of the L representing the eastward leg on the Choptank, and the final serif representing the two-plus miles
northward on the Tred Avon to the finish line.

Along the way there were landmarks which not only
performed their navigational function but served as familiar points of reference for the racers. The first of these was
Thomas Point Light, one of the bay's diminishing number
of old-style lighthouses. South of Annapolis, against the
blurred greenery of the Western Shore, it stood in the shallows near the mouth of South River, a white cottage on
struts, rocks piled about its feet. From the starting line
down to Thomas Point was approximately three miles.

From Thomas Point, the next landmark of note lay at
the end of a long diagonal in the opposite direction—all the
way across the bay. This was Bloody Point Light, which
stood on the Eastern Shore side near the southern tip of
Kent Island. Bloody Point Light was a burly cylinder of red
sandstone building blocks, hung with a spiral, black-runged
ladder curving from a few feet above the waterline up to the
reflector lamp on top. It marked an abrupt change of depth
in the water—from forty feet to three feet—and in the old
days was the site of many a shipwreck. Once Bloody Point
Light had come abeam, a boat had passed the seven-mile
mark and thus had completed a little better than one third
of the bay portion of the course.

In any sailboat race the greatest influence by far is
weather. Weather creates a race in its own image, gives each
race a particular coloration, heavily influencing maneuvers,
strategy, mood, comfort, victory and defeat. It brings variables that cannot be controlled. A boat may be tuned to a
uniform level of performance, a crew may vary little in its
race-to-race proficiency, yet both will always be subject to
the variables that sweep in from the horizons and pour
down from the sun and clouds.

That day the weather would approximately follow the
National Weather Service prediction. In the process it

would offer the variety so often characteristic of a summer's day on the Chesapeake. The morning would be overcast; soon after midday the skies would clear and the temperature rise. In the east that morning, the wind had already dropped down to the southeast. Here it would gradually diminish and die. After a period of calm there would be zephyrs from all around the compass, faint breezes first from one direction and then another. Finally the wind would set in from the west-northwest and pick up in velocity during the latter part of the afternoon.

But at eleven-thirty that morning it was still blowing from the southeast. Its speed was diminishing but still reaching as high as six and seven knots. This meant of course that it was blowing against the fleet, blowing counter to the fleet's course, and for the racers this meant tacking all the way down the bay, moving in an endless series of diagonals, long port tacks to the west and short starboard tacks to the east, white moths criss-crossing their way southward.

That morning, even though the boats had been funneled through a comparatively narrow starting sector, the fleet would become quickly and predictably scattered, ranging from one side of the bay to the other, a five-mile spread. There was also a goodly spread from north to south. The classes which had started early were already well down the bay. An hour after the starting gun for the final class some boats would be already well past Bloody Point, while others would not be as far as Thomas.

In addition to staggered starts and adverse and erratic wind there were always other forces that worked to scatter a fleet. Some skippers followed the Eastern Shore, some went to the west. This was so for a variety of reasons, perhaps simply because one might have done well in the past on one side or the other and had a preference for it, an affection, even a superstition. Skippers might hold a tack too long, or anticipate a wind shift that did not materialize, or shoot for a patch of air that disappeared before they reached it. A prime factor was the tidal current. Tidal current was strongest in deep water, hence with a favoring current a skipper often rode the deep channel in the middle of the bay. When the tide was flooding up the bay against him, he would go to the shallows, where the adverse current was weakest. Some skippers knew this and some did not. Some knew it and disregarded it. Some, balancing wind against current, decided that the strength of the wind in a particular sector was great enough to offset whatever adverse effect the tide might have in that sector.

One of the boats playing the Western Shore that morning was *Pottagold*, the powder-blue Cal-25 sailed by Gus Whitney and his estranged wife Judy, a tall young woman with broad shoulders and strong legs. She wore blue shorts and a faded blue sweatshirt with the sleeves rolled above the elbow. Her strawberry-blonde hair was tied in a blue bandanna. Gus wore blue denim cutoffs and no shirt. The blond fuzz on his chest matched the blond fuzz on his face.

Among the contestants that day there were many who would admire the smooth, skillful way the Whitneys handled their boat, the effortless, casual movements that came from long years of practice.

Pottagold had started the race on a port tack, switched over to starboard shortly after crossing the starting line and then a few minutes later switched again, taking off on a long port tack which it still held. Half an hour into the race, it was now far over on the Western Shore side, approaching Thomas Point Light and a little too close inshore to be comfortable.

Thomas Point was a favorite spot for fishermen. Two hundred yards from a cluster of fishing boats, *Pottagold* tacked over and headed once more out toward the middle of the bay, a sturdy little boat showing its glazed blue bottom paint as it heeled.

Until now the skies had been grey, with clouds rolling out behind them in long layers back toward the Bay Bridge, but just within the past few minutes the sun had broken through. As the boat slid on toward the middle of the bay on its starboard tack, the rift in the clouds grew wider and the sun now shone brightly, striking highlights in Judy Whitney's red hair.

At this point *Pottagold* was the leading Cal-25 and rapidly closing the gap on a Pearson-30, a class which had started five minutes ahead of the Cals.

Gus Whitney had the Pearson measured. He looked at the Pearson, then at the set of his sails. "In a little on the jib," he muttered.

Judy was an excellent crew member. She knew not to make sudden lurching movements, knew enough to move lithely and gracefully, to pick up her feet and place them down with care. She knew that in lighter air the jib should be let out some and that when the breeze freshened it should be brought in. She knew everything without being told, yet when she was given an order she carried it out swiftly and smoothly.

Gus and Judy had been separated since the previous autumn and in another few weeks their divorce would be final. Judy loved sailing and she loved racing, probably almost as much as her husband did. On land they argued a great deal. She had thrown jealous tantrums and he had gotten drunk and thrown tantrums of his own, but on a boat, in a race, they got along beautifully. The most compatible hours of their marriage had been spent in a sailboat, this sailboat, *Pottagold.*

When the sailing season began in April, Gus was living alone above a restaurant in downtown Annapolis, where he still lived. When he asked Judy to crew it struck her at first as a little far-out but then she asked herself why not, and all through the spring and summer she had been crewing for him. Not every race. He didn't always ask her but when he did she usually said yes. Sometimes they took a third person along but they were perfectly capable of handling the boat by themselves and always finished well up in the standings among the Cal-25s. Meanwhile they had gotten to be something of a joke around town—a couple clearly compatible only in a sailboat race; a husband and wife who had nasty destructive arguments in front of other people, even in front of their three-year-old daughter Jenny; a husband and wife who were separated and in the process of getting a divorce—and still went out and won races together. Gus may be willing to give her up as a wife, people said around town, but there's *no way* he's going to give her up as a crew.

By now they had sailed perhaps two hundred yards out into the bay, with the Pearson still ahead. When the Pearson tacked they followed suit and took out once more on a long diagonal once again toward the Western Shore, a course which this time would carry them well south of Thomas Point.

Judy was watching the Pearson. "Moving on him a little," she said.

Gus looked. "Maybe a little."

"Making trees on him," she said.

"Okay. Meanwhile . . . "

"What?"

"Go up and shake that starboard telltale loose."

On light feet Judy clambered forward. The telltale was a piece of light-blue yarn matching the light-blue hull. It had wrapped itself about the starboard stay so that it did not fly in the wind. Standing on top of the cabin to free it, she stretched high and wide. Her sweat shirt rode up, exposing an expanse of lightly freckled stomach.

"Thanks," he said.

"Like some coffee or anything?" She stood on the top step of the ladder and faced him through the open hatchway.

"No thanks."

Gus sat on the rail, holding the tip of the tiller extension with his thumb and index finger, holding it very lightly, handling the boat so easily and gracefully, eyes trained on the leading edge of the jib. Judy had been raised a Catholic and in catechism class when she was young they had talked a lot about being in a state of grace. With a sailboat, Gus was in a state of grace. From the time he was a kid, sailing was all he had ever cared about, all he had ever been good at. For him it was unfortunate that there had to be an economic side of life. He had been aggrieved to find that he could not spend his life doing what he loved most and did best—sailing a boat.

It was his tough luck, Judy often thought, and doubtless her own—and poor Jenny's—that he had chosen the wrong sport. All through the land, athletes were being paid to do what they did best. Although she could no longer be called an admirer of her husband she was still capable of resenting these other sports on his behalf. Her special target was professional basketball, her pet hate. It pained and even enraged her to think that $300,000 a year (and up to almost a million) could be paid to someone for stuffing a ball through a hoop.

It was remarkable about basketball. For a tiny initial outlay—a ball and a schoolyard backboard—the returns could be enormous. Sailboats on the other hand cost a great deal of money. With sailing the outlay was large and the monetary return absolutely nil. Nobody came to a sailboat race and nobody showed a sailboat race on television. In baseball, basketball, and football, bright young prospects were drafted and given fat professional contracts. From an early age, Gus had been a sensational sailor but nobody was drafting sailors. For the failure of her marriage, Judy sometimes blamed the incompatibility between the economic system and her husband's particular skill.

When she began to nag and pick a little and to point out some of the economic facts of life, he had begun to sleep with other women, young women, hardly more than star-struck children, as she herself had once been so star-struck by his husky body and the golden tan he always managed to acquire no later than Memorial Day. Having been there herself, she could easily visualize the way he propped up these kids in the cockpit, himself perched on the rail, wear-

ing only a pair of ragged white cutoffs, held up at the waist
with a piece of line, his hand light on the tiller; and they
sitting there, faces flushed with fresh sunburn and the
breeze caressing their flushed faces, hair in braids, tied,
probably, with red and green ribbons for port and starboard—how many girls had done that; thought it was an
original idea and done it to impress and please the skipper.
She had once. And the skipper, pointing to his lean hard
midsection and saying, "Listen, in case you'd like to learn
how to tie a bowline, here's the way it's done, here's one
right here."

And then taking them below to the foreberth, her private province and no one else's, and yet he had taken them
down there and spilled his lousy semen all over the nice
new maroon sleeping bag she had bought him for his birthday at Sam's Surplus, not even bothering to wash it off,
sometimes taking the trouble to drop anchor when he took
one of them down to the cabin and sometimes not even
bothering, just letting the boat drift with the tide. In one of
their truth-and-honesty sessions he had told her all this.
Thenceforward she would always be suspicious of any boat
glimpsed drifting with the tide and no one in view.

And then saying, as he had said, that in the final analysis
it was her fault for nagging and picking, for not genuinely
sharing his love of sailing, for not giving the marriage "suffi-
cient input"—a phrase he had read in a magazine or more
likely learned from a thirty-five-year-old female psychiatrist
he had been dating, a phrase he didn't even know the meaning of. He was saving all of his own input these days for
others—sometimes at anchor and sometimes just drifting
with the tide, the bastard.

She looked up at the sky. "This day can't make up its
mind," she said. The pools of blue narrowed and disappeared, then opened again.

"Yeah." He glanced at her quickly and then back
at the jib. "I guess this is as good a time as any to tell
you my news," he said. "Listen, in another month or so

we'll be divorced . . . "

"That's news?"

"What I was going to tell you is that I don't think I'll be coming back after the race, okay?"

"Why not?"

"I think I'll be heading out from Oxford tomorrow. You can take the boat back up, okay? I'll find somebody to sail back with you."

"Heading out where?"

"With Mel Fontaine. You know who I mean?"

"Of course."

"I asked him if I could sign on as part of his permanent crew and he as good as said yes. He's pulling out tomorrow. It should be a terrific experience. I may be gone a long time though. I thought I should tell you."

"Where's your stuff?"

"I put some things aboard last night before I went to bed. He told me to bring my gear."

She nodded solemnly. "How do you think Jenny will feel about all this?"

"Listen, this is the chance of a lifetime. He sails all over the world with that boat. Next summer he's sailing the Plymouth-to-Perth race—England to Australia."

Judy nodded. "I can't take the boat back though. My mother and Jenny are picking me up after the race."

"Okay, I'll find somebody else."

"Maybe you'd better."

"I guess we should probably sell the boat," he said. "So . . . this may be the last time we ever race together . . . so let's make it a good one, okay?"

Judy was looking at the tip of the mast. "Your main could come in a little," she said.

In the aftercabin of *Iceman* there were portholes on either side, and on sunny days Elaine, as she lay in the bunk, could look up and watch the reflection of the water flash and dart on the ceiling.

Now over the interior of the cabin the lamp cast a soft glow, blending with the grey light from outside. Elaine lay looking at the ceiling, her head propped against two thick pillows. She still wore the dark-blue fingertip jacket and her long bare legs were drawn up on the bunk.

She knew they were underway. The sounds on the boat were different once a race began. Her bunk was just beneath the cockpit and from above she could hear the drone of voices, the occasional click of a winch and once a heavy thump, as if someone had landed heavily. This was followed by an angry outburst from Fontaine. Aboard *Iceman*, particularly during a race, heavy movements were outlawed. Everybody moved lightly, with the grace and light step of a ballet dancer, at least they were supposed to. The crew was very efficient. Each of the guys had a specific task for each maneuver and they practiced precision.

Once again it was quiet above. Next to her leg, facedown on the bunk, lay a magazine, one of several that came in the mail pouch. She glanced at it, then stared at the ceiling. After leaving Harry's house the previous evening she had gotten back to the boat just ahead of Fontaine and when he came in she pretended to be asleep because she didn't want him to make love to her. She didn't feel like it and beyond that she was afraid he might notice something different about her. He knew her very, very well and she didn't want him to know or even suspect anything yet. She wanted to wait until after the race. It wouldn't be fair to tell him until after the race was over.

When she thought about telling him, she felt something funny in the pit of her stomach. Telling him would not be easy. Three years was a very long time and he had been very good to her. He had always said she could go when she was ready, but she wasn't at all sure he meant it. But he wouldn't hurt her, that much she knew. When she first went with him she felt it was only a question of time before she was dumped. In the terrible days just after Marioso she had known rich men who were content only with a succession of very young girls. The exploration of sex for them was an exhilarating pastime—but only in the company of youth and beauty. Much of the thrill was to corrupt; and without youth and beauty, without freshness, there could be no corruption. But it was not that way with Fontaine. She knew she was something very special to him.

The magazine was face-down on her stomach. She heard the whir of a winch, the swirl of water—and then as the boat tacked the grey sky tilted rapidly past the porthole. A moment later she heard a step on the companionway ladder. She looked at the ceiling, listening, but heard only the sound of the boat moving through the water, a faint creak, the sounds of sailing. Opening the magazine again, she continued with the article she had been reading on "women who are making it in a man's world," women who were physicists and architects and lawyers and doctors.

Directly forward of her cabin was the somewhat more spacious main cabin. In it were a stove, an oven, a sink, an avocado-green icebox, and a heavily varnished dining table. Settees were covered in black and green plaid and the walls with teak paneling. Sailbags were strewn about, one under the dining table, another slumped against the icebox. Above one of the settees hung a framed watercolor of a Victorian sailing scene.

On the cabin's starboard side there was a compact space outfitted for the use of a navigator. It contained a VHF radio-telephone, a depth finder, Loran, a radio direction finder, speed and distance indicator, compass, and other expensive electronic equipment suitable for ocean racing. Hanging shelves held charts, tide tables, and navigation books, as well as a neat array of dividers and protractors, parallel rulers, and sharpened pencils.

There was also a chart table and chair. The ship-to-shore radio was turned on, and seated at the chart table monitoring the set was a young crewman named Billy Henderson. Even during races, Fontaine kept the set constantly tuned to the marine telephone frequencies, primarily for the calls he might receive from New York, or from members of his family—his wife on Puget Sound, the children from wherever they happened to be around the country.

Crew members rotated in monitoring the set. Billy Henderson's face was burnished deep red. Although he was only nineteen he sported a heavy, drooping mustache. In his pink and white shirt he looked himself like a figure from a Victorian watercolor. His long legs were stretched out beneath the chart table and he sat low in the straight-backed chair, idly twirling a protractor about his index finger. The Saturday morning call traffic was heavy. Many of the calls concerned food and drink. A fisherman had just finished talking to his wife, asking her to have a six-pack of beer at the dock when he landed. "Are you through, Captain? Captain, are you through?" With a bored expression, Billy Henderson twirled the protractor and listened to the nasal voice of the Marine Operator: "Baltimore Marine off."

A second later she was on again. "Baltimore Marine . . . "

"Baltimore Marine?"

"Baltimore Marine."

"Oh. Okay, Baltimore Marine, this is the *Colly-model* and my call number is Alpha Romeo Zebra one-uh-two-uh-two-uh-nine-er . . . over."

"The name of your vessel again, please, Captain?"

"*Colly-model.*"

"Could you spell it please, Captain?"

"*Colly-model.* Charlie, Oliver, Double Leopard, Yesterday, hyphen. Mother, Oliver, uh, Daniel, Elephant, uh, Leopard. Over."

"Go ahead, Captain. Your call, please."

With a yawn, Billy Henderson reduced the volume until he could barely hear it and slid lower in his chair.

As he did so, the cabin door opened and Elaine stepped out wearing a white middy blouse.

"Hey!" Billy said. "You got anything on under that?"

"Yes," she said.

"Prove it."

Raising the blouse, she flashed the pants of a blue bikini. "Okay, that proves it," Billy said.

She sat at the dining table on the opposite side of the cabin, facing him.

"What's wrong, Elainsky?" the boy asked.

"Are you down here for the whole race?" she asked.

He shrugged. "I guess so." Getting up from the chart table, he moved past her to the icebox, yanked open the door, took out a large can of cola, ripped off its metal tab, and dropped the tab into a large black plastic trash bag beneath the sink.

Billy's feet were bare. So were Elaine's. On his way back to the chart table he tried to step on her foot. She yanked it back just in time. He tried again, missed again. "Let me alone," she said.

"What's wrong?" he asked, sitting again at the chart table.

She didn't reply. Moving to the icebox, she pulled out a slice of melon, put it on a plate, and sat down with it at the dining table.

"Didn't you have any breakfast?" Billy asked.

She shook her head and began scooping into the melon with a spoon, pausing now and then to stare into space, lips parted. Putting down the spoon, she sat with her elbows on the table. The table was an old hatch cover that had been laden with coat after coat of clear varnish, giving it a bright sheen. Her face was reflected faintly in the surface of the table.

"Elaine."

She didn't answer.

"Hey! Elainovitch!"

She looked at him. "What?"

"What's wrong?"

"Nothing."

"Come on—"

"Hey, Henderson!"

Billy was being called from above. With a shrug he climbed the companionway ladder and disappeared. Elaine toyed with her melon.

In a few minutes he was back, seated at the chart table and consulting a list of telephone numbers that was thumbtacked to the alcove wall. "Okay, okay," he muttered to himself.

Increasing the volume on the set, he called the Baltimore Marine Operator. She came on immediately. "Baltimore Marine . . . "

Billy spoke into the transmitter. "Yes, Baltimore Marine, this is the vessel *Iceman*, call number Whiskey Helen Dorothy oh-oh-five-er . . . "

Elaine was still spooning up fragments of her melon, paying no attention.

"The name of your vessel was *Iceman*, Captain?"

"*Iceman*," Billy said. "Shall I spell it?"

"No thank you, Captain. I've got it. Go ahead, Captain . . . "

"Okay, I'd like to place a call to Encino, California, area code two-thirteen, number 671-9825, person to person to Mary Ann Fontaine . . . My charge number is 237841."

Elaine was showing interest for the first time. She put down her spoon and listened.

"What was the name of the place, please, Captain?"

"Encino, just outside of LA. Area code two-thirteen . . . "

"All right, just a minute, Captain . . . "

The operator left the line. Billy looked at Elaine, raised his eyebrows, and shrugged. She scraped at the melon, then pushed it aside.

Drumming on the chart table with his fingertips, Billy waited. "Nine o'clock out there?"

"I guess so," Elaine said.

In a few minutes the operator came back on. "Sorry, Captain, that number does not answer."

"OK, Thanks, operator. I'll try later."

Billy got up from the table. "His daughter was on television last night."

Elaine nodded. "I know."

"Nobody even watched."

"He did."

"I'd have watched if I'd known about it . . . " Billy climbed the ladder and disappeared again.

Elaine got to her feet and headed for her cabin. As she closed the door behind her, she heard Billy coming back down.

Crossing the cabin, she stood at the porthole on the port side. Stretched before her eyes was the Chesapeake Bay. The overcast was breaking a little. Off to the left under the broken clouds moved a bright yellow sloop, two or three hundred yards ahead and standing close-hauled to the wind. She watched it for a while, thinking it might be Harry, then from the top of her dresser picked up a pair of binoculars and sighted through the window, bringing the cockpit of the yellow boat into sharp focus. At the wheel stood a man with thinning white hair and the look of a banker.

She was still looking through the binoculars when the door opened. Fontaine walked up behind her and looked over her shoulder. Taking the binoculars from her hand, he sighted through the window.

Elaine turned away and sprawled on the bed, bunching the pillows beneath her head and picking up the magazine again. "How are we doing?" she asked.

Fontaine put the binoculars back on the dresser. Even though he had just come down from the cockpit, his hair was in place, all the comb furrows showing. His hair was one thing she'd never been crazy about.

"We're doing well enough, I guess. How about you?"

"Okay," she said.

He was sitting on the bunk next to her now and his hand was on her leg, on the inside of her thigh, moving gently higher, lifting the bottom of the middy blouse. The magazine was face-down on her stomach. As he kept stroking her leg she didn't move. Their eyes met.

With a smile he patted her knee and got to his feet. Picking up the magazine, he glanced at what she had been reading. "Hey!" It was a word which conveyed surprise but not necessarily disapproval.

Patting her head, he tossed the magazine back on the bunk and closed the door behind him.

Thirteen

WHEN HARRY CROWDER sailed a boat, and particularly when he sailed a race, he was very much aware of his father. It gave him pleasure to think that he might be feeling some of the things about the water that his father had known and felt. There were mystical things about the wind and water and it pleased him to think of sailing as a mystique, guarded by the old-timers and passed on from generation to generation; passed on to him by his father. To sail with the old man had been to feel an awareness of all the familiar landmarks, to feel a sense of sharing them with all those who had plied the bay in the past. The old-time fisherman and oystermen, the British explorers in their sailing ships, the Indians in their canoes—all had looked upon the same hazes, the same bulges of land, the same river mouths, the same bordering strips of woodland in this corridor, this broad passage southward to the sea.

It was as if their accumulated knowledge had somehow found its way into his father's deep consciousness. To see the old man steer a course, spot a buoy, to see the sureness of his movements, one might think that he could see all the way down to the mouth of the bay and see every buoy and landmark along the way. To others, the buoys he sought seemed beyond the limits of human vision; yet he seemed to know unfailingly just where to look, to know just where invisible lines would form their invisible intersections—and there, many minutes later, ordinary eyes would spot a buoy.

An hour and a half into the race, *Sundance* was moving on a port tack, positioned near the middle of the bay almost as far south as Bloody Point Light. The wind was still in the southeast, gradually diminishing. To the right of the open hatch the race circular was still taped to the shiny white gel-coated bulkhead. One corner had come loose and flapped in the breeze. Mounted in the bulkhead were a compass and knot-meter. The compass reading was almost due southwest. The knot-meter, after reading almost five knots earlier in the race, now showed less than three.

For the sake of balance, to keep the boat sailing on its feet, meaning as nearly level as possible, Sam and Roy were posted on the high or windward side, the port side, trying to be comfortable in the narrow strip of deck space next to the cabin. Roy had a loose hand on the top strand of the lifeline, Sam's hands were thrust behind him on the cabin top, and their feet were hanging over the side. Roy had rolled up the ragged half-sleeves of his grey sweat shirt until they were tight up under the armpits. The only sound was of the bow sloshing into the mild seas with a steady gentle rhythm. On some boats a race was a picnic, a day's outing on the water. But racing to win was something entirely different. It meant long hours of concentration with very little conversation except an occasional word about compass directions, the wind, the speed of the boat, the set of a sail, and then once more an intense focused silence, broken by the occasional pop of a beer can.

Very often the long hours of striving took place in isolation, so that it was as if the boat were competing against itself. In protracted tacking maneuvers over a very broad body of water, it was not easy to judge how well a boat was doing against its competition. Judgment could rarely be so clear-cut as it would be, for example, in the case of two men running a mile, or two swimmers splashing along in parallel lanes. The competitive structure was far more complex. If there were boats nearby they were quite likely to be an entirely different class. An arch-rival might be very close as north-south progress was measured, yet in terms of distance he could be four miles away, far over against the opposite shore. To complicate matters further, Harry's boat and the boats competing against him were sailing with their own individual time allowances.

The sun had been in and out. Now it was gone again and the sky was a huge grey dome clamped down low over the grey water, tight to the horizon all around. There were sails to the left, sails to the right, sails ahead, and sails behind.

With a glance over his shoulder, Harry sailed on. Erect at the tiller, he was a tightly drawn string of effort, jaw knotted, lips a straight line. Behind the tinted glasses his eyes stared straight ahead and beneath the long bill of the khaki fishing cap which he now wore his brow was creased with concentration.

"Check me to leeward again," he called. The big genoa jib blocked from view whatever boats might lie to the right.

For the third time in the past fifteen minutes, Sam slid across the cabin top and placed his cheek flat against the deck, lifting the bottom edge of the jib a couple of inches and peering beneath it. "All clear," he said, rolling back again. He looked aft. "Some big boats coming up behind."

Harry nodded. This was to be expected. Class A had started last but it was the class that contained the largest and swiftest boats, many of them crack ocean racers such as *Iceman*, and with any reasonable amount of wind these could be expected to work their way fairly quickly down into and through the pack. The hull speed of a boat increased with its length and the size of its sails, and it was not at all uncommon for the big boats to reach Oxford well in front of boats which had left the starting line in Annapolis as much as an hour and a half ahead of them.

"See *Iceman?*" Roy asked.

Sam shook his head. "Not yet. Those are Class B."

"Keep that son of a bitch back there," Roy said.

"No way," Sam said.

"Beat him boat for boat," Roy said.

Sam laughed.

They all knew there was virtually no hope of beating *Iceman* boat for boat and very little hope for that matter of beating it on corrected time. According to their respective ratings, *Iceman* had to give them a handicap of forty seconds a mile. The race was approximately thirty miles long, which meant that to win on corrected time *Iceman* must beat *Sundance* by a full twenty minutes. If the margin was any smaller, Harry would win on corrected time but if the wind blew even moderately his chances were small.

The way he was sailing today was hardly helping. It was not the big boats that concerned him, it was the boats in his own class. After his very good start, something was not right, something was missing. His father would have said that he was sailing a lousy race and he would have been right. A long race was spent on the edge, on a very fine hairline, offering the fine edge of the sails to the fine edge of the wind. It was pursuing a fine edge all through the day, attaining it only in rare split seconds, yet all through the day there was a never-ending need to stay as close to the edge as possible, in constant search of the exact balance of wind, hull, sails, man.

The edge was elusive and today he didn't have the touch. The boat wasn't moving. For the past half-hour he had been aware of it and had been trying to pick it up—pick up the boat, pick up himself, but the sluggish feeling persisted. He knew that Sam was aware of it and possibly Roy as well. Sam had said nothing but a couple of times he had looked back over his shoulder in a way that seemed to convey quite plainly what he was thinking. Sam had sailed with him too often, knew him too well, knew the boat too well, not to know when something was wrong. He no longer seemed concerned about Roy. Roy was not the problem. It was the skipper.

His fingers light on the tiller, his eye on the leading edge of the jib, Harry tried to regain whatever it was he had lost. Touch meant concentration but he kept losing his concentration and after another fifteen minutes he gave it up and asked Sam to take the tiller.

Giving up the tiller was not something Harry ordinarily did. Moving back to the cockpit, Sam frowned. "You feeling okay?"

Harry nodded. "Yeah, I'm okay." From his perch on the high side, Roy looked back curiously. Harry handed Sam the tiller. "Just hold her as high as she'll go without pinching . . . "

"Yep . . . " Sam didn't need to be told. "Why don't you rest for a while?"

"I'm going to."

"Roy and I can handle her."

"Okay."

The overcast was again complete and the clouds seemed even lower. The air was more humid and it was getting warmer. Visibility was limited. Behind now, off the port quarter, was the outline of the Bloody Point tower. Ahead, still well to the southeast, was the fuzzy tip of Poplar Island, just becoming visible.

Harry went below, reached into the icebox and uncapped a beer. In the cabin there was six feet of headroom. At eye level was a small rectangular window. He stood at the window, slowly sipping the beer. Through the window he counted three boats to windward, toward the Eastern Shore side, their sails stark white against the grey sky, sailing one behind the other, all on port tacks, their slants identical. All three stood closer to the wind than *Sundance;* all three were ahead of it.

"Anybody want anything up there?" Harry called.

"No thanks," Sam called back.

"No thanks," Roy said.

To see the three boats through the window was like watching them on a small screen. For a while longer Harry stood there watching them, sipping the beer, hearing the slap of the water, the creak of the mast in its step, an occasional muttered comment from above.

Presently he turned away and lay on the seat, the beer can resting on his belly. His baseball cap slid from his head. He reached back for it and hung it over the beer can, then lay there looking at the ceiling. Racing a sailboat was of little importance. He knew this. His onetime wife had reminded him of it time and again. Yet sailing was all he had, it was his strength, his one ability, and it would be ironic if his touch should be taken from him. He would be like a fighter, he thought, who has lost his punch; a pilot reluctant to fly; a running back who has lost a step, a pitcher who has lost something off his fast ball.

He knew it was the telephone call from Marcia that had done it. It was as if the phone call had broken a spell that had lasted for almost eight lousy years. Now he wasn't at all sure that he wanted it broken because it was at least a spell he had learned to live with.

Harry was up, tossing the empty beer can into the sink and standing once more at the window. The three boats still sailed one behind the other. Sam had picked up a little on all three. They were passing the gateway to Eastern Bay, which led onward to the Miles River and the Wye and innumerable branches and creeks, islands and necks and coves and sloughs. Looking eastward, there was an impression of water beyond water, land beyond land, cove within cove. On the Eastern Shore so much of the landscape looked that way. The Eastern Shore was viewed by many as a paradise.

Not by Marcia. She considered it a miasmic, mosquito-ridden hellhole, lacking in opportunity, narrow in outlook, rich in bias. She was infuriated by articles portraying Eastern Shore people as "colorful, eccentric primitives." To Marcia they were simply greedy backwoodsmen, islanders who took from nature and gave nothing back, secure and untouchable on their island.

Harry disagreed. Eastern Shoremen were not islanders strictly speaking, although from centuries of being cut off from the rest of the world it was true that they had many of the characteristics sometimes attributed to islanders. Islanders were a special breed and in them, he felt, there was more good than bad. They were self-sufficient, independent, fiercely proud, and enormously able. They were what their island made of them, what the island demanded of them as men. They thought of themselves as superior to outsiders, yet he acknowledged that this superiority was not something they could always believe in. Their self-esteem after all had been built up on their own island, fed by their fellow islanders, not cauterized and hardened in the outside world, and proving themselves could be a process which never ended.

They could also be filled with hatred. Such a man was Harry's cousin Roland, a waterman, a hard drinker, a fiercely competitive man and one whose capacity for hatred was enormous. He was a man nourished by hatred. He was also very much a man's man and it was interesting to Harry that Roland, the man who seemed to represent all that Marcia most hated, was the one man in the family for whom she may have felt lust. If this was in fact the case, Roland was having none of it. His interest in women, even (or especially) in a woman such as Marcia, could not compare with the intensity of his fixation upon his rivals: sailing rivals, oystering rivals, rivals of any kind. Another man might regard the conquest of women as part of life's bounty. For Roland the reward and the bounty were in the besting, the defeating, the mashing down. To stride off with honcho strides, the girl slung over his back, was not for him. To be a lady's man would be emasculating. It would rob him of the strength he needed against men, the only adversaries that counted. It had been a very long time since Harry had thought of Roland in connection with Marcia.

"Hey, Skip . . . " Roy's face appeared in the hatchway. "We think we see *Iceman.*"

"Okay." Climbing the ladder, Harry looked astern. "Where?"

Roy pointed up the bay and toward the Western Shore. "Wow, look at the mother move!"

"I see five boats," Harry said.

"Okay, count from right to left. It's the fourth boat—the next to last one to leeward. Look."

Harry picked up the binoculars from the cockpit seat and raised them to his eyes. The big boat was moving well, huge sails drawing, the long black hull slicing the water. Like *Sundance* it was on a port tack but far far to leeward, well over toward the Western Shore. "I see him." He handed the binoculars to Roy.

Roy kept looking through the binoculars. "Son of a bitch still hasn't tacked out," he said presently. "I hope he keeps playing the Western Shore. The air's starting to look mighty spotty over there. Hey, men, I do believe Mr. Fontaine is sailing into a hole. Maybe he'll go in the tank—nope!"

"What's happening?" Sam asked.

Disgustedly Roy placed the binoculars back on the seat. "He's tacking. He's taking a hitch back out."

"Too bad." Sam shrugged.

Roy spat to leeward.

"Here," Sam said, offering Harry the tiller. "Don't you want it back?"

Harry looked ahead over the grey water. He shook his head. "Keep it," he said. "You're doing fine."

Fourteen

ON THE EAST SIDE OF THE BAY, about four miles below Bloody Point, lay three islets—Poplar, Coachman, and Jefferson, known collectively as Poplar Island.

The shoals off the Poplar Island shore stretched well out toward the middle of the bay, ending abruptly at the deep-water shipping lane, the ancient drowned bed of the Susquehanna. Near where the shoals gave way to deep water stood a red buoy, Red Nun 70. A contestant reaching Nun 70 was well down the bay—better than halfway to the mouth of the Choptank, where the course would turn eastward.

Nun 70 was a mark of the course. Although there was water enough to pass it on the shoal side, boats in the race were required to pass it on the deep-water side, leaving it to port as they proceeded southward.

Toward one o'clock, some three hours after the start of their MORC division, Walters Hackett and party were plodding along somewhere between Bloody Point and Poplar Island.

MORC boats were easy to spot. All classes were required to fly identifying insignia, a small blue and gold pennant attached to the backstay high enough to be readily identifiable, and another just like it at the bow. In addition to these pennants, the sail numbers of MORC boats were underlined with a red slash, a requirement peculiar to their class.

As one o'clock passed, Hackett knew he was sailing well to the rear of the fleet. Looking ahead, he might note a MORC boat here and another there, and he could try to nurture the illusion that he was still in the pack.

But looking to the rear, he could see no MORCs and for

that matter not many boats of any class. There was just a lot of empty water and to look back was an empty feeling.

On the encouraging side there were many boats far to the west, playing the Western Shore. Because he stood so much closer to the wind than they, he knew he was no worse off than many of them—and as sailing leads were measured, better off than some.

Thus the reason he had not done even worse was that he had stayed on the Eastern Shore side and the reason he had done this was that he had been zealously following the lead of Harry Crowder, doing what *Sundance* did, tacking every time *Sundance* tacked—until *Sundance* had gotten so far ahead that he could no longer see it.

From where the Hacketts now languished, Nun 70 was not yet visible to the naked eye but the movement of the boats ahead was a tipoff. There was a long string of them parading out from the Eastern Shore, slanting toward mid-bay on a course that would take them clear of the nun.

Among these, he knew, was Harry Crowder's yellow sloop, and once the jumble of boats cleared, Mrs. Hackett might be able to pick it up again with the binoculars. If not, he would simply continue to do as he knew Harry must be doing—short-tacking toward shore and then long-tacking southward again, until somehow he got where he was going.

For Mrs. Hackett, to this point the trip could have been worse. Although she knew the bay was capable of severe and sudden storms, it seemed so innocuous now, a wonderfully safe and landlocked pond, a safe calm passage between friendly shores. To seasoned ocean skippers in the race it probably was small-time. It lacked the thrill of the ocean, the imponderables, the incomprehensibles, the unknowns of the ocean, the fear. So far as Mrs. Hackett was concerned, this was all to the good.

As they moved haltingly and inefficiently down the bay, she was at times torn between her natural warmhearted, sympathetic nature—and her fervid hope that after a day of hell and humiliation Hackett would pack it in.

But could she be sure?

In the old days back in Rahway, when he had a tough decision to make, he always sought her opinion, grumbling if it did not agree with his own but then often accepting it in the end, never doubting that it had been his own in the first place.

In this recollection she felt there might be a valuable clue, a valuable reverse side of the coin. Maybe she was getting the sides of her coins mixed, but somewhere near Thomas Point it struck her that the surest way to harden his resolve was to continue to show what she truly felt about sailboat racing.

She was now in the process of shaping a new code of conduct. No more compressed lips. No more gasps of horror, no more cries of "ouch." Instead if possible she would offer pleasant comments. Whenever she thought he was looking she could compose her features in a pleasant expression. She would even try to show enthusiasm.

From the very beginning of the race there had been stress, but most of it had been between Hackett and his sister Kitty.

Mrs. Hackett was seeing a new Kitty. Since her divorce she was showing a more prickly personality than Mrs. Hackett remembered. She had changed just since Christmas.

"Look, Walters," Kitty said at one point early in the contest, "this is an elective, am I right? I mean you chose it of your own free will, didn't you? Nobody told you to take up sailing, did they?"

At the time they were dawdling past Thomas Point and as boat after boat passed them by, Hackett's face was becoming bleak. Clearly they were doing something wrong. His fingers held the tiller in a death grip, there was anger in his white knuckles, and fierce yet somehow unavailing concentration.

"What's wrong with us?" Kitty demanded a short time

later. "Look at all those boats over there whizzing past that Bloody Light, whatever you call it."

Now as they moved slowly toward the northern tip of Poplar Island, with the wind going soft, her impatience flared again. "I saw a book downstairs," she said, "and I'm going down and get it."

"Never mind," Hackett said. "The wind's dying, that's all."

"Well it's dying for everybody else too, isn't it? Are we the only people it's dying for?"

She went below. Returning with the book, she sat down, opened it on her lap, removed the gardening glove from her right hand and leafed through the pages. Presently she read: "Sheet tension controls the leach. This is perhaps the most overlooked factor in draft control . . . " Raising her eyes from the book, Kitty looked aloft at the mainsail. "Are we all right on that? Are we all right on sheet tension, Walters? I'm serious. I'm trying to get at the bottom of this."

Hackett looked over his shoulder. His lips moved. Another boat was coming up fast on his starboard quarter.

"How's our mast-bend?" Kitty asked, looking at the book again. "How about our slot?"

"Put that thing away," Hackett said. "Margaret, go down and get me a Coke, will you please?"

"Certainly," Mrs. Hackett said pleasantly.

When she returned he sipped from the can. "Anybody who learns anything young is at a great advantage, I know that for a fact," he said. "I'd be willing to bet that if anybody put me on a pair of roller skates this very night I'd be able to skate right off. Something inside me knows how to roller skate."

"Does anything inside you know how to *sail*, though?" Kitty demanded. She consulted the book again. "Listen, Walters, maybe we've got excess luff tension."

Mrs. Hackett looked at the sails and could see nothing amiss. So far as she could tell he was doing nothing particularly wrong beyond the fact that now and then they bumped into a crab pot and the fact perhaps that when he tacked the operation seemed a good deal slower than when others performed it. It was also true that when he tacked he seemed for several long moments to be pointing the boat where it should not be pointed, as though he had lost track of what he was doing. He seemed easily distracted.

"We seem to be going along quite nicely now," she said.

Draining the Coke can, he glowered at her—and then at Kitty.

On any given tack there is always a free jib winch. When one winch has the jib sheet wrapped around it, the other is free. They were moving slowly abreast of the northern tip of Poplar Island when Kitty gave the free winch a little spin.

Hackett, concentrating hard, looked up with a start.

Once again his sister spun the winch. Once again it produced the quick whirring sound characteristic of mechanisms which contain a ratchet, a sound that a tense skipper might easily find annoying.

A third spin. A third glare.

Although Kitty was spinning the winch with a seemingly innocent, even absent-minded air, Mrs. Hackett now began to suspect that it was not innocent at all. It was as if she were deliberately trying her sibling's patience.

As if she had been waiting all her life to get back at her domineering, industrially successful brother—and now, morally rearmed, newly militant, she was letting him have it.

Once again she spun the winch—a good long spin this time, with a nice long whir that didn't die for a good long while.

"Kitty . . . " Hackett said.

"What?"

"Maybe you'd like to go below and have a little rest."

"No, I'm just fine," she said, giving the winch a spin.

"It might be a long race," he said.

"Nope."

Spin.
"God!"
"What?" Kitty looked innocent.
"Stop spinning that goddamn winch!"
"This?"
"Yes!"
"Okay, you don't have to be so nasty about it, Walters . . ."

They moved slowly onward. Presently Hackett said, "Margaret, I was just thinking. This might be a good chance to go over some of the spinnaker arrangements with Kitty."

"*Spinnaker* arrangements?" Kitty repeated.

"Instructions," Hackett said.

"*Instructions?* Hey, Walters, what the hell *is* this—Lincoln Logs?"

"Walters . . . " Mrs. Hackett faltered. "Are we planning to put up the spinnaker? How can we? There's no wind. But whatever you say, of course."

"Don't ever say that to a man," Kitty said.

Hackett ignored his sister. "Okay, Mag, show her," he said. "Margaret will show you."

Frowning, Kitty stood surveying the assortment of lines which ran from the vicinity of the mast to the aft end of the cabin, some of them on into the cockpit. "There you have your foreguy," Hackett said. "Touch the foreguy, Mag."

Mrs. Hackett touched the line known as the foreguy.

"What's the foreguy?" Kitty asked.

"It's the line that holds the pole down and forward," he said.

"I see. Okay, the line that holds the pole down and forward."

"And here you have your pole lift. Touch the pole lift for Kitty, Margaret."

Mrs. Hackett touched the pole lift. "Pole lift," she said pleasantly.

"What's that do—lift the pole?" Kitty asked.

"Right," Hackett said.

"So you've got one lifting the pole and one pulling it down," she said.

"That's right." Hackett frowned. "Listen, you don't have to understand the dynamics of everything you look at. Just *accept* it."

"Right on, Walters—what's this one, Margaret?"

"That's the spinnaker halyard," Mrs. Hackett said. "It pulls the spinnaker up—way up into the sky." Her eyes widened.

"Let's look at it this way—" Hackett broke off and peered ahead. "Where's Harry? Anybody spot Harry?"

"I'm afraid not yet," Mrs. Hackett said.

"Okay, let's look at it this way. In setting a spinnaker there are one, two, three, four, uh, five lines, or ropes if you will, that we must deal with. You'll be on the afterguy."

Kitty looked dubious. "Maybe we should have gone over some of this before we—you know—started the race."

"We didn't have time," Hackett snapped. "If you'd gotten here yesterday and sailed with us up to Annapolis like I asked you to do—"

"I couldn't," Kitty said. "I told you I had to go to a meeting."

"Okay, so here we are," Hackett said. "Halyard. Sheet. Afterguy. Foreguy and pole lift. That's the crop, isn't it, Mag?"

"That's the crop," Mrs. Hackett said.

Hackett placed his hand on Kitty's shoulder. The set of her lips indicated that she did not particularly want his hand on her shoulder. "So you'll be on the afterguy, Kit, which controls the pole from back here in the cockpit. So in other words, you'll be on the pole. So just remember, when I say, 'Pole! Pole!' that'll be you. Or I may say, 'Foreguy! Foreguy!'—in which event you take this line here and release it by jerking it straight up out of its jam cleat. Do I make myself clear?"

"Do you—*what?*"

He looked at her for a second or two. "Of course when

we jibe, that's a special circumstance. Sheet here, afterguy here—but after we complete the jibe the sheet becomes the afterguy and the afterguy becomes the sheet. Does it sound too complicated?" Kitty had begun to gurgle with rage. "If you don't understand something, this is the time to sing out. . . . Now where in the hell is Harry?"

Fifteen

IN THE RACE THAT DAY many factors affected the outcome. The heaviest influence was an area of dead calm into which most of the boats sailed and came to a standstill, many of them in virtually the same spot.

Rhumb line is the name given the shortest distance between two nautical points. From Red Nun 70, the rhumb line for the course was a long diagonal to the southeast. After six miles or so the course would turn a corner and make the swing eastward into the Choptank.

Just before making the turn it would funnel the fleet down through a corridor between the southern tip of Tilghman Island and Sharps Island Light. In the area north of this corridor, the boats would encounter the doldrums predicted in that morning's weather forecast.

By one o'clock that afternoon, with the wind patchy all over the bay, some of the earlier starters were losing momentum and drifting to a stop as they approached the corridor. Here they would sit, gradually to be joined by more than half the fleet.

To the west was open water. To the east were the shoals off the lower part of Tilghman Island, and the pineland and sandy beaches of the island itself.

Ahead, nearly due south, stood Sharps Island Light tower, marking the remains of what as recently as the turn of the century had been a large island, complete with farms, cattle, and a summer hotel. Now these were all gone along with the land itself, wiped out by erosion.

Because of the storms and ice of recent winters, the light tower was tilted on its base. Aside from this pronounced slant, however, the tower at Sharps Island closely resembled the bulky red tower at Bloody Point, and the two were on an exact north-south axis, roughly eleven miles apart.

Although at one o'clock the vanguard was within sight of Sharps Island, many boats were still scattered all over the bay, some far to the west and many well to the rear.

By now the breeze was truly erratic. If one could have looked down from a hovering blimp, the water would have presented an irregular, hodgepodge pattern: a lightly ruffled path here, a slick patch there; a circle of dark ripples beneath a random puff; a scattering of catspaws; a wide spread of dead calm where nothing moved on the glassy surface but a dead fish on the tide.

Toward the Western Shore there was a large cluster of boats, MORCs, Cal-25s, Albergs, Tritons, Deltas, and Pearsons, all jumbled together. They were doing poorly. From the very first the going had been markedly better along the Eastern Shore.

Although Fontaine's *Iceman* was still moving, its sails were barely filled. It would pick up a puff, coast across a stretch of glassy smooth water, and pick up a puff again. Fontaine had kept tacking away from shore but continued to play the western half of the bay and *Iceman* had paid the price. Although it was not becalmed its progress had been badly crippled.

Boats hugging the Eastern Shore had prospered. In spite of what Harry considered to be his poor performance at the tiller, his decision to stay on the Eastern Shore side was the correct one. One reason for doing so was the tidal current. When the race began that day the tide was still ebbing strongly down the bay, but by noon it had passed its peak. Often after the tide loses some of its force in the main body of the bay there are strong currents still emptying out from the tributaries, and a sailor proficient at playing the tides can make good use of them.

With Sam at the tiller, *Sundance* had caught the full benefit of the strong tidal current still pouring out of Eastern Bay, the large body of water which separated Kent Island from the main landmass of the Eastern Shore. It had swept *Sundance* past Poplar Island and out around Nun 70. Once past the nun Sam had taken a short hitch toward shore, then tacked again and headed south.

Since taking the tiller, Sam had caught and passed two of the three boats ahead of them. An hour below Nun 70 the only boat in its class still ahead of *Sundance* was a brand-new white yawl named *Swift Chariot.* Now, with Sam still at the tiller and Harry and Roy handling the sails, *Sundance* began to close the gap until the white yawl was ahead by no more than twenty feet. At this point both boats were on short starboard tacks toward shore.

As *Sundance* sailed its course, Harry was aware that their every move was being closely watched from the other cockpit, knowing that when they tacked the other boat would immediately follow suit. "Okay?" Sam asked in a low voice. "Whenever you're ready," Harry said. "Okay, hard-a-lee," Sam muttered.

They tacked, swiftly and expertly, and *Swift Chariot* covered, tacking on top of them so that it now stood between *Sundance* and the breeze. *Sundance* had gained perhaps five feet on the tacking maneuver but was now blanketed by *Swift Chariot*'s sails. The two boats were sailing precisely parallel courses, separated by perhaps twenty feet of water, with *Sundance*'s nose roughly abreast of *Swift Chariot*'s forward hatch. Gradually *Sundance* gained and then, still sailing in *Swift Chariot*'s wind shadow, could gain no more.

A quarter-mile passed. A half-mile. Still the two boats sailed beam to beam, splash for splash, and it became hypnotic, the movement of the evenly matched hulls, the steady motion, the unchanging interval, the inability of either boat to gain so much as a foot.

Roy kept darting glances into the cockpit of the other boat and then looking straight ahead again, as if it would be according the sailors in the other boat too much stature to give them more than glancing notice. It was not uncommon —the spectacle of two sets of crew members in adjoining cockpits, sailing nearly cheek by jowl, each giving the impression that the other was not there.

Roy's eyes gleamed. "Taking him!" His voice was low, exultant.

Gradually *Sundance* had pulled abreast and was now beginning to inch ahead. A foot. Five feet. Sam kept his eyes fixed on the leading edge of the jib. He knew without looking that the other boat was falling behind, caught now in the backwind from *Sundance*'s sails. He didn't need to look. A helmsman knew by the sound, by the texture of the splashes, the velocity and tone, the sound of the bow against the water, just as he could tell by the change in sound when a boat was coming up from behind. This one was falling back. Finally there was the sound of the jib rustling. Roy grunted with triumph. Ten feet astern, *Swift Chariot* was going about, tacking away. For the moment it had surrendered.

Sam finally permitted himself a look.

"Nice going, Sammie," Harry said. "Nice going."

Sam seemed embarrassed. "Want it?"

"Hell no, you're doing great."

"Breeze is going," Sam said.

"Where's *Iceman*?" Roy asked.

"I don't see him," Harry said.

As they moved southward on the fading breeze, Harry picked up the binoculars. Far ahead, the Sharps Island tower was visible. In the distant grey mist its outline was a tilted shadow.

But short of Sharps Island the water glowed in a patch of sunlight. In the binoculars he could see boats barely moving. Their sails were soft. They had run out of wind.

Up in the area of these leading boats, up in the pool of light where the sun shone through the overcast, the weather was bearing out the early morning forecast with its prediction of light and variable and finally flat—prior to a wind shift.

After three days the east wind was blowing itself out.

Harry put the binoculars back on the seat. Within half an hour, *Sundance* was about out of wind, drifting slowly toward the ever-growing circle of becalmed boats.

By now some of the boats had been sitting in virtually the same spot for an hour and a half, with Sharps Island light standing like a tilted sentinel, a dark-red turret, down to the right, and the pine-rimmed shore of Tilghman Island to the left.

Now the tide had become important. It had quit running out. It was slack but soon it would turn and come running up the bay against them. The skippers knew this, and there was an impression of a fleet straining southward on the slack tide, straining to get around the shoals south of Tilghman Island and on into the Choptank before the tide began to flood and push them backward up the bay.

But it would require a breeze and no breeze came. In five acres of flat water sat half the fleet, with others still drifting in.

The remnants of the breeze had lasted precisely as far as this spread of dead water, giving each boat a ride this far and no farther. It was as if a boat's performance to this point had counted for nothing. The effect was to wipe out leads built up gradually and painstakingly during the first seventeen miles. The boats were brought level again. From here, when the wind came up again, it would be like starting over.

The sun was full out now, sucking the water up into the sky. With no breeze to blow it away, the water vapor overhung the flat sheet, turning the sky a milky blue.

Sun beating down, the expensive racing machines lay with sails adroop, lifeless in the water, the wind at zero.

Anyone who moved, who changed position, did so on tiptoe, or with lagging careful feet, speaking in low voices, as though low voices were appropriate to dead calms, as if low voices, like careful, tiptoeing movements, would preserve whatever imperceptible drift the boat might still be making.

From nature there was no sound save the occasional cry of a gull. Far out in the bay a motor was going at full speed. Its sound faded and disappeared. Against the stillness the subdued voices seemed loud and distinct.

On some of the boats people were having sandwiches, a beer, a soft drink. Others were scanning the water for ripples; checking the bits of yarn tied to their shrouds; wetting a finger and holding it aloft; searching for the elusive breeze —and alert as well for the first sign of being set backward by the soon-to-be-flooding tide.

Pottagold had been well up in the fleet and for a long while now it had been becalmed. For Judy Whitney there was no work to be done, nothing to do but sit and look for tiny swirls of water, faint traces of breeze. She spent the time thinking about the girl on Mel Fontaine's boat, Elaine. She knew all about Elaine. Everybody at the yacht club knew about her. People had been talking all week about Fontaine and his girl and the life they lived, speculating about the life they might be living, on how they spent their days and nights, telling what they had read in various magazines, talking about her glamorous life and the company she kept. Now for Judy this girl had special interest. She would be on the boat Gus was shipping out on.

Gus was stretched out on the cockpit seat. He had put on a shirt and his sunglasses lay on his stomach. Her hand on the tiller, Judy was looking for *Iceman*, not yet spotting it, but thinking about its graceful lines and the people on it. There was something about it that gave her the creeps. She would have felt this way, she thought, even if Gus had not been leaving to join its crew. The boat made her uncomfortable. All the boys with their smooth good looks, as though they all wore masks. And the girl. It was a creepy boat. It made her think of unsavory practices. It was a place where Black Masses might be celebrated. God alone knew what went on, down inside that boat.

Judy sighed. Reaching over the rail, she touched the water, let her hand trail slowly along the smooth hull. She looked about. Everything was so flat, so still. It was like being caught in the Sargasso Sea, she thought, except that here there was no seaweed, only some crab pots and jellyfish and concentric ripples, as now and again a fish or a snake poked its nose above the surface and ducked away.

Abruptly the stillness was shattered by the sound of a trumpet. Whiling away the time, a trumpeter somewhere in the fleet was running the scale, then playing the first notes of the cavalry charge, following this with *Auld Lang Syne*, evoking laughter all the way.

Idly Judy listened to the sound of the trumpet. There had been a trumpeter at the Fourth of July celebration at Oxford. Every Fourth of July after dark the yacht club at Oxford shot off fireworks over the river and she and Gus had sailed down with Jenny. Somewhere in the spectator fleet that night somebody had been blowing a trumpet, saluting each brilliant display as it lit up the sky.

Judy kept watching for *Iceman*. She had seen Harry Crowder's boat drift in half an hour ago and it now sat to her left, between *Pottagold* and the Tilghman shore. Fontaine must have played the Western Shore and gone in the tank.

Presently she heard somebody yell, "Hooray, look what's coming!" She looked up to see *Iceman* ghosting in at a long angle from mid-bay, headed for the pack.

With barely enough breeze to move, it drew gradually closer, drifting with other newcomers into the widening pond of lifeless water.

Its approach was causing a commotion. The reaction was mainly gleeful. With its record of wiping out the competition, the big boat was having a bad day. After his deferential treatment at the yacht club, Fontaine now was getting a dose of irreverence.

As it moved closer there were mock cheers. The trumpeter blew a garbled rendition of taps. Laughter and applause went through the fleet.

Gus stirred. "What's going on?" he muttered. From the thickness of his voice he had been sound asleep. Now he was up on one elbow, looking.

"Your leader just arrived," Judy said.

On a nearby boat a fat ruddy-cheeked man was clubbing his heavy hands together, cheering. The cheers grew as *Iceman* rode the last shred of the breeze and finally came to a dead stop in a patch of open water, off to itself.

It was separated from *Pottagold* by less than thirty feet, off the starboard bow. Judy searched its foredeck and then its cockpit. Fontaine stood at the wheel with an amused smile, apparently taking it all in good grace.

Elaine was nowhere in sight.

"I think I'll lie down for a while," Judy said. "Call me when you need me."

Gus didn't reply. He was staring fixedly across the water.

The cheering had subsided. Once again things were quiet.

Down in the cabin, sprawled on the scratchy black and white tweed cushions of the starboard berth, Judy closed her eyes. It was hot in the cabin and soon her brow was damp with sweat, her hair a mass of moist strawberry-blonde swirls. Her light-blue shorts were wrinkled at the crotch. Her legs were sturdy and freckled. She had been told she had the legs of a linebacker. She wore no socks and one of her blue canvas boating shoes was untied.

A ship's clock of polished brass hung above the small sink. She had given it to Gus for Christmas. In the stillness she listened to its rapid tick and thought about Gus. He had always talked a lot about moving to Florida, mainly because its weather permitted year-round sailing, and it was something she could understand. It might have been the answer, best for him and best for herself and Jenny, for she had always assumed that once he got there and got established he would send for her and Jenny.

On a ledge near the clock stood a framed color snapshot of Jenny, whose hair was the same shade as hers and whose face would be as freckled. In the previous year's race down to Oxford, Gus had finished first and won a silver bowl to go with the many silver bowls he already owned. After receiving the bowl he took it over to where the child stood with its mother. He bent over and kissed Jenny and Jenny placed a small caressing hand against his face. He picked her up and sat her on a wooden picnic table, and after a moment put the silver bowl in her lap and this was the snapshot: Jenny holding the silver bowl with both hands, looking up with a smile, a little red-haired girl in a pale-blue dress, framed by the trailing branches of a maple, and beyond her head the blue of the river.

As Judy's mother had often said, how could anybody be mean to a child, how could *anybody* be mean to a *child?* Judy looked at the snapshot, closed her eyes, opened them and looked away, holding back tears. Going to Florida was one thing; and as for divorce, she supposed it had always been inevitable. But to hook up with that damned boat, to cast his lot with those people, to elect to spend his *life* with them, doing the things they did—she couldn't bear the thought of it.

She could hear him moving about up in the cockpit. "Need me up there?" she called.

Gus was saying something in loud full tones, the voice he used when he was trying to impress somebody. "It's a thrill just to look at the lines of that boat, Mr. Fontaine," she heard him say.

"See you tonight after the race," she heard Fontaine call.

"Yes *sir,*" Gus called back.

From where she lay, looking up through the open hatch,

she could see him standing on the seat of the cockpit. He was preening. She had seen him in action and she could guess that the girl now had come out on deck and was watching, that he was trying to impress the girl. No doubt he was succeeding. He had taken off his shirt again and wore nothing but the white cutoffs held up with the old piece of rope. He had put on his huge sunglasses and his hair was tousled and sweaty and she could see one sturdy leg covered with golden fuzz, one tanned bare foot. He was tilting his head, probably showing his profile. She wouldn't put it past him. She wouldn't put anything past him. The stud at play. Her husband. She felt lousy.

Getting up from the berth, she stood on the bottom rung of the ladder and looked out. *Iceman* was not very far away. She could see Fontaine in the cockpit but there was still no sign of the girl. As she watched, Fontaine turned over the wheel to one of the boys and disappeared below.

Judy went down and lay on the tweed cushions again but she had only been there a few minutes when Gus peered down through the hatchway. "Tide's started to set us," he said. "I'm gonna throw the hook."

Sixteen

ALL THROUGH THE FLEET, anchors were hitting the water. The tidal current had begun to surge up the bay and boats slow to get their anchors over were beginning to be carried back up the Bay. Some skippers were using light sculling movements of the tiller to keep the bow headed in the right direction until their anchors were made ready and tossed over.

Soon virtually the entire fleet was at anchor, bows pointed south, straining backward on their anchor lines.

Without breeze, the water on the surface appeared lifeless, yet beneath the surface the tidal current was tugging hard and the anchor lines were stretched taut.

With the boats at anchor and the race in abeyance, some turned to swimming. All through the fleet there were splashes as crew members from boat after boat went overboard to cool off. Lean tanned young men and bikini-clad young women dived from the rail, climbed boarding ladders and dived again, waiting for the breeze that would set the race in motion again.

Elaine was in her bunk when she heard a lot of commotion up on deck, then heard one of the boys howling that the tide had begun to run. Soon she heard the anchor going overboard.

She had been dozing. Her cheek lay on the pillow. Her hair covered her face. When the door opened she didn't look up but through the strands of her hair she could see him standing now at the porthole.

"What's happening?" she asked. "Where are we?"

"Have a look."

She got up and stood at the porthole, looking at a string of boats with limp sails, and beyond them a strip of shore. Nearby there was a blue boat and on its foredeck crouched a blond boy in white shorts, fooling with the anchor line.

"Becalmed?" She turned away and sat on the bed.

Fontaine nodded. He was standing next to the porthole. She saw a body flash past and then heard a loud splash as one of the kids dived overboard.

Smiling, Fontaine moved aside from the porthole and stood with his back to the dresser.

Still in the white middy blouse, she sat on the bunk and watched his face.

Somewhere off in the fleet, from across the water, the trumpeter was blowing a few notes from "I Can't Get Started."

Tanned bodies kept flashing past the porthole and landing with a loud splash.

"A lull in the proceedings . . . " Fontaine smiled.

She was on her back now, her head propped up on the pillow, and for a moment her face was composed, her eyes reflective. She was looking at him, measuring him, knowing what was next, and knowing she didn't want it.

She picked up a magazine.

Still smiling, he moved to the bed and placed his hand on the inside of her leg.

"Don't you think you'd better save it for the race?" she murmured.

"No," he said. "I've got plenty for my age."

"For any age," she said.

He took the magazine from her hand and placed it softly on the coverlet. With a slow deliberate motion, his eyes never leaving hers, he slid the bikini pants down her legs and tossed them to the floor. She lay there, allowing him to do it, then lay back as he plunged and lunged into her, looking up at his flushed face, his unmussed hair, the slitted lids, knowing that what she was doing was perfunctory and knowing that he sensed it.

"What's wrong?" he panted.

She smiled up at him. "What do you expect in the middle of a sailboat race?"

"It's a dead calm," he said, never breaking stride. "We went—the wrong way. We—should have—stayed on the Eastern Shore side. That's where the breeze—was. It's what —comes—from not knowing the local—waters . . . "

She knew he was being funny but it didn't help, and she kept telling herself she wasn't really part of it, she was alone, she was just lying there, and the bodies kept flashing past the window and the air was filled with shouts.

He had collapsed. His face fell against her shoulder. She let it rest there for a moment, then squirmed out from beneath his body, feeling irritated in a way she had never felt before.

She went into the head and in a few moments returned, jerking on the blue bikini pants. He looked at her with puzzled eyes, then fell face down on the bunk again. Still face-down, he reached out a hand but she ignored it and left the cabin, closing the door behind her. A moment later she was fleeing up the companionway ladder and out to the deck.

She was greeted by the growl of a trumpet.

While people swam and waited for the breeze to return, Harry lounged in the cockpit of *Sundance*. Sam had gone below to rest. Roy lay on the foredeck, his head against the mast, his hands folded over his stomach. Nearby was Gus Whitney's *Pottagold*. Gus was adjusting and readjusting his anchor line, letting some out and then bringing it back in, all the while studiously ignoring Harry Crowder and *Sundance*.

Just beyond Gus's boat lay *Iceman* with most of its crew members in the water. Elaine was nowhere in sight. Fontaine sat for a while in the cockpit and then he too disappeared.

Across the water the trumpet was playing something aimless and desultory, a few halfhearted cynical notes of the cavalry charge and then taps and then, halfway through taps, quitting; losing interest, dropping the subject.

Harry kept checking for breeze. He stood in the stern, sweeping the water with the binoculars, searching for tiny prints, but the surface was flat southward as far as the eye could see, all the way to Sharps Island Light and beyond.

Placing the binoculars on the seat, he went below. Sam was stretched full length, his big blond head resting against the bulkhead. Harry sat opposite. Sam smiled. "Nothing's easy," he said.

"Right," Harry said. "*What* isn't?"

"Nothing is," Sam said. Sam had raised two younger brothers and a younger sister, never married, never complained, always said he was going to school at night and get a degree but he never had. "It really hit you hard."

"Maybe not," Harry said.

"Maybe it's not as bad as you think."

Harry nodded. "Maybe not," he said again.

Sam closed his eyes and laced his hands behind his head. "Maybe this isn't the time to say it but did it ever occur to you that maybe you should get married again—and have another kid?"

"I've got a kid," Harry said.

"Yeah . . . " Sam nodded.

Harry sat there listening to the splashing and yelling outside. "I think I've got a hangup about kids," he said. "I lost my own and it's made me a freak."

Sam was looking thoughtful. "Yeah," he said. But if you take that attitude . . . " He shook his head.

"I know," Harry said.

"It's none of my business," Sam said.

"It's okay," Harry said.

"You've got a lot to give."

"Not much," Harry said. "Not much that I know of."

"The hell you haven't."

For a few moments Harry was silent. "Well," he said finally, "you sure had this son of a bitch moving."

"For all the good it did," Sam said. "Pass all those boats and here we are all jumbled together again—what's all *that?*" He sat up with a frown.

There was a lot of yelling outside. Roy was part of it. Up on the foredeck he was yelling, "Hey! Whoooo-eeee!"

Sam got to his feet and went up on deck. Harry followed.

As a consequence of the dead calm and the random drift of the boats as they came to a halt, there was a circle of open water. Near the center of the circle sat *Iceman,* surrounded by a ring of boats. Like an arena stage, the deck of the big black boat was visible from all sides.

Elaine, fresh from the bed, her face still damp with perspiration, emerged from the cabin. As she stepped up to the deck and moved forward past the mast it was as if she had stepped onstage.

The white middy blouse was just barely long enough to cover the crotch of her bikini. Her legs and feet were bare and her hair was tousled.

Because of what she wore, the way she looked, because she was all alone on stage, but mostly because of the trumpet, some of the onlookers reacted as if she were a stripper who had just stepped out from the wings onto a runway. She had the attention not only of those watching from the decks of other boats but from those splashing around in the water.

As Harry followed Sam up into the cockpit he heard shouts of "Take it off!" followed by cheering and loud applause.

Roy stood by the mast. "Whoooo-eeeee!" he shouted again.

Each time Elaine moved she was pursued by the trumpet. Reaching the bow pulpit, she paused and stood motionless. Her face was flushed with anger. While she stood at the pulpit the trumpet was silent. The trumpeter could be seen now. He was on one of the Albergs, standing apparently on the foreberth, his head sticking up through the open forward hatch, trumpet aloft, catching the rays of the sun.

Still at the bow pulpit, Elaine raised a hand and brushed her hair back from her face.

The trumpeter responded with two quick notes.

Laughter.

Hand on the top strand of the lifeline, she was again motionless. The trumpet was silent.

Turning away, she moved aft toward the mast. As she walked, the trumpet cut loose with mad soaring notes and then slid down the scale with the gurgling sound of a dying animal.

Laughter.

Standing at the mast, she looked defiantly about the ring of boats.

"Let's see what you got on under that thing, baby!"

Again her hand went to her hair and again two sharp notes. Again she stood motionless, as if held captive by the trumpet; impaled.

"Can't you smile?"

Standing before the mast now, she let her head fall back against it, her face still defiant. The trumpeter began to blow bump-and-grind music.

Harry was watching with a frown now, his eyes clouded.

The trumpet blew high piercing notes, only to succumb and glide down the scale into a helpless heap of gurgling notes, as if devastated, wiped out by her sex appeal.

"Topless!" Roy was getting into the act. "Topless, baby, topless!"

Harry turned. His voice was sharp. "Hey, Roy! Shove it! Shut up!"

He saw Roy's eyes glitter and a flash of teeth. It was as if Roy had snapped at him.

"*Let her alone,*" Harry said.

Roy was looking again at the deck of *Iceman*.

From all around the ring of boats now there were cries of "take it off" and rhythmic clapping, accompanied by the guttural, snarling sounds of the trumpet.

The yelling grew louder and as it did so she stepped away from the mast, raised her hand high with the middle finger extended and stood there, jabbing it again and again into the air and all around the circle before darting back to the cockpit and disappearing below.

All the while, Sam had been standing at Harry's side. Now he turned quickly. Harry turned with him in time to see Roy on top of the cabin, arms dangling, crouched like an animal, his lips drawn back. "*. . . no son of a bitch talks to me like that . . .* " He sprang and while he was still in the air his fist caught Harry's nose. Blood spurted and as Harry closed with him he felt it gush down his chin. Harry pinned Roy's arms to his sides, holding him in a bear hug, then Sam took him from behind, locking his forearms around Roy's chest. Harry stepped back, holding his nose. Roy stood in Sam's grip, snarling and spitting with rage, his small dark eyes filled with hatred.

Still holding him in an iron grip, Sam pushed him down to the seat. Roy sat there panting. Saliva ran from his mouth.

Sam sat beside him, one arm over Roy's shoulder, his voice soothing. "Cool it, old buddy, cool it, cool it . . . "

Roy wiped away the saliva, then just let it run. Harry stood above him. Their eyes met. Roy looked away. The saliva dripped. Harry patted his shoulder and went below. With a paper towel he tried to stop the blood, finally tearing off a small piece and shoving it up his nostril. He opened a beer and began to gulp it and as he stood at the sink he could hear Sam still talking in a soothing tone and then Roy's voice, tight, angry, " . . . Antigua last summer all the broads in the whole fleet went topless . . . What's all the big deal? Chick's neurotic . . . Son of a bitch must be hung up on her. How in Christ was I supposed to know?"

Harry stood there, drinking his beer, taking out the pieces of paper towel and stuffing in new ones. He heard Sam still talking in the same soothing tones, talking and talking, and then silence and then Sam calling in a low urgent voice: "Hey! Here we go! Hey, Harry!"

Setting the beer can in the sink, Harry moved up the ladder. There was a breeze. It was coming in from the west, sprinkling the surface with light ripples.

"Okay," he said softly, "Sammie, bring up the anchor—slow but fast, if you know what I mean. Roy? Are you still with us? If you are, a little more slack on the jib halyard. Everybody walk real light . . . real light . . . "

Roy didn't say anything, didn't look up, but he was following orders. Harry picked up the tiller. With his free hand he gently trimmed the jib sheet and suddenly the jib filled and became a smooth curved bulge. Sam had broken the anchor from the bottom and they were moving through

Regatta

the smooth water even before he had finished bringing it over the side.

When it lay on the foredeck with its loops of line, Sam moved lightly back to the cockpit. "Lemme have this son of a bitch," Harry said. "I'll take it now."

"Good," Sam said.

Other boats were coming up with their anchors, getting underway with yelling and confusion and cries of "Starboard!" and "Watch your bow!" and "Keep clear, keep clear!"

Roy by now had the jib sheet in hand, playing it carefully. Harry was nursing the boat over the flat spots and they were making a faint bow wake.

Sam was looking to the west. "Hate to say it, but I don't think it'll last," he said.

But the breeze was gaining strength and the dead spots were filling in. The air had freshened. The water was dark blue with ruffles. The breeze felt cool on the face, at the temples, over the crown of the head.

By now most of the other boats had their anchors up and were underway, but *Sundance* had gotten a head start, stolen a march, and was slipping smoothly through the fleet, headed for the Choptank.

Part III

Seventeen

OF ALL THE ESTUARINE RIVERS OF Maryland's Eastern Shore, the Choptank is the longest and most imposing. The river is named for the unfortunate Choptank Indians, a gentle tribe whose traditional enemies had long been the Nanticokes and Assateagues, both from nearby, and the frequently marauding Senecas from up around Albany, New York. In the mid-1600's, the Choptanks began entering into treaties with white settlers and as the decades passed they went on exchanging their land for small annuities—believing perhaps to the very end that their principal enemies were the Nanticokes, the Assateagues, and the Senecas. By 1800 there were only four landowning Choptank Indians on the entire river, and soon these too were gone.

By most known accounts the outstanding feature of the Choptank Indian was the lack of purposeful energy sometimes characteristic of peoples who are especially well fed. If environmental factors weigh heavily in shaping the character and culture of a populace, it is interesting to note that in all the generations since the rise and fall of the Choptanks the populace has been very well fed. Bountiful eating is an Eastern Shore tradition; with some a pastime. In the opinion of at least one historian it is a land where the bounty of nature may cause one to lose one's way. Whether in spite of or because of this, the Eastern Shore is sometimes described as The Land of Pleasant Living.

The Choptank River is both long and broad. Because of shoals on both sides, the navigable part of its mouth is relatively narrow but once inside the headlands the river widens quickly.

The entranceway is flanked on the south by Cooks Point and on the north by Blackwalnut Point, the latter being the name given to the southern tip of Tilghman Island. Black-walnut Point gives way to a long stretch of shoal water which is guarded by Black Bell 7, known locally as the Gas Bell, a turning mark of the course and the mark which had seemed so near and yet so far during the long period of dead calm.

Sam had been correct. The breeze, so long awaited, would fade again before it blew in earnest but for now it was enough to get the fleet moving and soon upward of sixty densely packed boats were sliding down through the corridor and then, like bunched Roman chariots, wheeling slowly around the Gas Bell, five and six abreast.

As the boats rounded the bell and confronted the long-awaited waters of the Choptank, spinnakers were broken out. The new course was nearly due east and would remain so for roughly ten miles. The breeze was from the northwest, an ideal direction for a spinnaker run, but it was already dropping in velocity, thus making it difficult to keep the big sails filled. They would catch a breeze and assume their massive shapes, only to droop—to hang straight down from the masthead like a limp bedsheet dangling from the top of a flagpole.

As the spinnakers were hoisted one by one, a most interested onlooker was Margaret Hackett, even though it was true that she was still viewing the proceedings from a goodly distance to the rear.

Although the area of dead calm had been an area of pain and frustration to those frozen in it for so long, it was, to Walters Hackett, a sort of promised land where the elite gathered; a beautiful, longed-for, promised land that was always beyond his reach.

Like so many other boats in the fleet, *Silver Heels* had not made it to the area of dead calm, at least not while it *was* an area of dead calm. When the breeze finally came up and the fleet came to life, the Hackett party was still a couple of hundred yards short of the congested area. Mrs. Hackett felt that under the circumstances it was remarkable they had gotten as far as they had, especially since many boats were still far behind them, scattered all over the bay, and once again she felt thankful that they had played follow the leader with Harry.

Once the breeze came up, the Hacketts got going with fair dispatch, and as they rounded the Gas Bell they were somewhere near the middle of the fleet; that is, there were roughly as many boats ahead of them as there were behind, perhaps sixty of each.

Seeing the boats ahead putting up their spinnakers, Hackett now became crisp. "Okay, Mag," he said. "Time to break out the chute."

Thanks to the light breezes, to the God-given period of dead calm and thanks mainly to the fact that a spinnaker run had been out of the question, Mrs. Hackett's day had not been nearly so unpleasant as she had feared it might be.

Now her day collapsed. Just ahead lay a spinnaker attack that promised to make the one the previous night seem mild by comparison.

Hackett's designation of the spinnaker as the "chute" was a designation used by the sailing cognoscenti and was not inappropriate—for a spinnaker, it was true, was a sail somewhat reminiscent of a parachute.

Mrs. Hackett now told herself that a spinnaker was also something she hated more than she had ever hated anything in her entire life with the possible exception of water moccasins.

Composed of bright beautiful colors, a spinnaker as noted was used when the wind was more or less behind the boat, and this is what had given Mrs. Hackett comfort all through the morning and early afternoon—the fact that when there was a breeze it had been ahead of the boat, and that thereafter there had been no breeze at all.

What cruel trick of fate was being played upon her?

In full bulge, as even she could admit, a spinnaker could be a marvelous spectacle, floating out ahead of the boat, bell-shaped, hard-molded, hardly a wrinkle showing.

Regatta

Set properly, it was a thing of great beauty—but contrivances of the devil almost invariably had great superficial beauty.

During their practice runs on the Tred Avon that spring, Mrs. Hackett had found its beauty easy to overlook. For her it had become a sort of Fifth Horseman of the Apocalypse, a fearsome, monstrous living thing capable of hauling a boat to its destruction, of hauling seamen over the edge of the earth. In some of the instructional books her husband kept reading with such frowns of concentration there were frighteningly evocative words: hobby-horsing, hourglassing, jibing, yawing, broaching. There were sickening photographs of spinnakers flown in heavy air, the boat pulled over, skidding at great speed down the slope of a wave, rail buried, cockpit a sheer vertical drop with the crew clinging to the high side like the final passengers were said to have clung to the stern of the by-then vertical *Titanic.*

Stomach-curdling caption: *Boat out of control on leeward broach.* (Note: *Halyard jammed, making it impossible to lower chute.*)

And another photograph, uncaptioned but highly articulate, speaking volumes: flapping from the masthead a mere rag of spinnaker, a tag-end, a remnant, all that was left.

Now, looking through the open hatchway down into the cabin, she could see the turtled spinnaker, packed in its bag, ready for hoisting.

"Here's the stick, Mag," Hackett said.

Mrs. Hackett was now reminded, if she had needed reminding, of who would be at the helm. Hackett had to be free to hoist the spinnaker and pull and haul on the various lines and set the pole and whatever else it was that he did. So she, Margaret Hackett, was at the helm, at her age, with her biceps like cooked spaghetti, she whose previous athletic grounding included a single dismal semester at the Rahway Cycle and Health Spa. It was true that she had picked up a few fine points of helmsmanship from Harry

174

during spring practice on the Tréd Avon, and secretly she felt she might have a steadier hand than her husband, but this thought gave her small comfort now as she took the tiller.

In spite of the calm seas and the relative ease of working conditions, it was some little time before the Hackett spinnaker was aloft. Several things happened. For one, Hackett, squirming about on his stomach up on the foredeck and moving his legs haphazardly here and there, managed to kick the empty and unsecured spinnaker bag overboard and it soon had floated well astern.

There were other mishaps. The spinnaker pole on the first try was attached to the wrong side of the mast, making it difficult if not impossible to set the sail. Kitty, although she had been minutely instructed otherwise, wrapped the sheet counterclockwise about the winch, instead of the approved clockwise. When she tried again she managed to come up with a so-called wry turn, an undesirable and largely unintentional circumstance in which overlapping strands of line became twisted about the winch, causing it to become inoperative and, in extreme cases, necessitating that the line be cut with a knife.

Finally the spinnaker was up and spasmodically drawing.

It was axiomatic in sailing that whichever boat stood nearest a new breeze was the boat which would benefit soonest and most.

The faint breeze which had been drifting the fleet along at such a slow and erratic pace now steadied out. At the same time it moved up a degree or so to the northwest and it also increased in velocity, quickly turning the river from a pallid, unruffled sheet of grey into a lively gunmetal blue, full of stiff ripples.

Silver Heels, being at the rear of that part of the fleet already around the Gas Bell, was first to benefit. As the breeze struck, lifting the spinnaker and cooling their faces, Hackett laughed with a sort of manic glee.

It was a breeze which thus far was substantial only by contrast with the sluggish air which had preceded it. Still hardly more than five knots, it was enough nonetheless to fill the Hackett spinnaker, to turn it into the hard tortoise shell, the half a liberty bell which translated into speed— while the spinnakers on the boats ahead still had that dispirited, wet-wash look because the breeze had not yet reached them.

"Okay, Kit," Hackett shouted. "Go for'ard with the pole a little. Pole a little for'ard. Okay, hold it right there. Wait a minute. Aft a little. Little more. Good. Hold it right there."

Kitty noted that this was exactly where it had been in the first place but Hackett, in high spirits, ignored her. With his wife at the tiller, he was keeping very busy, not only handling the sheet but with his other hand tightening and loosening various lines here and there, pausing once to stand on the cockpit seat and bellow:

"Mag, I'll tell ya something! We're *moving* on these sons of bitches! We're really *walkin'* on 'em! She's got a *bone* in her teeth!"

"Isn't that nice!" Mrs. Hackett said with a pleasant smile.

Although it was hardly what she wanted to hear, it nonetheless seemed to be true. The breeze was still relatively light but it was steady, and the gap between themselves and the rest of the fleet had begun to narrow noticeably.

Soon some of the skippers up ahead were looking back over their shoulders—not, one might have guessed, because they considered Hackett a threat. His performance and method had made it clear that he could not be considered a threat, but he was of interest as a harbinger, as the herald of wind, the messenger of good tidings, bearer of a new breeze.

The *Silver Heels* people were coming from the direction of the wind. As sailing buffs had it, they were bringing the wind with them. In cluster after cluster, dead spinnakers lifted and filled and boats began to drive. The breeze moved rapidly on up the river, rippling the surface, bringing boats to life, freshening the air and dispelling the bright mist that had been overhanging the water ever since the early stages of the dead calm.

By now the Hacketts and Kitty were amid boats they had not seen since early that morning at the starting line. Hackett was thrilled. Mrs. Hackett was wondering how long she could sustain her foxy attitude.

"Mag!" Hackett was exuberant. His hair was up in white spikes, his voice high-pitched. "Have you ever *known* anything like this?"

"No, I never have," Mrs. Hackett said.

Eighteen

BACK AT THE STARTING LINE the people aboard the committee boat *Pandora* had been in no hurry to get away after the race began. For a long while they sat about in the cockpit, drinking coffee, discussing the weather prospects, and watching the sails of the fleet grow steadily smaller.

Some time after eleven-thirty *Pandora* weighed anchor and moved at a steady seven knots down the bay, sails furled and covered, motor droning smoothly. By two-fifteen it was within sight of the area of dead calm.

By this time Anthony Korbut had been asked by the boat's owner, one of the committee members, to take over the helm, and he had done so. It was one of the few times he had been at the tiller of a boat since he went to jail.

Intent upon giving the becalmed boats a wide berth, Korbut followed the inshore side of the channel, moving as close to the shore of Tilghman Island as he safely could. As he drew near, he cut the throttle, moving along at little better than a knot so as not to give the becalmed boats any wash, careful not to disturb any slight momentum they might still be nursing. Hands were raised in appreciation as he moved slowly by.

The committee members on the foredeck joked with the becalmed skippers and crew members as *Pandora* passed.

"Just wait until the tide starts to set!" one of the committee called cheerily.

"Expect you about midnight," another shouted.

The sun was out full now and at reduced speed it was very very hot. The committee was sprawled over the foredeck. One of the women clutched a portable radio, waiting for a Baltimore Orioles baseball game to start.

On the becalmed boats, Korbut knew, the heat by now was intense. He saw a man pull up a pail of water and pour it over his head. It was very hot. Some of the hottest moments of Korbut's life had been spent in sailboat races. Once, becalmed on the Sound, he had been close to a heat stroke. The only relief had been to put ice cubes inside his khaki cap and crown his grateful pate, reveling in the cool trickle of water that soaked the hair, soaked into the very brain. Racing was keen competition. It could exact the utmost in strength and judgment and skill, yes, but it could just as easily become guesswork, or it could become a travesty of sitting for long hours adrift beneath a boiling sun, this ritual of manhood now transformed into an exercise in sheer idiocy; grown men, adrift with ice cubes under their caps, waiting for a breeze that did not come.

Yet the tiller felt good in his hand.

Once he was well beyond the last boat, Korbut picked up speed again and soon dropped down into the slot between the shoals on the left and Sharps Island tower on the right. In another ten minutes he was rounding the Gas Bell and the last limp sails were out of sight behind Tilghman Island. When he could see them no longer, Korbut opened the throttle and moved at three-quarters power up the Choptank.

Regatta

Within an hour, *Pandora* was far up the river, nearing the mouth of the Tred Avon.

Where the Tred Avon joined the Choptank stood Choptank Light, which for many years had been one of the picturesque white cottages once so characteristic of the bay. It was now merely a skeletal girder-like structure topped with a blinking white light.

This light tower, still called "the lighthouse," was the final turning mark of the course. It would be left to port, rounded counterclockwise as the turn was made into the Tred Avon.

The lighthouse stood at mid-channel. There was plenty of water all around it and for those headed for Oxford and not bound by racing rules, it saved time to cut left well short of the light tower and run just wide enough to clear a black channel marker which guarded a long sandbar reaching out from the mouth of the Tred Avon.

Taking the shortcut and rounding the black marker, Korbut entered the Tred Avon and straightened his course for the yacht club two miles upstream. The Tred Avon's long beautiful sweep was spread before him now and under the soft grey oyster-shell sky it was filled with boats as far as the eye could see, some racing, some filled with spectators. To the right, small sailing dinghies moved slowly about a triangular course marked at the corners with orange flags. To the left, eight majestic log canoes were running toward *Pandora*, a remarkable procession of beautiful boats on a broad reach, their huge sails spread before the northwest breeze like white wings. The breeze was still light and their speed was deceptively swift as the slim hulls, so topheavy with sail, slipped over the faintly ruffled surface.

Everywhere there were spectator boats, idling along, watching, trying, sometimes haphazardly, to keep out of the way of those racing. Most of the spectators were moving in *Pandora*'s direction, headed downstream for the Choptank, where they would drift or drop anchor to watch the fleet as it rounded the lighthouse.

Regatta

Korbut steered sharply to starboard and then reset his course up the middle of the channel, giving all the room they might need to the log canoes, which were still running single file along the far bank with no indication that any one of them might be gaining on any other.

On that side of the river—the left, as one moved upstream—the scalloped bank was green and spongy. Beyond the shore stretched farmland rimmed with strips of pine. It was flat open country with a very big sky.

On the opposite bank, the right bank, the village of Oxford had begun to show up. From a distance the high curves of its densely leafed trees were fuzzy under the soft clouds, its spires still indistinct, but as *Pandora* moved steadily up the river, the village took form and its detail became sharper. Everywhere were signs of a village mellowed with age, a village from another time, with its huge old trees, the gazebos, the white houses with green shutters, the mounded clusters of very old boxwood. Freshly mowed back lawns ran all the way down to the river and people lined the shore, watching.

Korbut continued to work his way upstream. By now he could see clearly all the way to the jutting point of land where the yacht club stood. Just off this point was the red flasher buoy which would form one end of the finish line. At the opposite end the committee boat would drop its anchor and take up its vigil, and the racers as they finished would sail across the line between the committee boat and the flasher.

The end of the trip was at hand now and Korbut eased the boat in. It was greeted with good-natured cheers from spectators lining the sandy beach in front of the yacht club. Some of the committee members waved back. On the bow, the anchor had been made ready. Circling, looking over his shoulder, measuring his distance, Korbut eased *Pandora* toward the far shore until he guessed she was perhaps two hundred feet from the flasher. "Okay, let 'er go," he said and the anchor went overboard.

Regatta

As the anchor took hold, *Pandora* swung slowly with the wind, coming to rest with its bow pointed northwest, its stern pointed toward the yacht club. Here the committee, after its relaxing trip down the bay, would relax a while longer, waiting for the boats to begin crossing the line. Unless the wind picked up substantially, Korbut doubted that the vanguard would be appearing for at least another couple of hours. By now the boats must have some breeze, probably from the northwest. If it remained there and freshened a little, the fleet might have a good spinnaker run up the Choptank—and then a long tack up the Tred Avon to the finish line. If these were the circumstances there might be some wild tacking duels. The course up the Choptank to the lighthouse was almost due east. Rounding the lighthouse and turning into the Tred Avon involved a ninety-degree turn to the left. This meant that as the turn was made it would be necessary to take down the spinnakers and hoist the jibs for the 2.2-mile dash to the finish line. The course would be almost dead into the wind and there would be tacking all the way. Korbut could envision the entire river filled with white sails, with criss-crossing sailboats.

He got himself a beer and relaxed with the others in the cockpit. There was talk of the job ahead. With such a large fleet, such heavy traffic, the committee's task would not be easy—recording the finish of each and every boat, making sure of the name, sail number, and class, marking down the exact time of crossing; shooting off the cannon for the first in each class to cross the line; tooting the air horn for each of the rest.

Looking across the water toward the Oxford shore, Korbut saw an open boat pulling slowly away from the yacht club dock. It was finished in natural varnish, the shade of mellowed gold, a beautiful boat with a long powerful prow and the steering wheel amidships, very much resembling the sort of craft that Sir Malcolm Campbell, speed merchant of the thirties, set records in. Standing tall at the wheel was a woman in a pink gingham blouse and khaki skirt. Korbut recognized the boat and he recognized Roberta Lodge. Her head was high, thick white hair tousled, face tanned, and as she picked up a little speed the breeze flattened the skirt against her thighs.

She was headed out to greet the committee boat.

Reducing speed, she drifted alongside, the big boat's motor idling with a rhythmic, muttering lope that told of great power. "Where are they?" she asked. She spoke to the committee, to no one in particular, but her eyes were on Korbut.

"The wind dropped out north of Sharps Island," somebody said. "Everybody just sat. At least the ones lucky enough to get that far."

"And sat and sat . . . "

"They may still be sitting for all we know. We left them there almost two hours ago."

"They should have breeze by now." Holding his pipe over the side, Korbut knocked the bowl against his palm. "How did you find time to be out here?" he asked Roberta with a smile.

"I just *took* time," she said.

Bending, she placed a capable tanned hand on *Pandora*'s rail and pushed off. "Good luck," she said to the committee. She waved and headed down the river. Korbut followed her with his eyes as she gradually fed the big boat more speed.

Roberta Lodge was on the water because she had felt a strong need to get away by herself, even if only for a short time. There had been things all day long to claim her attention, all of them necessary to the performance of her job but some of them terribly trivial as well. There were, for example, a couple of dignified old gentlemen on her committee who felt that no man, young or old, should be admitted to the dance that evening without a necktie. She had said not a chance: it was hard enough to get kids to wear shoes, much less neckties. The old gentlemen had taken umbrage. Their

standards of behavior and dress were derived largely from
Ralph Henry Barbour and the Rover Boys. They felt she
had sold out to the philistines, sold out to the subversive
codes of the seventies.

She was clear of the worst of the river traffic but now
the log canoes, having finished their downwind run, were
coming back in her direction, headed back toward the yacht
club. As they tacked toward her side of the river, she gave
the boat some more throttle so that she would pass well
beyond the slant they were taking toward shore and be well
clear of their course.

Roberta smiled at the memory of the necktie argument.
Men were very amusing on the subject of codes; on the
subject of—manhood. She thought of her nine-month-old
grandson who only a week earlier had grasped the palings
of his crib and pulled himself for the first time to a standing
position. She and her daughter had cheered and clapped,
and such machismo! The look of pride on the funny little
lopsided face, the broad grin. What was in store for him?

Roberta gunned the motor. She felt the need for speed.
The boat lifted; the water fled by. She had needed this.
Probably she had no business being out here. Perhaps all
hell would break loose while she was gone but she had done
all she could for the moment. The committee boat had
arrived and was anchored at the finish line; supper arrangements were under control; the town cops were on the alert;
flowers and decorations were prominently displayed.
There were some fluttery, impressionable types who felt
something special should be done because of the imminent
presence of the great Mel Fontaine and his prestigious
oceangoing sloop. She had laughed them down.

The air rushed past her temples and she smiled with the
pleasure of it, smiled with pleasure at the long foaming arc
she was cutting as she made a wide curve around the black
marker standing at the end of the sandbar. So far as the
water could be owned, she owned it. She had always felt
that way and felt it now. It was hers to ride on, ride over,

it was her place, her domain. And of all the skippers in the race that day each, whether aware of it or not, must have been feeling the same acute and acutely satisfying sense of ownership. She corrected herself. Possession. Far better than owning was to possess without ownership. It was, she thought, the ultimate joy. In the same way, one possessed the sun and the stars, time and the sky—owning nothing.

Safely past the long sandbar, she cut her speed again. Enough speed for now. At slow speeds one saw the world. The sun was trying to get through the mist. There was a sheen on the water just as there had been that morning, the same muted beauty of sky and river. Suddenly her eye was drawn to a scene that took her breath away. A small skipjack was anchored in the shoals, clean, white, and graceful against the lime-green bank. Its sails were down and furled. Stretched taut over the boom was a pink and white striped awning which provided a canopy above the cockpit. Beneath the awning two bearded blond young men in basque shirts were laughing as they drank wine. With them were two honey-haired young women dressed in soft colors. The mist-shrouded amber light bathed the red wine in its glass jug. Roberta was reminded of a Renoir painting. Renoir had unabashedly painted beauty and happiness, the joy of a summer's day on the water. Too many people had too many reservations against happiness. Too many did penance.

With a final lingering look at the beautiful scene, she gunned the motor again. It would be awfully nice if she could see some spinnakers. She loved the very sight of a spinnaker and even more the sight of massed spinnakers. It was a sight that never failed to give her a thrill and in other years she had often stood and watched from the foot of her yard or even from her kitchen window, as the big boats rounded the lighthouse and headed up the Tred Avon, headed straight at her kitchen, bound for the finish line off the yacht club. Where else in the world could one stand at the kitchen window and look out upon upward of a hundred closely packed spinnakers, a pageantry of massed, multi-colored beauty, looking so huge and close, looking as though they were about to sail right into her kitchen.

But she knew enough about sailing to know that a spinnaker run up the Tred Avon required a wind out of the southern quadrant. It was on south winds that the massed spinnakers always moved up the Tred Avon. In the summer the prevailing wind was from the south but today's wind had finally settled into the northwest, this much she could tell, so that if there was to be a spinnaker run it would last only as far as the lighthouse.

Still idling along, she looked ahead, down the Choptank, and saw nothing on the horizon except a couple of fishing boats. Where was the fleet? Surely not still becalmed. She was following the deep channel of the Choptank now, headed slowly westward. Ahead the broad river was still covered with bright mist, the sun still trying to burn through. On and on she went, still at slow speeds, farther and farther, with a sense of doing something furtive, forbidden, following a whim, but if things were going to hell back at the yacht club, let them. She was going out to meet the fleet.

For her there was an old magic in the words, left over from long ago. On a beautiful day, to go out and meet the fleet was a beautiful thing to do and many times she had done it, taking a picnic lunch, she and her husband and the kids when they were little. But where *was* the fleet? She was five miles down the river now, more than halfway to the Gas Bell, and if they were getting any breeze at all the vanguard should be showing up by now. She opened the throttle wide and sped due west, then cut it again, lazing along and feeling the boat roll gently in the wash of its own making.

The haze still hung over the water and then—there! A light speck of color in the mist, a speck of orange and then soon there were others and still others—round spots of color showing up in the mist, some solid like lollipops, some striped, parti-colored balloons and pastel puffs, all still very far away.

Again she fed the boat speed, sent it racing toward the

spinnakers. Now she was seeing clusters and soon a long armada of color, a twisting spread of bunched spinnakers, greens and whites and blues and deep reds and yellows. At this distance they seemed to stand still, congealed on the river. Deliberately she cut her speed and let the boat drift along in neutral, its loping motor the only sound in the silence. The closer the spinnakers drew the faster they seemed to move, even though she knew the increased speed was only an illusion. As they drew abreast they were fairly flying, some hard and steady, others dipping and swaying with the motion of the boat as the bow was tossed by a wave.

From two hundred yards away, Roberta watched them pass by. It had the excitement of a parade without sound, a royal procession that might have taken place centuries earlier on the Thames. A pageantry reminiscent of the heraldic colors of a medieval army. It made her think of brightly striped tents, of banners and pennons and pavilions.

There was every conceivable color combination and there were no two spinnakers alike. Packed colors, curved sails, beauty. Never had she seen such a display of spinnakers.

For a while longer, still drifting along in neutral, Roberta watched them, committing the sight to memory.

Then she gunned the motor again and sent the boat flying back toward the lighthouse. After a half-mile or so, she slowed again and looked back over her shoulder. The fleet was receding fast, back into the haze where she had discovered it. There was nothing visible now but a few tiny spots of color, the tiny bright balloons, the tiny pastel lollipops, and soon these too disappeared back into the mist.

Roberta gunned the motor and streaked for home. At top speed her boat did better than thirty knots and in ten minutes she had rounded the black channel marker and was speeding up the Tred Avon. Cutting the motor, she passed close to the committee boat.

"They're still about five miles down the river," she

called, "but they've got a breeze and they're coming fast."
Korbut waved. She waved back and moved the boat at
half speed across to the yacht club.

Nineteen

To MANY the area of the Choptank has a special
beauty, the river so wide, the land so flat, the topography
so uneventful. The south shore—on the right as one moves
upstream—is virtually unbroken. From a distance it resem-
bles a child's drawing, with a huge sky and huge expanse of
water separated by a long strip of horizon hardly thicker
than a pencil line.

The north shore is heavily indented and on this side the
river is fed by numerous tributaries, most notably Broad
Creek, a very large body of water with many tributaries of
its own. Broad Creek is a blue-ribbon residential area. Its
own banks as well as those of its coves and inlets and feeder
streams are lined with expensive homes, beautiful estates.
From a passing boat there is an impression of depth and
dimension. Everywhere the shore is scooped out with
creeks and hollows. Distant coves nestle deep back within
the land. Blurred loops of greenery follow the curved edges
of the coves, and the progressively lighter shades of green
tell of the receding distances.

On her foray down the river, Roberta Lodge had pro-
gressed perhaps a quarter-mile beyond the mouth of Broad
Creek when she withdrew to watch the spinnakers pass.
Here the boats in the vanguard had covered not quite half
the Choptank portion of the course, the mouth of Broad
Creek marking approximately the halfway point.

It was soon after Roberta raced away, leaving the spinnakers once more hidden in the mist, that the fleet was

overtaken by the impact of the frontal system that had been heralded earlier above Sharps Island—when the front's leading edge stirred up the breeze that ended the long period of dead calm.

Now, just after four o'clock, Harry Crowder had Broad Creek on the beam when he felt *Sundance* lift with fresh wind. By the time the creek had fallen astern, the wind, still out of the northwest, was piping up toward ten knots and seemed likely to go higher. The humidity was quickly gone. The cleansing breeze drove the mist from the air and scoured the sky. River and sky now glittered a deep blue. The bright colors of the spinnakers stood out bold and clear. Sharply etched white clouds raced eastward above the spinnakers, clouds and sails all headed in the same direction.

Unlike the bay portion of the race, where the constantly tacking fleet was fanned out from shore to shore, the movement now was more of a procession, a parade of closely bunched boats with little lateral spread, this being true of a spinnaker run by its very nature—for with the wind from behind, a boat is blown straight ahead like a leaf over the face of a pond.

There was additional help that afternoon from the tide, which was flooding strongly. The city of Cambridge, fourteen miles or so upstream, is a deep-water port, a frequent port of call for ocean shipping, and the channel of the Choptank reaches a depth of forty feet and more, producing a very strong tidal current. The boats for the most part were moving in single file or clustered in parallel lanes. With a following wind in the sails and a favoring tide surging beneath their hulls, they were dead on course, compass reading 093, headed straight up the river for the lighthouse —the girdered tower which, with the haze now melted away, would soon be showing up as a faint blur in the distance.

Harry's head start in breaking out of the dead calm had stood him in good stead. Going around the Gas Bell, he was ahead by a sizable margin. In the lull that soon followed, the fleet drifted with limp sails. Picking up a zephyr here and there, he had coaxed *Sundance* over the flat spots toward the south side of the river. When the rest of the river was flat there was often breeze close to shore. Moreover the tide changed earliest in shallow water and by sailing along in water no more than six and eight feet deep he was able to pick up the early force of the current.

Running along the shore, he had added to his lead and when he felt the current was reaching full strength he had angled away from shore toward the middle of the river. Now he was closely following the deep-water channel, riding the flooding tide, and as the breeze picked up his speed increased. The wind was coming in over his left shoulder. His mainsail was trimmed far out to starboard and held down tight with a vang which stretched from boom to deck. His yellow and black spinnaker was a smooth mold, flying beautifully out ahead of the bow. Flecks of light danced on the water, long ribbons and darts and pinpoints of light, constantly lengthening and shortening as the light shafts rode over the ripples, dazzling the eye. Harry again wore sunglasses and the long-billed fishing cap. Every now and then he touched his nose. His eyes kept watering. His nose hurt but he didn't think it was broken.

Ahead there was open water. To the right was the south shore. Far to the left, heading badly off course, was a boat flying a spinnaker, a boat with a grey hull. Harry was afraid that he recognized the *Silver Heels* of Walters Hackett. If it was Hackett there was nothing he could do about it except wonder what in the hell he was up to.

"Sammie—sheet!"

Sam sat on the cabin top playing the spinnaker. As Harry spoke he had already noticed the leading edge begin to collapse and was already trimming it, bringing the big sail full again.

"Flying!" Roy sat all the way aft on the port side, ready to ease or trim the spinnaker pole as needed. His face was

intense. He was jubilant about their lead and seemed to
have forgotten completely about the fight. To judge from
his attitude it was as though nothing had ever happened.
Harry would have been only half surprised to hear Roy ask
what was wrong with his nose. It was strange but he had
no time to think about it now. He was intent upon the race.
For whatever reason he felt like sailing the boat again.

Sam was pointing astern.

"Look what the hell's coming!" he said.

Harry looked. *Iceman* was sweeping up from behind.

The big boat had dawdled through much of the race.
The erratic wind had permitted little more. Light air was
not its forte and there had been wrong choices. Fontaine
had chosen the wrong side of the bay and almost gotten
buried. He had straggled in late to sit with the pack in the
dead calm; and in the first hour or so after getting around
the Gas Bell he was still lagging.

"What's wrong, Fontaine? Can't you get that thing
cranked up?"

"Is that the way they do it in the big time?"

There were taunts, some good-natured, some with an
edge.

"Time to do your stuff, Fontaine."

"Time to get it on, Melsy."

In whatever walk of life, some people love seeing a titan
humbled. In the fleet that day there were many who found
it a nice joke that *Iceman* was still back with the ordinary
mortals. Many would have been pleased to see Fontaine
mess up. To them it was pleasant irony that the mighty
Goliath was hurting so badly, and for those sailors who
lived around Oxford the pleasure was all the greater for the
fact that out in front, leading the pack up the river, was a
man with local connections, a local David of sorts—a little
old, perhaps, but still a local David in a small boat with two
in crew.

There were others who, even while enjoying Fontaine's

plight, would have been just as pleased to see him win big. They had come that day expecting to see him do his thing. They wanted to admire the marvelous racing machine from the Seven Seas, wanted to believe in Supersailor in Superboat.

These now were suddenly getting their wish. As *Iceman* passed the mouth of Broad Creek it began living up to its reputation. Suddenly the huge black spinnaker was packed full of northwest wind and the boat was moving through the fleet like an express train.

Down in her cabin, Elaine felt the moment when the wind struck, felt the impact of wind against sails. There was a noticeable lift, the hull quickened, the boat came to life. It was familiar to her. She had felt it many times before.

"Pole aft!"

"Pole aft!"

She heard the sharp crack of Fontaine's voice and the calm acknowledgment from the crewman posted on the afterguy. There was the grind of a winch, the intensified creak of the rigging, the rush of water past the hull, a surge as a gust of wind lifted the spinnaker.

He was passing boats now, knocking them one by one back into the ruck. Over the years she had talked now and then to his competitors and she had been told what it was like to be passed by *Iceman*. One had told of a night race, describing a rushing sound he could not identify, like the far-off sigh of wind moving through a distant woods. Then he realized that it was *Iceman* coming up from behind and whoosh! . . . it was gone on past.

Other skippers could say they were not sailing against him boat for boat and technically they were not. The separate classes, the handicapping system, provided distinct lines of competition. But it hardly mattered what they said, he was still the star of the show. He was the figure of glamour, the object of envy. To own The Boat, to be The Man. To be rich enough, early enough—but of course it took more than mere money. Money could buy such a boat but it took a special man to dare to own one and then to tame it, to make it perform.

Standing at the porthole, she could see the spinnaker. It had always seemed hardly conceivable that something so modest in size as a sailbag could contain such a vast expanse of sail—a spinnaker that seemed half an acre of black nylon, filling the sky with its huge bell-shaped contour.

She knew enough to know that the boat was performing well. The kids were good. They were putting to good use the many hours they had spent at sail drill—off Lauderdale, off Boca Grande, Jamaica, Haiti, wherever the boat happened to be. The wind was doing its part and the work of the crew was a model of precise synchronized movement. Fontaine was at the wheel, in his element, doing what he did best, piloting his spaceship, devouring the competition. With the utmost of kindliness, with as much compassion as lust, he had devoured her as well.

But by now her irritation was gone. Once more she was thinking how hard it was going to be to tell him she was leaving.

When Harry heard Sam's shout and looked back he immediately spotted *Iceman*'s spinnaker—unmistakable, the enormous spread of black nylon, the smooth taut bulge, with the lethal-looking weapon emblazoned between its shoulders. It was still a good hundred yards astern but it was picking its way through the fleet, passing boat after boat, gaining swiftly. *Sundance* would be overtaken. He knew at a glance that it was only a question of time.

Harry looked ahead. The spidery legs of the lighthouse were beginning to take form now, probably less than two miles away.

He glanced over his shoulder again. The thing to do, if he could do it, was to hold him back, delay him. If he could keep him from getting too far ahead on the spinnaker run he might have a better chance with him in the Tred Avon, where the course was more confined, the river not so wide, the shoals more of a factor, a place where local knowledge was important. In the Tred Avon the wind, as they moved northwest, would be almost dead against them and they would have to tack all the way up the 2.2-mile stretch to the finish line. In tacking maneuvers over a relatively narrow course there were many opportunities. Wind oscillations. Wrong guesses. Mishandled sails, poor tactics, unexpected currents. A person could get lucky.

But if Fontaine got away now on the spinnaker run, if he held a huge lead as he went around the lighthouse, there wouldn't be much chance of doing anything with him in the Tred Avon because he would be too far ahead.

Even so the day would hardly be a total loss. Taking into account his handicap allowance, Harry knew he would beat *Iceman* handily on corrected time and would, barring a mishap, win first-in-fleet. Astern there were bigger boats, A and B boats, messed up as *Iceman* had been by the dead calm and the erratic breezes thereafter. They too were gaining but not very rapidly, and unless he messed up in the Tred Avon he was almost sure to win on corrected time. He was holding his own against all but *Iceman.*

To win on corrected time would be a fine victory. For Fontaine it would be a painful loss but he would at least salvage the prestige of being first boat in the fleet to cross the line. But to lose boat-for-boat, to lose head-to-head to a so much smaller craft with its dinky three-man crew would be an ignominious loss and one Fontaine would hear about from his wealthy peers, his cohorts in the world of big-time ocean racing.

Harry's decision was made. "If he passes to windward, we'll take him up," he said.

"Let's not count on it," Sam said. "He won't be that dumb."

"We'll see," Harry said.

With boats on the same tack, the racing rules award the right-of-way to the boat to leeward, or in any case to the boat being overtaken. These were the rules that prevailed as the boats were heading off into the southeast breeze at the starting line that morning, and the rules applied in the same way to boats on a spinnaker run.

With the wind over their left shoulder, Fontaine and Harry were both on port tack. Fontaine, approaching from the rear, was the overtaking boat and Harry therefore had the right-of-way.

Under these circumstances, even though it meant sailing slightly below his course, the prudent choice for Fontaine would be to pass to leeward—pass, that is, to Harry's right.

Even though Harry's sails would block him momentarily from the wind, the size and speed of Fontaine's boat, the momentum he had built up, would carry him right on through with little trouble—and because the rules did not permit the leading boat to bear off below its course to the next mark there would be absolutely nothing Harry could do about it.

Fontaine's other option, the show-off tactic, the flashy, machismo tactic, was to pass to windward, meaning to Harry's left. Passing to windward is often the only way for an overtaking boat to get by, particularly if two boats are evenly matched, but this was hardly true in Fontaine's case. With his big fast boat he could go to whichever side he liked.

Harry was guessing he would go to windward. It would be an unwise choice but Harry had a hunch it would be the choice Fontaine would make. Harry's hunch was that Fontaine would enjoy showing him up simply because he had had the effrontery, or the luck, to be leading the pack.

There was also Elaine. She had said Fontaine was too conceited to be jealous and that he didn't care what she did. Maybe he still knew nothing of the time Harry had spent with Elaine in Jamaica. On the other hand maybe he did and maybe he didn't like it. If so, this might be an added reason why Fontaine would like to make him look bad.

For the overtaking skipper, the tactic in passing to windward is to blanket the leading boat, to take his air, to block him from the wind; to collapse his spinnaker, reduce his speed and shoot on by, leaving him dead in the water and struggling to get back into the race. This was the inglorious fate Harry now envisioned for himself.

But a boat being overtaken to windward has a legal option, a defensive maneuver. Since his is the right of way, he can at the strategic moment head up high of the course, swing his bow over and carry the overtaking boat up with him—in sailing parlance "luff him up." Under the rules, no statement of intent is necessary, no warning to the overtaking skipper is called for. The overtaking skipper's is the burdened boat and under pain of disqualification he must keep clear to avoid a collision.

It was this tactic to which Harry referred when he said that if Fontaine passed to windward "we'll take him up."

"Watch him," he said now.

"Coming hard," Sam said.

Harry took a quick glance. By now there were no other boats separating him from Fontaine. The big black spinnaker was out in the clear, ahead of the pack, gaining fast, less than fifty feet astern.

"Keep watching him," Harry said.

"Watching him," Roy said tensely. "Watching him . . . getting closer . . . watching him . . . "

"Keep watching . . . "

"Getting closer . . . closer . . . hell, he's going to leeward . . . wait a minute . . . *no he's not.* He's changing his mind!"

"He's taking us to windward," Sam said. "Watch it!"

Harry darted another quick look. Fontaine was now hanging off his stern, off his port quarter, already blocking his wind and ready to come on by.

"Okay," Harry muttered. "Ease the pole forward. Sheet in a little. Okay. *Now!*"

To be effective, the luffing maneuver could not be gradual. It had to be sudden. With the spinnaker trimmed forward, Harry rounded up into the wind with a spurt of speed, his bow swung to the left, and Fontaine was confronted with an obstacle—a boat almost broadside to his course, blocking his path.

Fontaine reacted slowly. Just in time he swung his bow up, putting the two hulls parallel, both pointed now toward the north shore. On the big boat there was great confusion. Crewmen were lunging, Fontaine was barking, the huge spinnaker collapsed, flapping wildly.

Harry waited only long enough to see the monster black sail fold and collapse. Swiftly he fell away from the wind. Roy pulled the pole back where it belonged, Sam trimmed the sheet and in a matter of seconds they were once again moving swiftly straight ahead, back on course.

Iceman was not capable of such a fast recovery. For a few moments it was stopped almost dead. Because it was less maneuverable and because its sail handling was more complicated, it took time to regain its bearings.

Gradually it was brought under control but by this time Harry's spinnaker was filled and he was moving swiftly up the river, the lighthouse now less than a half-mile away. Roy let out a whoop. They had opened up a lead of thirty feet before *Iceman* could get its spinnaker back under control, regroup, and swing back on course.

But now once again it was coming on. If Fontaine chose to try passing to windward again, Harry could luff him up again and again but this time Fontaine decided against machismo. As he could so easily have done before, he set a course to leeward and came swiftly up on Harry's stern, ready to pass on the right instead of the left. This time Harry knew there would be no stopping him.

Iceman kept gaining. Now the two boats were nose to stern; now they were cockpit to cockpit, hull to hull, separated by ten feet of water.

Fontaine glanced over. His nose and mouth were smeared with white sunburn ointment. "Nice going back there," he said with a smile. "Nicely done." With his left hand he saluted.

Harry nodded. "Thanks," he said.

Roy looked sullen. Sam concentrated on the spinnaker.

"I should have done this in the first place," Fontaine said with another ingratiating smile.

As *Iceman* moved by, he kept on smiling. Looking back over his shoulder, he gave a salute of farewell.

"We've still got a chance," Harry said. By the luffing maneuver he had delayed being overtaken and by now the lighthouse was a scant two hundred yards away. He could see the glistening rocks piled about its feet.

Iceman was pulling steadily away. Twenty feet ahead. Thirty. Harry gave his orders. The big jib would go up first. Fifty feet from the lighthouse the spinnaker would come down. As the jib was trimmed in, he would swing wide around the lighthouse and head for the Tred Avon.

"What the hell is happening over there?" Sam was pointing.

Harry darted a quick glance to the left. He saw *Silver Heels,* the grey ghost, a quarter-mile away, rounding up into the wind, spinnaker flapping wildly, then falling away from the wind and filling its spinnaker again. By now it was far, far off course, very much out of the race, having not only failed to honor the lighthouse as a prescribed mark of the course but not even observing the black marker which stood at the mouth of the Tred Avon as a navigation warning. It was already well inside the black marker and as Harry watched in disbelief it started bumping across the shoals.

"My God," he breathed, and then could watch no longer. He was close enough to the lighthouse now to see the swift foaming current spilling around the rocks. Fontaine's spinnaker was down and his huge genoa jib already up. He was sailing dangerously close, cutting it very fine.

"Crunch!" Sam muttered but there was no crunch. Fontaine was past the rocks, rounding into the wind, his jib already drawing. Twenty seconds later, Harry too was around the lighthouse and pounding along in his wake.

The Tred Avon leg lay ahead.

At this juncture, aboard the ill-starred *Silver Heels,* Walters Hackett was frozen to the foredeck, his wife was frozen to the tiller, and his sister was down in the cabin throwing up.

It was of course unrealistic to believe that on this, his very first race, Hackett would fare well, yet for that wonderful interlude when his spinnaker was first to catch the new wind there were indications that it might be a banner day.

His finest moment had come perhaps a third of the way up the Choptank, when the new wind kept driving him forward until he had moved into the very vanguard of the fleet. Improperly trimmed sails and other deficiencies of seamanship had combined to drop him back to some degree but for a long while he was still in the pack, with boats right and left and fore and aft. All the bright sails were packed hard with breeze and all were gliding along at a good rate of speed—a real sleigh ride, in the words of Hackett, whose propensity to use sailing jargon seemed to intensify as his sailing fortunes waxed.

After Broad Creek, Mrs. Hackett, still at the helm, decided that what they were doing was no longer reminiscent of a sleigh ride so much as it was reminiscent of some of the chilling photographs in her husband's how-to-sail books.

"Walters!" Kitty's voice had a note of concern. Since Broad Creek, her bravado had lost some of its edge.

"Steady on," Hackett replied.

Fifty yards of foaming water fled by.

"Walters!"

"Steady on," he snapped. "All right, if you're all that scared, I'll take it. Gimme the tiller, Margaret."

Gratefully Mrs. Hackett handed him the tiller.

"I'm going down and get some milk or something," Kitty said. "My stomach doesn't feel so good."

"There's some nice low-cal root beer down there," Mrs. Hackett said.

"Some what?" Kitty's head popped back up through the hatch.

"Some low-cal root beer," Mrs. Hackett said.

"For God's sake," Hackett muttered.

"I don't really like low-cal things," Kitty said. "Do you have any regular root beer? By any chance?"

"No, just low-cal," Mrs. Hackett said.

"For God's sake!" Hackett bellowed. "Do you have to keep talking about goddamned *root beer?*"

"I'm sorry I came," Kitty said, disappearing again.

"That's your problem," Hackett muttered.

"We've been doing so nicely," Mrs. Hackett said. She closed her eyes. Even with her eyes closed she could still see the spinnaker, beautiful and lethal. Such beautiful colors. Such a soft baby blue.

She felt a lurch and opened her eyes. "Walters, maybe—" she ventured.

She didn't have time to finish. At that moment the wind gusted and moved sharply forward. The spinnaker whipped over to starboard, flattening out like a jib, and the boat rounded up into the wind in a fearsome near-broach that brought a hoarse shout from Hackett and a cry of protest from below.

The hull righted itself but the incident had the effect of driving the boat to the left, well off course.

Beneath the white spikes of his hair, Hackett's ruddy brow was creased with anxiety. He was now sailing the boat in what might have struck an uninitiated observer as a careless, swaggering way, as though he were a sort of nautical Musketeer or Bengal Lancer, and one might have concluded that he was feeling giddy with pleasure at the way they were hurtling through the water.

This would have been a misinterpretation. The fact was that he was showing signs of dementia praecox. He was a man about to go to pieces. They had put up the spinnaker at a time when the breeze was gentle and while the breeze was moderate they had been able to handle it. But now, since Broad Creek, the breeze was stronger and stronger and it was all too much for him.

Again now the wind whipped forward and for a moment they were a fiberglass-and-flesh-and-blood representation of the fearsome photograph—boat pulled far over, rail buried, cockpit a sheer vertical drop, Mrs. Hackett clinging to the high side, and Hackett at the tiller, seeking traction for his feet.

A moment later the boat jerked in the opposite direction, righting itself with a lurch. Hackett was breathing heavily. "Take it, Mag," he said, thrusting the tiller at Mrs. Hackett.

"Are you sure?"

"Yes. Take it. *Take it!* Gotta get the spinnaker down—*before we go over!*"

From below there was the first retching sound of the day.

Summoning unsuspected reserves of tenacity and bravery, Mrs. Hackett clasped the tiller between her reluctant fingers. She found that something unusual was happening, something beyond her brief experience as a helmswoman. The boat was trying to round up into the wind of its own accord. She gripped the tiller very hard, shoved it with all her strength, trying to throw the nose to the right, away from the wind. Even so she found she was being carried farther and farther off course, toward the north shore, which was certainly not where they wanted to go because the lighthouse was well to the right and all the other boats were over in that direction. They were no longer with the fleet. They were off to themselves, a lonely grey boat, and the trouble was that no matter how hard she shoved on the tiller the boat, when it wanted to, rounded right up into the wind and sailed for a while toward shore before she could get it straightened out again, and she supposed this is what the book had meant when it spoke of a boat under spinnaker being out of control. The fact that they were not going around the lighthouse with the rest of the boats was of no concern whatever. Disqualification was of no importance. What concerned her now was safety, the fear that the boat might run smack into the shore, although this of course would have its compensations since she could then, if the water was shallow enough, simply get off and walk ashore, and what did it matter if where she walked was a soybean field near no area of civilization that she could recognize.

Farther and farther off course they sailed but Hackett didn't seem to notice. This surprised her, but then abruptly she saw the reason for his self-absorption: having clambered on all fours to the foredeck, he had uncleated the spinnaker halyard and was now staring at the top of the mast with the deeply perturbed look of a man expecting something to happen which hadn't. Although the halyard was hanging loose, the spinnaker was still aloft, its destiny uncontrolled. "It's stuck," he shouted. "It won't come down! *It's stuck!*"

At that moment, under the impact of a particularly strong gust, the boat once more rounded up into the wind, with the same fearsome result as before, this time hurling the miserable Hackett to the foredeck, where he lay on his stomach, grasping the base of the mast with both hands. "Keep the wind behind you, Mag!" he shouted piteously. "Don't go to weather! For the love of God, don't go to weather!"

"I'm trying not to," she replied. "I can't control it . . . "

Spinnaker snapping and thrashing, they were sailing straight for the sand bar. Across it they bumped . . . and bumped . . . and bumped a third time, and this is what Harry had witnessed just before he rounded the lighthouse. On they bumped but did not run hard aground. No such luck. They were in clear water, on a boat that was running amok.

Down below, Kitty, between retchings, was moaning that she was never coming again, calling her brother a "mad-mun" and once shouting in a harsh voice, "Mother was right!"

Mrs. Hackett stared straight ahead at the piteous figure on the foredeck. Flat on his stomach, he was still clinging with both hands to the foot of the mast, eyes wild.

Margaret Hackett with her spaghetti biceps at the tiller;

her husband hanging on for dear life; his sister down below, puking her heart out. The three of them, inexperienced and getting on in years. Too late to say that they had no business being there. Too late.

Mrs. Hackett knew now that it was all beyond her control. She would go where wind and sail would take her. She closed her eyes and thought, Oh to be a child again, oh to be where the woodbine twineth.

Twenty

BY THE TIME Fontaine and Harry rounded the lighthouse and headed into the final lap of the long race, the Tred Avon was relatively clear.

It was by then almost five o'clock. The log canoes and small one-design sailboats had finished racing for the day and were gone from the river. Spectator boats stood by near the lighthouse to watch the fleet go around. Others idled along in the Tred Avon itself but their skippers could see that the vanguard of the fleet would soon be filling the river and they were on the alert, ready to get out of the way when the time came.

Some in fact were already veering off to make way for the runaway grey sloop *Silver Heels,* a few perhaps in the mistaken notion that it was still in the race and should be given racing room; others merely fearful for their own safety, hardly knowing which course to follow, so erratic was its behavior. Those with knowledge of sailing were mystified as well by the fact that it was still flying a spinnaker when the wind was almost dead on the nose.

Its haphazard tactics, its zig-zags and demipirouettes, its helpless progression up the river, were in sharp contrast to the appearance of the leading boat, Fontaine's, and the boat pounding along in its wake, Harry's, both on the same slant, their lee rails nearly buried, big jibs drawn tight against the lifeline.

Already into the river, well past the black marker that stood at its mouth, both boats were on port tacks, the northwest wind coming at them from the direction of the hamlet of Bellevue, which lay ahead and to their left, directly across the river from Oxford.

Thus once more, as had been the case that morning going down the bay, they were facing an adverse wind. Its direction made it impossible for them to sail straight up the channel to the finish line and their present port tack was carrying them at a long angle toward the Oxford side of the river. Their progress would be by a series of tacks. Starboard tacks would carry them at a right angle toward the barren shore on their left. Here, high on the wind, they would tack away from the shore and, once more on port tack, head as closely as possible up the middle of the river, aiming for the committee boat anchored in the distance; yet because of the wind direction they would again be driven gradually off toward the Oxford shore. When they ran out of sailing room they would tack and move once more up to the far shore and start the process all over again.

Two thirds of the way up the river, Harry was still trailing *Iceman* by a good three hundred yards. By now *Sundance* was moving at great speed, hurtling along like a runaway log in a sluiceway. Harry glanced back at the stern wake billowing out behind the boat. Great sliding billows of grey water, streaked with running courses of white foam. An instant earlier they had been on top of those billows, and new billows were already under the boat, sliding swiftly astern; the billows went on forever as the gleaming yellow hull slid past the marshy scalloped shore, past an old house, a duck blind.

He was feeling the tension now, eyes trained on the leading edge of the jib, and beyond the jib the boat ahead, the big black speedster, the high-gloss finish of the tapered black transom, with *Iceman* in flowing gold letters.

It was past the two-thirds mark that *Iceman* overtook *Silver Heels*, which now was floundering along not far from the left bank of the river against a lush backdrop of soybeans. Although it presented no obstacle, Fontaine saw fit to shout a warning as *Iceman* sped by. "Keep clear!" His voice floated back over the water. He was pointing a finger at the grey sloop and then pointing astern. Other boats were around the lighthouse by now and were beginning to fill the river.

Harry looked fore and aft. "Take it a second." Handing Sam the tiller, he moved up next to the cabin and as they sailed abreast of *Silver Heels* he peered across the water. It was obvious what had happened. The Hacketts couldn't get their spinnaker down and it was alternately flapping empty and then filling and running away with them. The halyard was stuck—and so was the sheet or the afterguy, or both.

He cupped his hands. "Mr. Hackett!"

Mrs. Hackett, hand on the tiller, had lost her white hat. Her mouth was a straight line. Hackett was kneeling on the foredeck, one hand clutching a starboard stay. The other lady was not in sight.

"Stuck!" Hackett howled.

"Jerk it!" Harry shouted.

"Stuck!" Hackett repeated, not hearing.

"Jerk it! Jerk it!" Roy yelled as they moved by. "Jerk it!"

Harry raised both fists and jerked downward. On the other boat no one moved. For a few moments longer he looked astern. At the moment *Silver Heels* was not making much speed. Its spinnaker was flapping violently. Soon the big sail might snap a line, lose a fitting or, mercifully, be blown to shreds.

The Hacketts were falling astern. With a final look, Harry took the tiller back from Sam and concentrated again on the race. When Fontaine tacked again, Harry tacked behind him, once again crossing his foaming wake a substantial distance behind. In a good wind a boat the size of

Fontaine's might average eight knots. *Sundance*'s maximum, its hull speed, was seven knots, maybe a fraction more. Until now he had matched Fontaine tack for tack all the way in from the lighthouse. Now he made a decision. It was time to gamble. He would split tacks. "Okay, let's let him go," he said.

Roy and Sam were perched on the rail on the high side, facing forward into the stiff breeze. Sam nodded without turning. Roy frowned but said nothing.

As Fontaine continued sailing off on another long port tack toward the Oxford side of the river, Harry prepared to come about. Another skipper, seeing this, might have covered but once again Fontaine was taking the path of supreme confidence, obviously certain that with his superior boat speed he would have no problem.

Harry gave the order and *Sundance* tacked away toward the opposite shore. The tide was still coming in hard, flooding up the river, and the power of the current was greatest in the middle. He was gambling that the loss of tidal drive would be more than offset by staying high, running along the shore, tacking back up to it as many times as necessary and not coming down for good until he could be sure that his next long port tack would take him across the finish line. It was what his father would have done. "Across the river's where the wind is." Harry had heard him say it many times.

As he explained his strategy, Roy interrupted. "I don't like the idea of being on port tack at the finish line," he said. "Suppose he's on starboard. If we cross he'll have the right-of-way and cream us."

"Right," Harry said. "I'm gambling that we'll be far enough ahead so that right-of-way won't matter. So let's do it."

"Let's do it," Sam said.

Roy shrugged. "Okay—let's do it."

They tacked a short distance toward midstream and then almost immediately back up to the high shore again. Twice more they tacked, Sam and Roy handling the sails with speed and precision. Harry kept glancing toward the committee boat, measuring his distance, measuring the angle, eyeing the space that stretched between the committee boat and the red flasher off the yacht club. The finish line. They were once more on starboard, headed up to the high shore. Briefly the wind had moderated but now it was picking up force again. Harry was looking over his shoulder, still gauging. "Okay . . . " His voice sounded calm. "Ready about . . . hard-a-lee . . . Okay, going for it!"

They tacked. The wind was stronger, and still stronger. It was blowing hard. Within twenty feet the boat was slashing through the waves like a knife, rushing through the foaming, swirling grey-white water like a game fish; spray flashing off the bow and lifting high and soaring all the way back to the cockpit. Roy was exulting. He was making low noises of joy in his throat. Sam's eyes were shining. There was a rhythm now, the deep sound made by the hull thumping the water and then the water spraying with a high-pitched treble sound, and it developed into a bass-treble, thump-splash that went on and on.

It had the thrill that came with the peak of effort; the pounding and the knowledge that there could be nothing beyond, nothing better, nothing harder, the mast slanted, the wind on the nose, sails trimmed in tight, Roy and Sam on the high side, leaning outboard, trying against the force of the wind to keep the boat in balance, to keep it sailing on its feet, but the wind was heeling it over more than Harry wanted it heeled over; with his free hand he jerked the mainsail loose and let it go an inch, two inches, and then jerked it down tight through the jam cleat again. The boat was sailing more nearly level now, sailing better, sailing faster.

Harry was aiming for the left end of the line, aiming for a point just left of the committee boat. He feathered the tiller, sending the boat a hair up into the wind, breathing, "Lift, lift," nearly a prayer, asking the breeze to move up a little, asking for extra assurance that he would have the room he needed to make it between the committee boat and the red flasher. But the wind was holding steady, both its direction and now its velocity. No oscillation, no gusts, just the hard steady breeze with a trace of chill from the northwest, the Canadian air they hadn't had all summer, coming down on the northwest wind in mid-July.

Roy was looking across the water toward *Iceman.* "Go on, you bastard, run aground," he muttered. "Run aground."

Fontaine was on port tack, running out of room on the Oxford side. Now he tacked swiftly. The big boat was a thing of beauty. It looked like something on the cover of a boating magazine, its sails like a sailmaker's advertisement, trimmed in hard, slot perfect, a slice of a slot, and beyond its sails the heavily leafed trees and the white houses of the village and to the left the yacht club and in front of the clubhouse a sandy white beach lined with spectators.

It was all coming down to this now, the whole race coming down to two boats angling in at ninety degrees, and if it came to a collision course Harry would have no choice but to yield the right of way, to fall off and go behind *Iceman* and the race would be Fontaine's.

"Got him," Roy said. "We got him. We got him. We got him. *We got him.*"

"Maybe." Harry was trying to stay calm but he could not keep the exultation out of his voice. *Iceman* was losing wind and laboring. *Sundance* was still flying. It was clear to him now and clear to anybody with eyes to see, that *Sundance* would cross ahead of *Iceman* with twenty feet to spare.

There would be no question of calling for right-of-way. The two boats were not close enough for it even to be at issue. Even so, Fontaine tried and Harry could only think that the crack ocean skipper, the Big Man, thought he might have a chance of psyching out the yokels.

"*Starboard!*" Fontaine called.

Yet it sounded more like a lament than a warning, more like a dirge than a demand for crossing rights. It had a hollow sound. Roy stood up on the cockpit seat and laughed at him as they crossed well in front of his bow.

From the other cockpit there was a flash of Fontaine's face. As they went by he was looking at them very gravely but without expression, as if he might have been looking at a buoy.

Not so his crew. They looked glum. Now they could only watch as Harry shot through the gap and crossed the finish line.

The gun sounded. First in Class C. First in fleet.

Roy whooped.

From the beach there were cheers.

Fontaine tacked and ten seconds later he too had crossed the line. He too got a gun, the first Class A boat over.

Sundance was twenty yards past the line, still driving. Roy's eyes were glazed with triumph. Sam ducked below and returned in a flash with three cans of beer, popping them open as he handed them around.

"Okay," Roy said, "let it all flap. *Let it all flap.*"

Sipping his beer, Harry looked off to the left. The Hacketts and their grey sloop were running along the Bellevue shore. Their spinnaker was now full more often than it was empty and they were moving very fast.

"Guess we'll have to do something about poor old Hackett," Harry said. "If he's not careful he'll kill himself."

"Wait'll he runs aground," Roy said. "That'll stop him soon enough."

Harry set his beer on the seat. "Let's go help him." He gave his orders. They would sail up and try to come in along the Hackett boat's rail from the leeward side.

Five minutes later they were hovering off the stern. "Mrs. Hackett . . . " Harry called. Mrs. Hackett looked benumbed. She had the look of a woman who had spent many years in purgatory. She managed a thin smile. Hackett was still up next to the mast, kneeling now and hanging onto the lifeline. "We're stuck, Harry!" he bellowed.

"I can see that, Mr. Hackett." Harry handed Sam the

tiller and moved up close to the mast, where he grabbed one of his shrouds and leaned far out. "I'm coming aboard, Mr. Hackett."

A gust of wind drove *Sundance's* bow off. Harry looked back, Sam nodded. He was coming up again. "A little closer," Harry called. "Little closer . . . "

He stepped across, grabbed a stay and was aboard *Silver Heels.* Within a matter of seconds he had gotten the knot out of the afterguy. The line ran free and the spinnaker flew wildly aloft, its power gone but its flapping noisier than ever. Slowly, painstakingly, he got its folds under control and gave a jerk. The stuck halyard came free and he pulled the big sail down to the deck. A few minutes later it had been shoved down into the cabin, the mainsail was lowered and furled, the engine was running, and *Silver Heels,* with Harry now at the tiller, was heading for the slip from which it had departed the morning before, when it began its memorable odyssey to Annapolis.

Hackett sat in the cockpit. He looked older than Harry remembered him. Old and very much subdued. "Sorry we had to put you to all this trouble, Harry old boy." He frowned and looked back down the river. His eyes had a reminiscent gleam. "She sure had a bone in her teeth there for a while though, didn't she, Mag?"

A worn face appeared in the hatchway.

"Harry," Mrs. Hackett said. "I'd like you to meet Mrs. Crawford, Mr. Hackett's sister from Connecticut."

"How do you do, Mrs. Crawford," Harry said.

"Oh, my!" Mrs. Hackett said, kissing Harry's hand.

Twenty-one

JUDY AND GUS WHITNEY ON *Pottagold* were around the lighthouse and well into the Tred Avon when they heard the far-off sound of the gun, borne down the river on the wind. Judy assumed the gun was for *Iceman*. It had to be, the way the big boat had gone pounding through the fleet coming up the Choptank. She knew it was ahead going around the lighthouse because she had seen its spinnaker. With its spinnaker up it was easy to spot but now in the Tred Avon the boats ahead of them were tacking all over the river, and at that distance with so many sails it was impossible to tell but she was positive the gun was for *Iceman* and she wished it had not been.

"That must have been *Iceman*," Gus said. He cocked his head at the sound of the second gun. "Somebody must have been right on his tail."

Judy nodded. Gus looked over his shoulder. "See any twenty-fives?"

"Nope," she said. "We're way ahead."

Until now they hadn't talked much. Judy had decided she would not get sentimental. This was the last time they would ever be on the sturdy little *Pottagold* together, in fact it probably would be the last time they ever sailed together, but she was not going to mention it. She refused to be sentimental about it because there was nothing to be sentimental about. If she could get sentimental and weepy about the last time she and Gus would ever sail together, then God knows she could get sentimental over anything. She was not going to pray. She had decided this long ago. In early spring, after he moved out, she had prayed to Mary to bring him back but soon stopped. It seemed to demean the Mother of God to ask her to bring back such a bastard.

Gus was making the last race a very good one and so for

that matter was she. After breaking out of the dead calm they had gotten their spinnaker flying and moved up the Choptank ahead of all the other Cal-25s and ahead of most of the MORCs and even ahead of some of the A, B, and C boats. There was nothing special about this. They sailed well as a matter of course, almost as a matter of reflex. They seldom made a mistake, even without a third person to help with the spinnaker. He was sailing and she was crewing, something they had always done well, whether in their farewell race together or a race in the best part of their marriage. Wherever that had been. Maybe their marriage had never had a good part, because it had been one long unholy mess. Except when they were sailing. There was the afternoon they took Jenny out for the first time. Jenny's first sail. Gus, the dumb bastard, had been really happy that day. Never had he seemed to like Jenny so much as he had liked her that day. Life was sailing. Sailing was life. Just a while ago, after they all got around the Gas Bell and *Iceman* started roaring through the fleet—the expression on his face as he saw it go by! Such a look. Such reverence. If Gus could own a boat like that before he died, his life would be complete. It showed all over his face. And she knew that short of owning one the next best thing was crewing on one, a very close thing to paradise, the damn fool.

"So you're leaving in the morning . . . " She knew she had to mention it sometime. All through the race she had barely touched upon it—and he probably hadn't even been thinking about it. He'd been concentrating on the race. Now as they tacked up the Tred Avon, steadily lengthening their lead, he seemed to relax.

He nodded. "Sometime tomorrow. Maybe not until afternoon."

"Think you'll be able to get somebody to sail *Potta* back?" she asked.

"Sure. I'll find somebody. No problem."

"Okay . . . "

"I guess we should sell it, huh?"

"I suppose so," she said.

"Maybe tonight I'll get in touch with Harding. He always wanted it. Whaddya think—ten thousand?"

"I guess."

"Where's Riley?"

Judy looked over her shoulder. "Way back. We've got him by half a mile."

"Okay. Listen. I've been thinking. I don't think it's such a good idea for me to tell Jenny goodbye. It might upset her. Besides . . . I'd just as soon not have to—face your mother. Do you mind?"

"Up to you," she said.

"I've been thinking," he said. "I'm sure we get ashore a lot. Lauderdale and places like that. So I was thinking Jenny could come down and stay with me for a few days once in a while. You could put her on the plane and I could like meet her."

"Yes," Judy said. "I guess so. I guess she could. I guess she's old enough."

"The stewardesses take care of them," he said.

"Yes."

"You'll be hearing from me," he said.

"Okay."

"Jib in a fraction."

Judy turned the winch handle. The winch clicked twice.

"Right there," he said.

In silence they tacked up to the high shore and then tacked out again. It was all going too swiftly, she thought. The finish line was too close, coming up too fast. She wasn't quite ready for the race to be ending. Soon she would be in a car, riding back to Annapolis. That's the way it probably would have been anyway, even in ordinary times. She always went on back to be with Jenny, and Gus always stayed overnight and sailed the boat back the next day. He liked staying. He liked the atmosphere. He liked the rafting-up and the boat-hopping and the beer drinking and then he always sailed the boat back the next day.

But this time somebody else would be sailing it back.

There were eleven divisions in the race that day and during the course of the afternoon the cannon would sound eleven times. Occasionally two boats would finish neck and neck. There were others where the winning boat sailed over virtually in private.

That's the way it would be with the Cal-25s and *Pottagold*. The finish line was less than two hundred yards away now and they would speed across on their present tack. There was nothing ahead but open water.

A hundred yards more and it would all be over.

Gus was offering her the tiller. "Wanna take it across?"

She shook her head. "You do it. It was your race."

"Yours too."

"You sailed a good race."

"I guessed wrong after we went around the Gas Bell," he said.

"You came out of it fine."

They slid over the finish line. "Shoot it," Gus said. "Hey, *shoot* it!"

Belatedly the small cannon fired. Judy looked over her shoulder. On the foredeck of the committee boat a man knelt next to the cannon. Taking a pipe from his mouth, he smiled in apology, then raised a fist. Gus waved. The man waved. Judy waved. People in the committee boat cockpit waved and Judy waved again.

Beyond the finish line, Gus kept on sailing, easing the sheets a little to cut their speed. "Kiss Jenny for me," he said. "Tell her I love her."

Judy bit her lip. "Do you want me to help you get the sails down?"

"No thanks," he said. "I think I'll sail around a little and watch the others come in. See what's going on."

She looked toward the yacht club. Compared with the clubhouse at Annapolis, this one was unpretentious. The grounds were crowded with spectators. Barefooted kids, their races all over, were dragging Penguins up the slope of the beach. On the dock there was an electric hoist. A Star boat was being lifted from the water and placed on a trailer, water streaming from its enameled hull. It would be towed to one of the lots reserved by the town for overnight parking. Judy knew all about it. When he was younger, Gus had a Star and when he was still younger he had a Penguin. She had crewed for him in both of them.

"So . . . " She paused, then began again. "You can drop me right over there, I guess." She pointed to the yacht club dock.

He tacked and headed for the dock. "Well, next time we see each other—" He paused. "We won't be married, I guess."

"If there is a next time," she said.

"There's bound to be a next time. What the hell."

"I suppose you're right. Okay. Well . . . " She went below and a moment later came back up with a faded Pan American flight bag, but she had not bothered to change. She still wore the wrinkled shorts and the faded blue sweatshirt, sleeves rolled above the elbows. She touched his knee lightly and then moved up to the bow as the boat nosed into the dock and the stern eased back against a couple of pilings.

"So long, *Potta,* " she said, patting the bow pulpit. Then, grabbing the top of a piling, she leapt ashore.

From the cockpit he called, "Hey, Jude . . . "

She stood on the dock on her sturdy freckled legs. Her eyes were dry, wary, skeptical.

"Nice race," he said.

She nodded. "Nice race," she said.

"You're the greatest," he said.

She blinked.

"Sorry things worked out the way they did," he said.

He moved forward then, all the way up to the bow. She dropped the flight bag and grabbed the forestay, holding the boat in and at the same time trying to hold it off, because the wind and wash were threatening to bump it against the piling. "You'll be fine," she said. "It's just what you've always wanted. Maybe it's just right for you. Okay?"

She let the forestay go, picked up the flight bag and

turned away. She had gone maybe twenty steps when he shouted again, "Hey, Jude . . . "

She turned.

"You're the best crew I ever had," he said. A tear trickled down through the blond stubble of the beard he was trying to grow.

Then he was dropping a line over the piling and jumping ashore, moving quickly after her. She stood squinting. He took her in his arms and for a minute she thought he had changed his mind . . . and what if he had? It was out of the question. It was never any good, it never had a chance, a marriage with nothing in common but sailing a boat, winning sailboat races. Preposterous. Really preposterous. Stupid, crazy, but she'd take him back in a minute and she knew it. *Hail Mary, full of grace, the Lord is with Thee, Blessed art Thou amongst women* . . .

But he was turning away and stepping back over the lifeline, getting back on board, lifting the line from the piling and shoving off. "So long, Jude . . . good luck . . . okay?"

Holding the flight bag, she stood there squinting into the sunlight and then turned away.

Part IV

Twenty-two

ONCE PAST THE FINISH LINE, *Iceman* had kept going right up the Tred Avon, pausing only to drop its sails. Still in her cabin, Elaine heard the engine start and then the rattle of the sails as they came down. Her door was ajar and faintly she could hear the nasal tones of the marine operator on the ship-to-shore circuit. From down the river there was the boom of the cannon as the winner in one of the other classes sailed across the finish line. Overhead the shuffling of feet had stopped. Voices were restrained. *Iceman* had lost and what she was hearing were the subdued sounds of a losing boat as it went up the Tred Avon under power at a slow, steady pace.

Fontaine hated losing and it was probably because he had lost that he had kept going on up the river. He did not want to swing back into the anchorage where he knew he would be confronted by the other skippers as they came in one by one and dropped anchor nearby. She knew he did not want to see the smiles or hear the taunts. He wasn't ready for that. She knew from experience that he needed time to recover.

From her cabin she had been aware of the tacking duel up the Tred Avon and very much aware of the finish. She was looking from the porthole when she heard Fontaine howl "Starboard!" and when she saw that Harry would clear *Iceman*'s bow by a huge margin she moved to the opposite side and saw the surge of the yellow hull through the water, the foam swirling out from its wake just before it knifed over the line.

Now *Iceman* continued to glide up the quiet, gradually narrowing river, past banks of greenery and beautiful houses set on emerald lawns. She stood at the porthole looking at the houses and the greenery and the sparkling blue water, waiting for Fontaine. She hadn't expected him to lose the race. Telling him would have been easier if he hadn't lost.

When she heard his step she turned from the porthole, and as he entered the cabin she moved close and put her arms around his neck. "Sorry," he murmured. "I couldn't possibly."

"Nobody's asking," she said.

"Thank God for that." He smiled. In his hand was a can of beer. He always looked older after a race. His face was drawn and his eyes were bloodshot. He had pulled the shirt off over his head and even his hair was messed up. She felt sorry for him and this, she knew, would be a big mistake.

He stood there barechested, sipping the beer. She looked him in the eye. "Mel . . . "

His brows were knit. "What's wrong?"

"I'm leaving," she said.

He took a deep breath and let it out slowly. "I'm too tired to react," he said.

"I'm sorry. I didn't count on your losing."

"Are you glad we lost?"

"No, I never want anything bad to happen to you," she said. "You don't deserve it."

He was sitting on a blue sailbag in the corner just to the right of her dresser, his elbows on his knees, the beer can held in both hands.

She tried to make it light. "Just think," she said. "You can get somebody else. Younger. And have the fun of— doing it all over again."

"Not funny," he said.

"I didn't mean it to be funny."

He was looking down at his feet and now raising the beer can to his mouth.

"I owe you a lot, Mel," she said. "Almost everything."

"I can't marry you," he said.

"I know that. I wouldn't want you to."

"I could put you on the stage."

With a sad smile he was looking at his feet again.

She shook her head. "You know I wouldn't be any good."

"You can do anything now." He tilted the beer. "Anything."

"Mel . . . I could stay on and on until I'm thirty years old, being your girl . . . but I can't . . . "

"I've never expected you to." He looked up. "Who is it?"

"I think you know. Don't you?"

"Crowder?"

"Yes."

"Because he beat me in a sailboat race?"

"No. Of course not."

"Is he in love with you?"

"He will be."

Fontaine smiled. "You really think he's the one?"

"Yes."

"Are you sure?"

"Yes."

"If you go to him I'll kill him," he said. "I'll get somebody to blow his brains out."

"You're not serious," she said.

"Of course not," he said.

"You wouldn't."

"No. I wouldn't."

He got up from the sailbag and stood at the porthole, looking out at the river. "I always said when you were ready you should go. And I still feel that way. I'd just like to know that he's right for you." He turned from the porthole. "Do you mind if I talk to him?"

"Of course not."

He sat on the sailbag again, looking at his feet. "I can be the king and you can be the princess," he said, "and we'll see if he can pass the three tests."

"What three tests?"

Fontaine shrugged. "He's already passed one. He just

beat the hell out of me."

She moved quickly to his side, knelt on the sailbag and threw her arms about his neck.

"I'm too tired to think about it now," he said. "It has to sink in."

When he looked up from his feet there were tears in his eyes. She had never seen tears in his eyes and she groaned. "Mel . . . "

Rising, he threw the beer can across the cabin. For a long moment he stood at the porthole and when he turned his eyes were dry.

"I love you," she said.

He patted her head, glanced once more through the porthole, and strode from the room. When she heard him go above, she fell on the bunk and for a while she just lay there, looking up at the ceiling, feeling her eyes grow moist.

Presently she swung her feet to the floor, sat on the edge of the bunk and then, with a deep sigh, went out to the main cabin.

Billy still sat in the alcove, slumped on one elbow, looking bored, listless, curling and recurling a lock of his flaxen hair over his forefinger.

"We got creamed," he said matter-of-factly.

She nodded. Opening a jar of iced tea mix, she spooned some into a tall glass, half-filled it with water, opened the refrigerator and dropped in some ice cubes.

"Keep me company," Billy said.

She sat at the table with the shiny varnished surface and sipped her iced tea, staring into space.

"What's the matter?" he asked.

"Nothing."

"Are you bugged about the trumpet player?" Billy grinned. "If you go out on deck with nothing on, what do you expect?"

She was still staring into space. Then she plucked an ice cube from her glass and threw it at him. "Up yours, Charming Billy," she said.

"Ho ho ho," Billy said. "Hey, you been crying? What's with your eyes?"

"Nothing."

He looked at her closely. "Well . . . she still hasn't called back."

"Who?"

"Mary. Ann. "

"Maybe it's just as well," she said.

He had spoken the name in a loud voice, spacing the words and hitting each one hard. Now Fontaine's face appeared in the hatch. "Is that Mary Ann?"

"No sir," Billy replied.

"I heard you say 'Mary Ann.' "

"I was just talking to Elaine," Billy said. "I was just saying she hadn't called back yet."

"Try her again." Fontaine's face disappeared.

"Don't," Elaine muttered.

Billy glowered. "Whaddya mean, *don't?*"

"Don't call her," Elaine said.

"What are you—stupid or something?"

Elaine sat sipping her tea as he got the marine operator on the line and placed the call again to California.

As the phone began to ring, Fontaine descended the ladder, glanced at Elaine, and stood at Billy's side.

This time a young woman answered. Fontaine took the transmitter from Billy. "Hello, Mary Ann?"

"Just a moment, Captain." The Marine Operator cut in. "Is this Mary Ann Fontaine?"

"Yes."

"Go ahead, Captain, your party is on the line."

"Hi," Fontaine said. "Is this Miss Jeanne Roselle?"

Elaine winced.

From the other end of the line there was silence.

Billy disappeared into the forward cabin.

"Mary Ann—it's Dad . . . "

"Yep." The voice was flat. "What do you want?"

"I saw you last night and I just—"

"—anyway, for God's sake!"

"What? Hey. Mary Ann. Sweetie. Wait a minute, you're not coming through. You're cutting across me. You're cutting right through me. Over."

"That's not a bad idea."

"I can't hear you unless I'm ready to listen. I can't hear you until I release the call button. Wait until I say 'over' each time and then start talking. But not until you hear me say 'over.' Otherwise we might as well not be talking."

"That's not a bad idea either."

"Come on, sweetie . . . over . . . "

"Like I said, what do you want? What are you calling for?"

Elaine had been sitting there, sipping her iced tea. Now she got up and went into her cabin but didn't close the door. She could still hear both voices.

"I saw your show last night," Fontaine was saying, "and I just wanted to say I thought you were fine. Just great. I was proud of you. Over."

From the other end there was silence.

"Mary Ann? Do you read me? Over."

"I read you," she said. "Is that all you want?"

"I was pleased by the way you handled your part. It wasn't an easy part. Over."

"I don't really care what you think. Can't you understand that?" The voice was suddenly choked. "I don't give a good goddamn *what* you think."

"I'm sorry you feel that way, Mary Ann. Very sorry."

"It's the way I feel," she said.

"Have you had any other reactions? Any reviews? Over."

"I'm going now," she said.

"Don't go yet. Hey! Mary Ann! Don't go yet."

Click.

"Mary Ann?"

Silence.

"Mary Ann? Are you still there? Sweetie? Come in. Over."

There was only silence.

Through the open doorway, Elaine could see him sitting there, holding the transmitter.

The marine operator's voice came on. "Are you through, Captain?"

Fontaine was looking at the floor.

"Are you through, Captain?"

His eyes were still on the floor.

"Captain . . . are you through?"

He took a deep breath. "Yes, operator. Thanks. *Iceman* off."

"Baltimore Marine off."

Fontaine hung up the transmitter and touched a button. The set went dead.

Still he sat there in the alcove, his head lowered.

Finally he looked up. Through the open doorway he saw Elaine watching him. For a moment their eyes held. She moved toward him. Without a word he got up and climbed the ladder.

She went back into her cabin and lay on the bunk. In a few minutes the anchor went over. It was another hour before she heard him give the order to raise the anchor and head back down the river.

Twenty-three

THE YACHT CLUB at Oxford was a one-story structure that rambled informally along the shore of the Tred Avon. That day, after the change in the weather, the sky covering it was deep blue with rapidly moving puffs of white. From a staff in the yard the American flag stood out in the northwest breeze.

A short distance upstream from the yacht club the earlier finishers had taken down their sails and dropped anchor in a large curved bay off the Strand, the same capacious anchorage where British ships had stood offshore in great numbers three centuries earlier.

On taut anchor lines the boats pointed into the wind, sterns facing the village. People were sitting on deck, drinking cocktails, eating snacks from plastic plates, and rehashing the race. Damp towels and articles of clothing were draped over lifelines, drying in the sun and wind. By now, shortly before six, the anchorage was already crowded, even though many boats were still out on the course. The Tred Avon home stretch was filled with boats completing the race, slanting in against the northwest wind. Close-hauled and heeled over, they were tacking one by one across the line. Spectator boats still lingered along the far shore. Now and then the report of the cannon reverberated along the river, saluting a winner in one of the slower classes.

After leaving the Hacketts, Harry had swung back to the Strand and dropped anchor, and now he and Sam and Roy were having another beer to celebrate their victory. Roy kept looking for *Iceman*. When the race ended Harry had seen the big boat move past the finish line, and while he was occupied with the Hacketts he had assumed Fontaine would turn back and join the fleet, but obviously he had gone on up the river. The Tred Avon offered no outlet. There was nowhere to go except for small coves and tributaries, all of them dead ends, and the river itself ended just short of the town of Easton, roughly ten miles upstream.

Presently Roy put on swim trunks and went overboard, splashing around near the boat for a while and then swimming off to visit some of the other boats.

"Whew!" Sam said when he was gone.

"It could have been worse," Harry said.

"What do you want to do about your nose?"

Harry shrugged. "I don't know."

"You should see if it's broken."

"Maybe I will a little later."

"Maybe you should go to Easton to the hospital."

Harry nodded. He slumped lower. The anchorage was continuing to fill up. Anchored off to itself was a large exotic-looking vessel built all of teak, with a very high prow and an elevated afterdeck. So-called "character" boats often showed up at regattas and the transom of this one proclaimed it to be out of Bangkok. On deck, slung here and there, were hanging baskets filled with vines. There was no living being in sight except a large black monkey which ran swiftly up and down a network of rope shrouding, paused to peer out over the assembled fleet, and then ran up and down the shrouds again, running and peering, running and peering.

The monkey reminded him of Roy.

"Do we tell his family?" Sam asked.

"That he hit me in the nose? No. The hell with it."

"Maybe they should know."

"They already know enough. They know what he's like." Harry's eyes were on the monkey. "The poor bastard, maybe I shouldn't have yelled at him."

The ferryboat from Oxford to Bellevue crossed at a point not far beyond the finish line. Harry watched as it made its slow crossing, patiently picking its way through the river traffic. Downstream to the left, an empty log canoe was being towed past the yacht club, its masts lashed lengthwise to the hull.

Close by, a group of mallard ducks glided about among the anchored boats, squawking for handouts. A slice of white bread hit the water. The mallards paddled swiftly over and pounced, picking the bread quickly to pieces; then, squawking again, they paddled out of the way as a small outboard motorboat bore slowly down on them. A slender young girl, no older than twelve, was running a taxi service to the yacht club, using the outboard as a tender.

"Hey, Laura! . . . " She was being hailed. Picking up speed a little, she moved on through the fleet.

Harry was feeling the fatigue now, tired and let down after the long race and the tension. He didn't feel up to much more than sitting there and watching the boats come in, watching the spectacle. In the cool breeze and the clear bright sunlight he sat there watching the monkey, the ferry-boat, the mallards, hearing the low hum of outboard motors, the sounds of automobile horns from the town, the cries of pleasure from the kids splashing around in the water. The smell of cooking was in the air. On some of the boats, hibachis had been attached to the transoms, and steaks were broiling over charcoal briquettes. Smells also drifted over from the yacht club where a couple of women in white aprons were barbecuing chickens on open-air grills. For most people, however, eating was a long way off. First there was drinking to be done, and around the fleet the shouts grew steadily louder as the cocktail hour lengthened. For many, this was the best part of the regatta, the social part, the boat-hopping. The race had been just an excuse to be here, to feel part of the scene, part of a brotherhood.

A boat was passing close by. Somebody in the bow pointed an air horn at *Sundance* and sounded a long blast. Then a yell. "Nice going, Harry!"

Sam had been lying on the cockpit seat. Now he sat up. "Who was it?"

"I couldn't tell," Harry said.

From other boats closer by there were some desultory cheers and another horn blast.

Harry slumped again. He had won a lot of sailboat races. This was undoubtedly the biggest victory of his life. This hadn't occurred to him until now and he sat there thinking about it.

He touched his nose. "I guess I should go ashore and get somebody to look at this. Wanna drop by the club?"

"Sure." Sam looked at his watch.

"What time do you and Roy leave? What time's your ride?"

"Eight," Sam said. "What time you leaving tomorrow?"

"I'm not sure."

"Gonna stay to get your trophy?"

"I haven't made up my mind."

"Maybe you should," Sam said. "We can put it in the office. Impress the customers."

Harry nodded. Still he sat there, gazing out over the river. Sam watched him. "Cheer up, for God's sake," he said. "You just won first-in-fleet."

"Right." Harry shrugged. "Sorry." He got to his feet. "Okay, let's go over to the yacht club and capitalize on it. Drum up some business. 'Patronize Crowder's boat yard and you too can win races like Crowder.' Here we go . . . "

"Don't knock it," Sam said. "There's a hell of a lot of truth in it."

"Right. Hey, Laura!" Harry whistled between his fingers.

"Here she comes," Sam said.

When the child pulled alongside they stepped in.

"Yacht club?" she asked. She had on a short blue gingham dress and her funny twisted little face was smoothly tanned.

"Right." Harry helped her push off.

"Is that your boat?" she asked as they moved away.

"His," Sam said.

"Is your name Harry?" she asked.

"Yep."

"You won the race, didn't you?"

Harry smiled. "He did."

She looked at Sam, then back at Harry. "Fontaine tried to starboard you, didn't he? But he couldn't. I saw it."

"Hey!" Sam said with admiration.

Harry looked at her with amusement. "Do you sail, Laura?"

"My little brother and I have a Penguin."

"How do you make out with it?"

"Not very well."

"You will," Harry said.

"Hey, Laura," Sam said, "will you be here to take us

back out to the boat?"

"Sure," she said. "Just call me. Just holler, 'Hey, Laura' and I'll hear you." She was looking at Harry again. "Don't you live in Oxford?"

"I used to," he said.

"I thought so," she said. "I thought I'd seen you before. Don't you have a son named Roger?"

"Yes," Harry said. "How did you know?"

"I saw him with you last summer. He and I were talking one day."

"No kidding?" Harry smiled. "What about?"

"I don't know. I forget. But I remember his name. Roger."

"I'll tell him," Harry said.

"Was he on the race with you?"

"No," Harry said. "Okay . . . thanks, Laura." He handed her two quarters.

"Bye, Laura," Sam said.

They stepped up to the dock and she pushed off, headed out toward the fleet again.

Harry and Sam made their way to the yacht club entrance. Inside the clubhouse it was very noisy, very aimless. People rushed in and rushed out. A moment later the same people were back. At the single public phone there was a long line. Harry forged ahead. "Where we going?" Sam asked.

"Over here," Harry said.

"Over where?"

"Over here," Harry said.

"The bar?"

"The bar, right."

At the bar, people were jostling for elbow space and everybody was yelling at once. "Sure this is a good idea?" Sam said.

"It might not be," Harry said.

He felt Sam's hand tighten on his shoulder.

"Sammie, you're a good man," he said, "but take your

hand off my goddamned shoulder."

"You've come a long way," Sam said.

"Right," Harry said.

Sam removed his hand. "How's your nose?"

"It hurts. We're having a drink."

"How do we get one?"

"Maybe we don't." Harry got one elbow on the bar and then the other. Sam shoved in beside him. "They're only serving setups," Harry said.

Sam looked at the rows and rows of bottles on the shelves behind the bar. Each bottle bore a name scrawled in black. "How about all those bottles?"

"They belong to the members," Harry said.

The bartender was working hard. He was pink-cheeked and chubby, and his pink vest swung open and his curly blond hair was damp with sweat. Harry caught his eye. "Barton," he said.

The bartender turned and surveyed the shelves.

"Cutty Sark," Harry said. "Right there. Second shelf. See it?"

The bartender plucked the bottle from the shelf.

"Make it a double," Harry said. "Couple of doubles with a little ice."

The bartender peered at the label. He looked up. "You Mr. Barton?"

"I'm Crowder," Harry said. He pointed to Sam. "This is Barton."

Sam nodded. The bartender dumped Scotch in two glasses. "Don't go away," Harry said. "We might want another one."

"Yahoo!" said a voice from behind. "Yahoo! Nice going, Harry."

Harry drained his glass and set it on the bar. People were slapping his back. Diving into the ice cubes, the bartender looked up. "Barton?" he asked.

Harry nodded. "Barton," he said.

The bartender dumped more Scotch into his glass and

as Harry picked it up Sam pulled him away. "Let's see what this is," Sam said. They crossed the room to a large plate-glass window which provided a view of the finish line. "Aground," Sam said.

A green sloop was aground on a sandbar which reached out from the yacht club beach near the red flasher, and the wind was blowing directly against it, helping to fix it fast. The jib had been let go and flapped in the breeze, rustling and snapping with a series of loud reports. People were watching from the window and from all up and down the beach. Their faces were coated with light from the falling sun.

Harry sipped his drink, making this one last. "What are you going to do tonight?" Sam asked.

"I don't know," Harry said. "I think I've got a date."

"Who?"

"Fontaine's girl."

Sam looked at him closely and then at the glass in his hand. "You serious?"

"I don't know," Harry said.

From the stranded sloop two crewmen jumped overboard. Standing in water up to their waist, they shoved at the bow.

"Do you or don't you?" Sam said.

"I don't know," Harry said. "I might have."

"How about your nose?"

"I'm going," Harry said.

"To the hospital?"

"No, there's a doctor up the street."

There was a loud cheer as the boat came free. The two crewmen were taken aboard again and with sails trimmed the boat moved away from the sandbar and headed for the finish line. The skipper and crew looked grim. As they crossed the line there was another cheer which only made them look grimmer. To them it was not funny, it was ignominious. It had been a long hard day.

They were among the late finishers but by no means the

tail-enders. Boats were still tacking up the Tred Avon—and far down the river, not yet as far as the lighthouse, there were still a few boats flying spinnakers; boats which had been stranded far back in the bay during the period of dead calm. Harry sipped his drink and peered down the river at the distant spinnakers. In the softening light they looked beautiful and a little sad, like toy balloons floating at the end of a very long parade.

It was past seven when he left the yacht club gates and headed for the doctor's office. Across the river the sun was dropping and the sky was flushed with evening light. Sam had gone back to the boat.

The doctor's office was three blocks away. The doctor was a local G.P. who always had office hours on Saturday afternoons but when Harry got there the door was locked.

He turned and retraced his steps. At the end of the main street, overlooking the river, stood a large yellow-beige hostelry known as the Robert Morris Inn. On its veranda people stood in clusters, drinks in hand. Others stood out front, mostly in the street, moving aside now and then to let cars pass. An incline led down to the ferry dock and beyond lay the fleet. A few masthead lights had been turned on. Some people were still swimming and a skinny kid was skidding around through the fleet on a surfboard with a small yellow sail.

For a while longer Harry stood there, looking, feeling the Scotch and liking the way it felt. He was about to head back to the yacht club dock and hail Laura when he spotted a husky girl in denim cutoffs and a faded blue sweatshirt with the sleeves shoved above the elbows. He recognized her as Gus Whitney's wife. He had seen her a couple of times when she came by to pick up Gus at the boat yard, but she hadn't seemed to recognize him that morning on the way out to the starting line and she didn't seem to know him now.

She was standing there looking out toward the fleet, and

her eyes were damp. It occurred to Harry that being married to Gus would be enough to make anybody's eyes damp.

Behind her a car honked and the crowd in the street moved slowly aside to let it through. Gus's wife turned, waved, and started moving toward the car. At the wheel was a woman in sunglasses, maybe her mother, and on the seat next to the woman stood a little girl with red hair and a freckled face who looked just like Gus's wife. It had to be their kid because when she saw Gus's wife head for the car the little girl started squealing and clapping.

As the car moved slowly off through the throng of pedestrians, Gus's wife was still looking out over the river. The little girl was standing on her lap, smiling with delight and patting her cheek.

Harry headed back to the yacht club. It was nearly quarter of eight by now and the streetlights had been turned on in the village. Reaching the yacht club dock, he looked around for Laura and in a few moments he saw her boat headed in his direction with two passengers—Roy and Sam.

"We had to leave," Sam said as they drew near. "Did you see him?"

Harry shook his head. "He was gone. The office was closed. It's okay."

Sam and Roy stepped from the tender up to the dock. Sam held out his hand. Harry brushed it. Sam was looking at him closely. "Take care of yourself, for God's sake," he said. "Don't do anything stupid."

Harry shrugged. "Okay."

"Like I say, you've come a long long way."

Roy was pulling some change from his pocket for Laura. Now as he turned, Harry stepped forward to meet him. "Roy . . . " Harry held out his hand. "Thanks for everything."

Roy tapped his hand. "Put it to 'em, didn't we, Skip?"

"You sailed a good race," Harry said.

"Sure." Roy shrugged. "What did you expect me to do —screw it up for you?" He grinned and moved away. Sam followed and they disappeared into the crowd.

Harry turned to the tender. The little girl had her hand on a piling. "Can you take me to my boat, Laura?"

"Sure. Hop in." She smiled. "*Sundance,* right? The winning boat, right?"

Harry smiled and touched her head as he stepped in. "Right," he said.

When they reached his boat he patted her head again and said, "Good luck with your Penguin."

"Thanks," she said. "Oh, *thanks,*" she said again as he handed her a dollar.

Climbing aboard, he went below, found a cheese sandwich left over from lunch, came back up and sprawled once more in the cockpit.

The wind had dropped some and the water was smoother now, filled with glints and bars of light, sworls and eddies of grey and deep blue.

Across the way, lights had been turned on in the yacht club parking lot. Inside the clubhouse a band was testing its amplifying equipment: A rasp, an amplified hum rising to a screech, loud over the water and then dying.

He had just finished half his sandwich and thrown the rest to the ducks when he saw *Iceman* coming back down the river, headed for the anchorage. Its long black hull was unmistakable, even in the deepening twilight. Mainsail perfectly furled, sliding smoothly along under power, it turned from the channel and moved through the fleet, and when it found space rounded up into the dying breeze and dropped anchor. Slowly it swung back on its anchor line. Its masthead light came on.

In another five minutes the sky was dark. Harry was headed below for something else to eat when he heard the purr of a small outboard motorboat. It was moving slowly toward his stern and the beam of a flashlight was playing over his transom. "Is this *Sundance?*"

"Right," Harry replied.

The boat eased in closer and the flashlight shone on the

water. "Are you Harry Crowder?"

"Right." In the deflected light, Harry could see the figure in the stern now, a teenaged kid, a towhead with a bowl haircut. Standing on the seat of the motorboat, the boy reached up and grabbed *Sundance's* rail. "Mr. Fontaine sent me," he said. "He'd like you to come aboard *Iceman* for a drink."

"He would, huh?" Harry stood for a moment, looking across the water. "Okay, I'll be right with you."

"I'll wait," the boy said.

Twenty-four

HARRY STEPPED BELOW, turned on his masthead light, retrieved his blue shirt from the quarterberth where he had slung it and went above again. Stepping over the lifeline, he eased into the motorboat and they moved away.

Fontaine was waiting for him. Standing on the cockpit seat, he raised a hand in greeting as the boat approached. A section of the lifeline had been dropped to provide a gateway for easy boarding.

"Greetings," Fontaine called.

Harry grabbed the top edge of a huge winch and pulled himself over the rail.

"Harry Crowder? Mel Fontaine. Welcome aboard." Fontaine offered his hand and Harry shook it. "That was a great race you sailed this afternoon, Harry. Really superb. I admired it." Fontaine was wearing a Mexican shirt, white with pleats and ruffles, hanging over his dark trousers.

"Thanks," Harry said.

Fontaine held up a frosted aluminum glass. "I'm drinking gin-tonic . . . or would you rather have something else? God, the way you took us up and collapsed our chute back there in the river . . . " He shook his head. "I should never have tried to take you to weather."

From below there was a loud burst of Latin-American jazz—all percussion, brass and marimbas, quickly fading as the volume was turned down. The way Fontaine was dressed he looked a little like a marimba player himself. "Gin okay, Harry?"

"Do you happen to have a little Scotch?"

"Scotch it is . . . Right back." Fontaine went below and Harry stood in the cockpit, overwhelmed by the size of the boat. As he sighted forward over the cabin top, the deck seemed to go on and on, receding, disappearing into the darkness. He looked at the dials and the winches and the rigging. It was a marvelous boat, an incredible boat, and that afternoon he had beaten it, head to head. It kept surprising him how little he cared.

"Water?" Fontaine called.

"Just a little ice," Harry called back.

He wondered if he might be feeling better about winning if he had not had two double Scotches. Maybe worse. If he hadn't had the first two he wouldn't be asking for the third but there was no danger. He could handle it, or maybe he couldn't, or wouldn't.

Harry shrugged and sat down as Fontaine appeared with his Scotch. It was not in a frosted aluminum glass and he felt grateful for this because he hated the taste of Scotch in aluminum glasses. "Cheers," Fontaine said, raising his own frosted aluminum glass. "To *Sundance!*"

"Thanks," Harry said. "Thanks a lot."

Then he was drinking and Fontaine abruptly was asking a lot of questions.

"Done much ocean racing?"

"No," Harry said.

"Mostly right here in the bay?"

"Right," Harry said.

Quickly the questions became more personal. "I understand you own your own boat yard."

"I own the business. I rent the yard."

"How long have you been in Annapolis?"

"Couple of years. A little more."

"And before that?"

"My father had a yard over on Trappe Creek. I worked with him."

"Does he still have it?"

"He died a couple of months ago."

"I'm sorry to hear that. Did you go to college?"

"Yep." Sipping his drink, Harry found the edge of the glass between his teeth.

"Where—here in the South?"

"No. New England."

"You've been married before . . . "

"Yes."

"Divorced?"

"Yes."

"Kids?"

"One. A boy."

"And you and Elaine met at Montego Bay . . . "

"Yes."

"While I was away . . . "

Harry nodded. "That's right."

He looked up from his glass. Fontaine was gazing off across the water and in the faint light there was a twinkle in his eye. He didn't look at all like a marimba player.

"What else do you do well, Harry?"

"Nothing else," Harry said. "If that."

"Where do you want to go? What do you want to do with the rest of your life?"

"I haven't given it much thought lately."

Fontaine started saying things now that required no answers, telling anecdotes about sailing and long races and trips to foreign waters, foreign ports, large turtles, storms at sea, bargains in silk suits, roller reefing.

Now Harry had an impression of a man who was doing all the talking and yet at the same time was doing a lot of sizing up. Two compartments in the same guy, one transmitting, one receiving. He felt Fontaine was doing a lot of receiving and wondered what he himself could be sending. Not much.

He was feeling the Scotch again, it was taking hold, and what he was thinking of mostly was whether he was in fact going to fall off the wagon, glancing at the bottom of his glass, checking to see how much Scotch was left, wondering how soon he would drain it and ask for another; and thinking that if he fell off the wagon now it would be Marcia's fault and Philip's fault; and that if he fell off the wagon *now, this* time, it might be really bad, he could easily go to hell this time. Things might get so rotten that he'd look back on these eight lousy years he'd just spent as a really good period of his life.

"Certain women can dominate your life simply by being neurotic," Fontaine was saying. "You rise and fall by their neuroses. You live for their moments of lucidity. When those times come, you enjoy them, glory in them even, and then go through long periods of misery while you wait for them to come again. I don't know how it was with your marriage, but that's the way it was with mine."

He fell silent, waiting. Harry felt resentful, hostile. Even though he had won the race he was being patronized. Fontaine was waiting for him to say something about his wife, about his marriage, but he wouldn't. He wanted to give back nothing that mattered. Why, then, had he bothered to come? For a drink. The jokester within. The jokester had sent him because it was an easy way to get another drink.

"I hope it wasn't that way with yours," Fontaine said. "Another drink?"

"I've still got some," Harry said.

"How well do you feel you know Elaine?"

"Not very well," Harry said.

"When I met her she was a twenty-year-old girl from

North Carolina. Never even finished high school. Didn't even know the language very well. In three years she's changed a lot."

Fontaine was on his feet now, standing at the stern, looking over the water. He turned back. "She's a remarkable girl, a wonderful girl, highly intelligent. Warm. Compassionate. She's everything a father might want his daughter to be."

Fontaine fell silent. On one of the rafted-up boats there was the sound of a banjo, a snatch of song. The song died. People called back and forth over the water. Nearby somebody was splashing around on an air mattress.

"Drink?"

"Still got some," Harry said. His glass was empty.

A door closed. Abruptly the cabin below was filled with orange light and Elaine was silhouetted in the hatchway. She paused for a moment, then mounted the final two steps. "Good evening, Harry," she said.

"Hi," Harry said.

Her feet were bare. In her hand she carried a pair of spike-heeled shoes. She wore the jeans and the clinging white shirt that she had worn when she came to see him on his patio.

She sat next to Fontaine, letting her hand linger for a moment on his knee, and then leaned forward with a smile. "Congratulations, Harry. Congratulations."

"Thanks," Harry said.

"Would you like a drink, honey?" Fontaine asked.

"No thanks, I'm fine."

She started talking about the race, then about the river and town and the way the boats looked in the dark. Fontaine's manner had changed with her arrival. He seemed keenly aware of everything she said, of every movement, every gesture, not with an attitude of jealousy, Harry thought, but certainly one of ownership, and pride; with the manner of one who very much enjoyed what he owned. The daughter he had wrought. Created. Educated and polished. And spent three years sleeping with. Harry tilted his glass and got nothing.

"This is Harry's home town," she was saying.

"I could tell these were his home *waters,* " Fontaine said wryly. "I could tell that this afternoon, very damned well."

At times he felt they were watching him together. Small intervals. A second of silence here, a few seconds there, and it was as if, united, they were using the silence to study him.

Over at the yacht club the band had begun to play. The music was floating across the water and she was looking in the direction of the music, her slim neck, the tilt of her head, the puff of hair, silhouetted in the orange light from below.

Without looking, Fontaine tossed his empty glass over his head through the open hatchway. It landed below with a metallic sound and rolled to a stop.

"Harry promised to take me to the dance," Elaine said.

Harry looked at her over his empty glass. "I did?"

"Yes." She smiled, reached across and patted his knee. "You and I are going to the dance and Mel is staying here."

"I've got a kid coming to see me," Fontaine said. "He's shipping on with us. He's from Annapolis, maybe you know him. His name is Gus Whitney."

Harry nodded. "I know Gus."

"He sails a Cal-25. He raced it down today. I haven't heard how he made out."

"He probably won," Harry said.

"Good sailor?"

"A very good sailor," Harry said.

Raising the hinged lid of the cockpit seat, Fontaine reached inside and came up with an air horn. Aiming it at the sky, he sounded two short blasts and one long.

Almost immediately the same outboard motorboat was bobbing alongside, and the same young man was holding it close without bumping *Iceman's* glossy black hull. "Robin," Elaine said. The boy reached up to help. Holding the shoes in her hand, she slid down into the boat.

"To the yacht club, Rob," Fontaine said. "Step in, Harry."

Harry tilted his empty glass to his mouth, set it on the seat, and stepped in.

Fontaine stood at the rail, smiling down. "Come aboard on the way back," he said. "We'll have a nightcap."

"Thanks," Harry said.

Elaine blew a kiss, and the little boat moved toward the floodlights that shone on the yacht club dock, toward the sound of the music. Harry looked over his shoulder. *Iceman* had disappeared into the shadows.

Twenty-five

INSIDE THE YACHT CLUB they confronted a solid wall of bodies. The band thumped beneath a roar of voices. The crowds were thickest around a bulletin board where the race results were posted, and at the bar. Slowly they worked their way through the crush, her hand lightly at the small of his back, his hip, his shoulder, trying not to break contact. Faces in the crowd were eyeball to eyeball. Heads swiveled. She was attracting attention from men and women alike. As they passed the bulletin board with the race results, her lips moved close to his ear. "Don't you want to see your name?" she asked. "I know what it looks like," he said. At the bar those able to get drinks were finding it hard to turn and break through the thirsty supplicants pressing in from behind. Hands rose, holding drinks high, out of harm's way.

Beyond the jam-up around the bar, the crowd thinned out and the lighting grew dimmer. The dance floor, a small rectangle at the far end of the building, was bathed in deep lavender light, and to the left of the bandstand doors opened out upon a dark patio. Compared to the crowds around the bar, the dancers were very few. Most of them were young and barefoot, the girls with long straight hair, the young men with beards. The band was very loud and a boy with a helmet haircut was howling into a microphone, "Gotta thing . . . gotta thing . . . gotta thing . . . " repeated over and over without variation, bar after bar, the mode that summer in lyrics.

On the darkened floor she turned to face him. He had not danced since college and had never been any good at it. "I'm not much for dancing," he said. His words were slurred. He was still feeling the Scotch. At one time three drinks would have had little effect but he'd had a long layoff. "In fact, I'm lousy."

"Who cares?" she murmured.

As they moved together he was acutely aware of her body, the rise of her breasts, the smoothness of the jeans over the hips, the slimness of her waist. With the stilt heels she was almost as tall as he was. Clumsy as he was she moved with light grace, with a wonderful sense of anticipation, always a split second ahead of his touch, ahead of pressure, so that her body seemed weightless. The soft glow from a lavender spotlight bathed her shoulders, hollowed her cheeks. She eased her hips gently forward, pressing against him, and then wrapped her arms about his neck, looking into his eyes. "I'm going to be your girl, Harry," she said.

"Like hell you are," he said.

"Yes I am, Harry." Again she eased her hips forward, still looking into his eyes. "Yes I am."

"My God . . . " Drawing apart, he stood looking at her without expression, then led her slowly from the dance floor out to the patio. Picnic tables were scattered about the patio and people were sitting in the dark, drinking and talking. She led the way to an empty table and sat on its slatted wooden surface, resting her feet on the bench.

Through the open doorway, the dancers could be seen

writhing and twisting in the dim lavender light. Off to one side of the floor, Gus Whitney danced with a girl with long blonde hair and cutoffs. They were moving slowly along the rim, barely moving to the fast pounding tempo of the band. Gus's white shirt was unbuttoned to the waist. He was holding the girl at arm's length, looking down at her with a high-voltage smile, but as they reached the open doorway he ignored her. He was looking over her shoulder, out toward the patio, and Harry realized that Gus had seen Elaine and that he knew who she was. They would be on *Iceman* together and Elaine would represent the challenge of his lifetime, the dumb bastard.

As Harry watched he felt an impulse to swing on him and he knew it was the Scotch, yet it was also because he was lazy and because he was leaving his sad middle-linebacker of a wife and the little red-haired girl, his daughter.

Around the patio, voices rose and fell and drifted into silence, and rose again in ripples of quiet laughter.

Gus stood in the doorway. His head was tilted back. He was sniffing the air, looking all around the darkened patio. "Fee fie fo fum," he said. "I smell pot. I smell el grasso." He smiled in Elaine's direction.

"Hey, there's somebody for you," Harry said in a low voice. "Gus Whitney. He's shipping on."

"I could never like anybody that young," she said.

"He'll be right on the same boat with you," Harry said.

"No he won't. Because I won't *be* on the boat." Lightly she punched his arm. "I'll be with you."

Slipping down from the table, she sat on the bench. "Harry, I'm sorry about last night at your house," she said. "I came on much too hard. Okay, but I was serious about what I was saying. I'm leaving Fontaine, leaving the boat. It may not be a big thing to anybody else but it's a hell of a big thing to me."

Gus had gone back inside and was dancing again, moving out of sight.

"I have to tell you this," she said, "whether you want to hear it or not. I've been waiting six months to talk to you and I'm going to say what I have to say. I'm leaving him. Are you listening?"

"Yes."

"Are you drunk?"

"No."

"I'm scared of what's happening to me. I'm becoming—him. Not myself. Hell, I've never really *had* much of a self before but now I think I've got a chance to have one. A chance, at least. Do you understand what I'm trying to say, Harry?"

"Yes."

She was talking louder now against the sound of the band. "There's nothing I can do for him—except be his toy, his sex toy, his daughter toy, whatever it is I am." Her voice rose again. "I'm nothing but an appendage and I don't like it. I have no job, no function. Even in the races I don't have anything to do—*this goddamned band!*"

She touched his hand. "Come on."

The patio led down to a stretch of lawn. Off to the left lay a strip of beach. To the right, around the corner of the clubhouse, was the dock.

With her hand on his wrist, they turned the corner and moved out toward the edge of the dock.

"Too bright," she said. Looking toward the water, she smiled. "Poor Robby . . . " Her appearance at dockside was all it had taken. The motorboat was approaching from the darkness. The boy with the bleached hair had a line in his hand. He was looking up at Elaine. With a smile she shook her head. His eyebrows went up and he smiled back, then shrugged. "Sorry, Robin." As he turned away, she kicked him very gently in the seat of the pants. He grasped one spike heel and then her ankle and gently shook it, as if he were shaking hands, then sent the boat gliding back into the darkness again.

"Why do you keep touching your nose, Harry?" she

asked. "Every time I look at you, you're touching your nose."

"Right," he said. "Don't you ever touch your nose?"

"I was looking at the town from the water this afternoon," she said. "It looked so peaceful. Could we walk?"

"You don't want to sit here?"

"No. I want to walk."

"With me, you mean?"

"Yes, you bastard, with you. Does your nose hurt or something?"

"No."

In silence they walked through the yacht club gates and up the incline to the street. People still stood in front of the inn, talking in small groups.

Beyond the inn the street grew darker and steadily darker. Dim lights burned in the houses.

"What's wrong, Harry?" she asked quietly. "You're not like you were in Jamaica. You're not even like you were last night."

"I guess not," he said.

"What—?" She was having trouble with the stilt heels and the uneven brick sidewalk. "Wait a minute . . ." Stooping, she took off her shoes and carried them in her hand. "That's better."

As they walked she looked left and right, peering into the darkness. "Is the town always as quiet as this? What time is it?"

"About eleven-thirty, I guess," Harry said.

"Why are you being such a bastard, Harry?"

"Maybe because I *am* one," he said.

"Is it because you don't like me telling you these things? About my leaving Mel and everything . . . ?"

He didn't answer.

"Do you hate Mel?"

"Should I?"

"That's up to you. Without him, God only knows where I'd have ended up. On the scrap heap. In an alley. A whore.

Beaten up by some pimp. My arms full of needle holes. But because of Mel Fontaine none of that has happened to me and I'm grateful to him and I always will be."

She fell silent. A dense canopy of trees arched overhead. Their leaves rustled softly in the faint breeze. A slim bare-foot girl in a white dress had crossed the street at an angle and walked for a while just ahead of them. Now she turned in at a gate. When they reached the gate, Elaine paused and looked in. The house stood four-square, three stories high, fresh white paint gleaming in the dark. The barefoot girl seemed to vanish down an aisle of mammoth boxwood and then appeared again, rapidly climbing a flight of steps. She opened a screen door, stepped into a shadowed foyer and disappeared.

Elaine stood a moment longer, then turned away. "Imagine being raised in a house like that," she said. *"Imagine!"*

"I can't," he said. "The town wasn't like this when I was growing up."

They walked half a block in silence. Next to a dark store stood a lighted phone booth. He looked into its interior and touched his nose. He told himself that even though he might badly want another drink he probably would not have it. He was sobering up now and as he sobered up he concluded that his nose for sure was broken.

Elaine was talking again. "Down in Montego Bay," she was saying, "when I told you about what my father did to me—it really turned you off, didn't it? I mean you were very sympathetic when I was telling you about it but afterward it really turned you off."

"What turned me off—" Harry paused and got a fresh start. "What turned me *off* was hearing you say that it turned Fontaine *on.*"

"He's honest," she said. "He's very honest. A lot of my appeal for him is—a father-daughter appeal. He knew this from the very first and after a while he brought it out in the open and admitted it. We talked about it and decided it was okay. What the hell, Harry. The world is full of older man-younger woman relationships. It's not exactly *unusual,* you know."

Her voice grew bitter. "That's the way it *is* with some girls, Harry. They have to be *content* with father-men. Father-men rape you but they also take *care* of you . . . "

She became silent again. Head high, face without expression, she seemed now to drift through the darkness as if under a spell. On they walked through light and shadow. Some of the doorways were lit with coach lamps and there was an atmosphere of colonial restoration. Now and then before one of the doorways, before a lighted window, Elaine's step lagged and she stood for a moment looking at the front of the house and right into the rooms when the curtains at the windows were not drawn.

"It's very strange looking into a room at night," she said in a faraway voice. "Like looking into a dollhouse. Dollhouses always give me the saddest feeling. Seeing the little figures in the rooms. The father always has on a tuxedo and his hair is always parted in the middle and there's always a maid with a white cap and a black uniform and a feather duster in her hand. Little chairs with nobody sitting in them, and a little tiny light fixture hanging from the ceiling."

In the darkness she turned suddenly and faced him. Her voice was low and intense. "Harry. *Harry . . .* " Her arms were spread. It was as though her whole body was opening before him.

"You don't want me, Elaine." Grasping her arm, he started walking back. "I'm the last person you want."

"Wrong," she said. "Wrong."

Harry took deep breaths. His head was clearing and his nose hurt like hell. Block after block they walked in silence, back the way they had come. They made their way past the inn and moved down the incline and passed through the yacht club gates again. Inside the building the band was still playing but the grounds now were nearly dark. The outside floodlights had been turned off, leaving only a single naked bulb burning over a rear entrance of the clubhouse.

In the dim light couples stood on the dock, walked on the beach, leaned together in the shadows.

"Thanks for the walk." Her voice was bitter.

"You're making too much of it," he said.

"Too much—of what?"

"Too much of us. I don't get it. We saw each other once in Jamaica and that's all."

"That was enough for me."

He led her past the clubhouse and kept going.

"You're making it very tough for me," he said. They had reached the shadows beyond the dock, where the dock gave way to a bulkhead. Just offshore stood the red flasher that marked the finish line of the race.

She sat on the edge of the bulkhead and he stood behind her in the sand. "Let me tell you something about myself," he said. "I'm not for you. I'm not for anybody. I'm one of the dumbest bastards you can imagine. And one of the dullest. I'm not worth a damn. Sometimes it's all I can do to get up in the morning, all I can do to get dressed, to set one foot after the other, all I can do to drive over to the goddamned McDonald's to get myself a hamburger for supper. I'm no good for you or for anybody else."

"I can help you," she said.

"The hell you can! Why would you even want to? What's the attraction? Because I beat your old man in a sailboat race? Don't be a damned fool . . . "

He rubbed his hand hard over his cheek and sat beside her on the bulkhead. "Look," he said, "I'm sorry. What happened to you when you were fifteen years old was a lousy thing—but it *wasn't my fault!*"

She picked up his hand and drew his fingers to her lips. "Whoever said it was?" She let his hand go. "Whoever said it was?" she repeated softly.

Out in the channel a powerboat was moving slowly by, its cabin lights blazing. Harry watched as it went down the river. She was looking at him. He touched her hand. "Why do you want anybody at all?" he asked. "If it's being an appendage that bothers you? You'd be doing the same thing all over again—just switching him for me. And it would be a lousy switch. You said he'd try to keep you when the time came, so let him. You'd be better off with him, believe me."

"It would be different with you," she said. In the blink, blink, blink of the red flashing light her face was calm. "We could help each other, Harry. I know we could. I'm not really helping Mel. In some ways he's a man who's beyond help. In most other ways he doesn't need any. With you I could be a person. I wouldn't be swallowed up."

It sounded stilted, as though she had gotten it from a book or magazine, and he felt sorry for her. Looking back over the river, Harry reached back into the sand. He picked up a fistful and let it sift through his fingers, picking up some more, digging his fingers into the cool sand. Over in the anchorage a hundred masthead lights twinkled in the darkness. With the humidity washed away by the new wind, the stars were clear and sparkling.

The band was silent again and this time it must have quit. He looked over his shoulder. People were leaving. Headlights were coming on and cars were pulling out of the parking lot.

"I could help you, Harry," she said.

"How?"

"By loving you. And in other ways."

He was still grabbing the sand, grabbing and sifting, over and over, looking out over the river. He threw a handful into the water. "Let me try to explain it *again*. Listen to what I'm saying. I'd be no good for you. I'm dull. I'm stupid. I stay depressed and stupefied. I come out of it long enough to sail a boat race because that's the only thing that can bring me out of it, the only thing I'm willing to leave it for. The *only thing I'm good at*. Are you with me so far?"

The red flasher blinked. She was biting the tip of her finger.

"Like a singer. Or a trumpet player. Somebody hooked

on drugs who comes out of it only long enough to sing for a couple of hours or play the trumpet for a few hours and then gets stupefied again and goes back into a dark hole. That's the way it is with me and sailboat races. Can you understand that?"

She was still watching his face, saying nothing.

"Today for a while I couldn't even sail the goddamned boat. I couldn't make it go, and I started to panic. I thought I'd lost the only thing I have and that I'd be left with nothing but myself and today for a while it scared hell out of me. Tonight I don't even give a damn and maybe that's even worse."

"I could help you," she said.

"Why don't you stop saying that? If you don't want Fontaine, then go find somebody else. You're a sexy kid. The way you look you could get almost anybody you want. He's made you what you are, he's polished you up to face the big world. The sky's the limit. Go find yourself a movie star, go find yourself the president of an oil company, get your name in *People* magazine."

"I've had all that and I don't want it. I want you."

"Then you must be insane."

"Everybody's got hangups, Harry. Maybe you're mine."

"You don't know what you'd be dealing with," he said. "I'm not worth a damn."

"You don't have to be perfect. Who's perfect? Do you think I'm perfect? Do you think you're the only rotten person around? My God! Ever since I was fifteen years old I've been some man's whore. Until I met Mel I was in the pits. The real pits. There's nothing I didn't do. Nothing I wasn't asked to do. And I did it."

Her voice was intense now, choked with anger. "And that book that told me I was doomed—cursed—because of what my father did to me. Do you suppose there's ever a day that I don't think about *that?* When I saw him at my sister's funeral this spring I got sick, literally sick."

He was listening in silence.

"You think you're such a bum. My God! Compared to

the men I've known you're a boy scout. When I saw you in Jamaica last winter I knew it was you I wanted. I didn't know it right away but I knew it after we left. I realized it when I knew you were in that broken-down boat, sailing all by yourself back to Florida. Then I knew it and I told myself I was by God going to get you. I knew you were what I wanted."

"In God's name, why?"

"I don't know. Maybe because I felt good about myself that week in Jamaica. Maybe because of the way your eyes looked when I told you about my father. Maybe because you didn't want to screw me any more after I told you about it. Maybe a lot of things. Maybe because you reminded me of somebody I knew when I was eight years old."

When the red flasher blinked he could see that her lashes were damp now and her eye makeup was beginning to streak.

"The trailer across the road," she said. "I told you about it but I'm sure you don't even remember. The beautiful trailer where my girl friend lived, the trailer I envied when I was a little girl because it was so much nicer than ours. Her father always wore clean khaki pants and a clean khaki shirt and he worked very hard and he was nice to kids, very nice to me, and he told me I was beautiful and I loved him . . . *Christ!*" Her voice was harsh. "*Forget it!*"

She was on her feet and moving away, carrying her shoes. He watched her go and then slowly followed. Moving out to the edge of the dock, she whistled softly and Robby emerged from the darkness on cue. His running lights were on—red and green eyes in the bow, a white light on a staff in the stern. The stern light gleamed on the slender ridges of his wake.

She got into the boat and shoved away from the dock. Robby was still idling the motor, looking up at Harry. She looked over her shoulder. Her voice was tight. "Do you want to go back out?"

"Why not?"

She tossed him the bowline and he pulled the boat close and got in.

"I'll take it, Robby," she said.

With Elaine steering, they moved through the darkness. Fontaine was sitting in the cockpit of *Iceman*. As they approached, he looked over his shoulder and then got to his feet. "Greetings," he called.

Robby stood balanced on the forward thwart and as the little boat slid by he yanked himself up over the side and into the cockpit.

"Have a good time?" Fontaine asked.

Elaine put her hand against *Iceman*'s hull and shoved off, advancing the throttle a little. "I'm taking Harry back to his boat," she called.

"Okay," Fontaine replied. "Good night, Harry—and nice race."

"Thanks," Harry said.

In the dim light, Fontaine's face looked curious. The boy had already disappeared below.

"Which way is your boat?" She was shading her eyes, peering ahead.

"I'll take it," he said.

Without replying, she slid aside and climbed forward, sitting in the seat just ahead of his. Harry gripped the steering wheel and moved slowly through the mass of anchored boats. Reaching *Sundance*, he slowed down but instead of stopping he gained speed again and picked his way through the fleet until he had moved beyond the last boat and was in clear water.

Once in the channel he headed downstream. The red flasher fell behind. Gradually he moved the throttle forward. On the Oxford shore the lights of the houses were moving by.

She looked over her shoulder, then turned back again and settled into the seat.

They were moving faster now and as their speed increased the boat began to lift. He jerked the throttle forward as far as it would go and the bow rose from the water. He stared straight ahead, trying to pierce the darkness with his eyes. Far down the river was the flashing white light that he knew to be the lighthouse but in between there was only the darkness that kept rushing up at him and rushing by. He gave a quick glance at the sky. It was like a river rushing back over their heads.

She let her head fall back, looking up at the speeding stars.

Gradually he eased the throttle down. Their speed faded and they were bobbing in the gentle swell of the black river.

He circled then and moved back through the darkness, cutting the throttle again as they neared the anchorage. When he reached *Sundance* he looped a line over his starboard winch and sat there, motor idling.

She pivoted to face him, then faced forward again. "You love me, Harry, you know you do." She let her head fall back against his knee.

Out in the channel a boat had passed and they rocked a little in its wash. The tip of *Sundance*'s mast moved gently back and forth among the stars.

"I'd love to have your child, Harry," she said softly. "It would be a good one. It wouldn't have whore's blood. I promise you."

He touched her head and pulled himself up over the side, into the cockpit of his boat. Lifting the line from the winch, he cast her off. As she moved away he sat in the cockpit, watching her go. He saw the little boat disappear into the shadows and then, a few minutes later, saw it swinging out behind the big one, tied behind *Iceman*. By then she had disappeared.

Twenty-six

AFTER SITTING FOR A WHILE in the cockpit, Harry went below but found it impossible to sleep. For more than three hours he lay awake in the foreberth, feeling every motion of the boat, hearing the lap of the water and the faint creak of the rigging. Finally he went up on deck and stretched out on the cockpit seat, looking up at the thin veil of clouds that now covered the sky.

By the digital watch on his wrist it was four o'clock and then four-fifteen. Still sleep did not come. He was sitting up by now, looking out over the water at the silent anchored fleet.

At four-thirty he took off his watch and shirt and lowered himself over the side. The water was soft and warm. For a few minutes he stayed close to the boat, slowly treading water, then began to move away, diving and swimming beneath the surface with a slow frog kick, coming up each time with a muffled splash, floating face-down for a second or two and then diving again, moving gradually toward shore.

When he had cleared the last of the anchored boats he turned on his back and floated. Overhead there were slits in the clouds. The stars were in and out. He closed his eyes, floating, relaxing. Soon he could stand. Water lapped his neck as he stood facing the sloping seawall that curved with the shore.

Where he stood it was still dark but in the northeast now, up the river to the right, stretched a long band of filtered light, broken by clouds. Out in the channel the dim white blur of a workboat was sliding down the river, the reflection of its port light a red stake riding vertically in the dark water.

Floating and swimming, he made his way slowly back.

As he approached *Iceman*, he paused and began to tread water again. The motorboat was still tied off its stern. In the main cabin there was a dim light. Silently he circled the boat, pausing once to tread water and listen. There was no sound and he turned away.

As he climbed back into *Sundance*'s cockpit the sky was turning grey. He looked toward the village. In the deep grey light the houses along the shore were stark white, the way they had always looked when he went out as a boy with his father, moving down the river just at dawn, on their way out to the oyster beds.

He was looking at the row of houses that stood along the strand. By its silhouette, its steep gable, he recognized the rooming house where his father had spent the final years of his life, dividing his time between the house and the boat yard and his log canoe.

Still in the wet trunks, Harry slumped in the cockpit, thinking of his father and of Marcia, thinking that two nights ago on the telephone she had spoken nicely of his father, and that he had listened and been pleased and even grateful.

. . . thinking that he loved the kid, but how much of the pleasure and anticipation of seeing him had been in the thought, the possibility, that it would be Marcia who brought him on the plane, as she had done that one time at Friendship? And how much of the pleasure in telephoning lay in the hope that he would be talking not only to the boy but to Marcia?

. . . to be so impressed by the woman who had been his wife that he could not escape whatever it was. He should have hated her but he had never been able to. Without his even knowing it, she had become entrenched in his mind as the paragon by which he judged all other women.

After all these years he was still in love with his wife. All these years he had been waiting to wake up from a bad dream and when he woke up they would still be married, and the baby would still be eighteen months old, staggering around in his blue tennis shoes.

"God," he said softly. "Oh my God . . . "

He continued to sit where he was. When he looked at his watch again it was six o'clock. The sun was up, still blocked by the village, but some of its rays were getting through, finding slits and corridors between the boat sheds and the houses and casting long shadows over the river.

People were beginning to stir. In the next boat a grey-haired man sat in the cockpit with a mug of coffee, reading a book. As Harry got to his feet he looked up curiously, smiled and said good morning.

"Good morning," Harry said.

The sun was above the trees now. Its rays were catching the tips of the masts. The sky was no longer pale. Directly overhead it was turning a soft blue.

Stepping up to the rail, Harry dived overboard, swam slowly ashore, and walked down the main street. Against his wet skin the air was chilly but when he walked through the patches of sunlight he felt warm.

When he got to the phone booth next to the store it was six-thirty. He hoped Marcia would answer. It really wouldn't bother him too much if it should be Philip but he hoped she'd be the one.

She answered after the second ring. Her voice wasn't sleepy. It was sharp and alert, on top of things, and he could picture her face, but where was the phone? Next to the bed . . . or maybe down in the big kitchen. He knew there was an enormous kitchen because Roger had told him so. An enormous kitchen with an enormous fireplace, big enough for a small rowboat.

"Harry! What is it? Is something wrong?"

"No," he said. "Nothing's wrong."

"Then why on earth are you calling at six-thirty in the morning?"

"Because I wanted to tell you something," he said.

"What is it? Couldn't it wait?"

"No," he said.

"What is it?"

The words came up from his chest. "Go to hell, Marcia," he said.

"*What?*"

"Go to hell, you bitch. That's what I called to tell you. Go to hell."

He hung up.

At eleven-thirty that morning, Mel Fontaine lay on *Iceman*'s foredeck in his swim trunks, sunning himself. His eyes were closed and he was dozing when he heard her. Even though she moved lightly and almost without sound, he could sense her presence because he knew it so well.

He opened his eyes. She lay next to him. Her hair was pinned up and she was wearing her blue bikini and her eyes were washed clean of makeup.

"You finally got up?" he asked.

She said nothing. The heat was intense. The sun beat down, striking sparks from the chrome chocks and the big chrome cleats at the bow.

"Are you planning to keep me in suspense?"

When she didn't answer he lay there waiting.

There was just enough breeze to make the sun bearable. It was cooling one side of his face, one side of his body, drying the sweat even as it formed, but on the side away from the breeze the sweat ran from his armpit and trickled down his ribs.

He opened his eyes. She was tracing her finger over his nose, following the line of his nose with her fingertip.

"Not good?"

She turned on her stomach and pillowed her head on one slim tanned arm, looking into his eyes. "Not good," she said.

"You're putting me on," he said. "Are you?"

"Would I?"

Grunting, he closed his eyes again. Presently her hand touched his chest. "Who's that blond ape back there in the cockpit?"

Raising up with his elbows, he looked. "That's Gus Whitney." He lowered his body again. "You don't like him?"

"No."

"Why?"

"I think he's got ideas." Her voice became imitation haughty, an imitation of a grande dame. "I think . . . he *aspires* . . . to get into my *pants.*"

Fontaine chuckled. "You think so, huh?"

"I think so, yes. And furthermore . . . "

"Yes?"

"He keeps putting o's on the end of his words and it makes me sick."

"Like what?"

"He told Billy he liked to be called Gus-o, that people in Annapolis called him Gus-o."

"Gus-o . . . "

"And last night at the yacht club he sniffed pot in the air and referred to it as el grass-o."

"Gus-o. My God."

"And if he messes with my pants do you know what he's going to get?"

"What?"

"A knee right in el crotch-o."

Fontaine exploded with laughter.

Her head was on her forearm again but she was facing the other way. "Don't let that son of a bitch sail on this boat," she said.

Fontaine was still smiling. "I'll get rid of him." He touched her shoulder. "How are you otherwise?"

"Fine," she said.

"How about Harry?"

"Nothing," she said.

"How do you feel about it?"

"Okay," she said.

Her knee was bent and he looked at the smooth curve of her calf, the texture of her flesh. He looked at his own stomach, wishing that it were harder and leaner and younger. He wished he could be as rich and powerful as he was with a body twenty years younger.

A seagull beat up into the breeze, hung suspended and then sideslipped away, skimming the water. He watched it.

Before she came out on deck he had been thinking about his wife and about the daughter who hated him, and about his father who, when he was still very young, had told him to learn shorthand because it would be a stepping-stone to the promised land.

Here he was in the promised land, without wife and without daughter and soon to be without the mistress who was a substitute for them both.

So he had convinced himself, but was it true? King Solomon in his wisdom had renewed himself with young virgins. Maybe he had never loved her. Maybe what he had felt was simply a raw need for adulation and young sex. Love had been burned out of him by enormous success and enormous failures. By his own making she was the reward for the successes and she was solace for the failures. He was a man at bay, and she represented the next moment—all the nervous next moments of his days.

His cheek pressed to the deck, he looked at the delicacy of her forearm and told himself that he loved her as much as he was capable of love. Perhaps more important, he deeply feared being without her.

"How about this afternoon?" he asked. "Do you want to hang around for the trophy party?"

"It doesn't matter," she said.

He smiled. "Well I do. And I want you to go with me, and I want you to look spectacular."

She was on her back now.

"Don't leave," he said. "Okay."

She pressed his hand.

"Listen, I feel something very strong," he said. "I feel that if you leave me I'll get old. Fast. And—I guess I don't want to get old."

She was looking up at the sky, and now as he watched

he saw tears fill her eyes. For a moment he dared think they were there because she was touched by what he was saying, but then he couldn't be sure.

"My God!" he said. "You actually love that kid, don't you?"

She got to her feet and walked slowly forward.

He was up on one elbow. "Don't you?" He felt he was choking.

She was leaning against the bow pulpit, half sitting on it, her face outlined against the hot blue sky.

At one o'clock that afternoon, Tony Korbut was in Roberta Lodge's kitchen doing her breakfast and lunch dishes. He had never minded doing dishes, in fact he rather enjoyed it. He had once read that a lot of very intelligent, extremely accomplished men relaxed by doing dishes and he saw nothing demeaning about it.

While he did the dishes she was at her desk in the next room, the louvered, colorfully furnished sunroom that she called her Florida Room, going over her list. The cocktail party on her lawn would begin at four. It would be catered but she was still poring over a list which she had headed Things to Worry About. He stood at her shoulder, a plate and dish towel in hand. Her head was bent over the list and she was murmuring, " . . . trophies . . . liquor . . . cheese . . . flowers . . . chairs for—" Here she ticked off the names of three very elderly, very frail local women who had nothing to do with the regatta or with boating, but whom she had invited to the party because they didn't go out much.

Korbut returned to the kitchen, put the plate in the finished pile, and picked up another. Before arriving for lunch, he had spent a good part of the morning with the Washington *Post* and the Baltimore *Sun*, sitting in the deeply shaded town park on a bench overlooking the river. It was the way he had spent many summer Sunday mornings.

That morning, after finishing with the papers, he

planned how it would be. First he would make his confession. He would tell her he had been in jail for cheating on his income tax. There was something ennobling about a confession and she would not fail to be impressed. Then he would ask her to marry him.

With the dishes done, he sat on the arm of the white sofa and watched her, thinking what a truly handsome woman she was and what a strong woman. He needed a strong woman. She had looked wonderful the previous afternoon in her boat, with her hair blowing back and the khaki skirt flattened against her legs. Now she wore her black-framed glasses and the same skirt and a white blouse with tiny purple fleur-de-lis.

She was aware that he was sitting there gazing at her. Looking up with a smile, she asked, "All finished with the dishes?"

"Yep."

"Thanks, Tony."

"Okay. Listen, Roberta . . . I've got something I'd like to tell you."

She nodded. He got up from the arm of the sofa and stood next to her. She took his hand and smiled and as he kept talking she kept smiling. He paused to gauge what the smile might mean. Certainly affection. It was a warm gentle smile. He kept talking. " . . . paroled after five months . . . " The pressure of her hand increased. " . . . I was well thought of . . . I did a blueprint of the entire plumbing system, every last pipe in the whole prison. I was always pretty good at mechanical drawing. The warden was very pleased with it. The warden liked me. I was one of his favorites and when I came up for parole he told me he would be sorry to see me go—what's wrong?"

She had removed her glasses. She patted his hand. "I know all this, Tony," she said. "Not about the warden and the pipes but I know you were in prison. Everybody in town knows."

Stunned, he sat again on the arm of the sofa. "You're not

serious." He shook his head in disbelief. "How? How do they know?"

"News travels," she said.

"How could it have?"

She smiled. "That's the way it is with news. It's like an underground. It gets here somehow. People learn where the skeletons are buried . . . but they don't confront you with it. The person himself, or herself, never knows. They talk about it among themselves, so there's never any accusation, or any redemption, but on the other hand plenty of privacy."

"My God," he said.

"People know that's why you gave up sailing. They don't see why. They don't see any connection. Some of the biggest bastards in the world sail boats."

He took a deep breath. "My God," he said again.

"Don't worry about it," she said. "Now maybe I'd better get going with some of these—"

"Wait a minute, Roberta."

She had been halfway across the room but now returned to her desk and looked at him curiously.

"I'm not quite finished," he said. He shook his head. "This isn't easy. I thought I was confessing something you didn't know. I had it all planned. I was going to make this big confession and you were going to think it was all very noble and high-minded, and then . . . "

He broke off and looked at the floor with a smile.

"Yes?"

"Then I was going to say now that you know the worst about me—will you marry me? But now the whole thing's shot to hell because you already knew the worst about me. Okay—how about it? Will you marry me, Roberta? Let's get married, what do you say?"

She sat looking into his eyes, still smiling the same gentle smile.

"Look," he said, "you've had a husband and I've had a wife. We've each led a life but—we're both here, we've both got a certain number of years and we might just as well live them as pleasurably as possible."

She nodded. "Let me say something first about this jail thing, Tony. Stop letting it gnaw at you. You're alive, you're breathing, you're healthy, you've paid your debt to society and nobody is ostracizing you—in *fact* . . ." She began to smile again. "There are certain people I know, certain Republicans mostly, who would consider it an honor, a real badge of honor, to go to jail for income tax evasion . . . As for the rest of it . . . "

He sat waiting, watching her face.

"I like your company, Tony. I enjoy doing things with you, going places with you, I think we get along real well. By the way, I think you should by all means start to sail again. I love to sail and I wish you'd take me . . . "

She paused and shook her head. "But I couldn't possibly marry you. Marriage at our age is so—*legal*. So *financial*. So many papers to draw up. I've got all my papers straight, everything's in order. That horrible thing you have to draw up to reduce your inheritance tax—I couldn't possibly go through all that again. And my daughter is at peace because she knows everything's straight and all drawn up and she knows there's no danger that somebody I meet in the last part of my life will get some of the money that she thinks belongs to her. She's just as tight as she can be about money and if she thought I was going to get married again I think she'd have a nervous breakdown and I really can't blame her. So I really can't marry you, Tony, but it's certainly not because you've been in jail . . . "

He nodded. "Okay . . . "

"Even if you were—Robert Redford . . . "

"Okay."

"Or *anybody.*"

"Okay."

"Are you really and truly wife-hunting, Tony?"

"No, not necessarily. It's just that I do like you very much and I guess I get lonely. I want a place to be at night."

"Come here," she said. "Any time. Okay?"

He smiled. "Okay."

"And now let's get ready for this party. We've still got a regatta going on."

At three-thirty that afternoon, Margaret Hackett was sitting in a lawn chair behind her house, waiting for her husband to return. He had left shortly after one o'clock to take Kitty back to Annapolis, where she would pick up her car and drive back to Connecticut. She did not expect him back much before five.

At the foot of the yard, safe in its slip, lay their boat, the *Silver Heels*, bow foremost. It looked so docile, so tamed. Yesterday a monster pterodactyl, a flying reptile; now a bird with its wings quietly folded.

Yet she knew that so long as it remained in her husband's possession it was a menace, a threat to her way of life, if not to life itself.

The previous evening after Harry Crowder had helped them get the boat to its slip they had eaten a quiet supper. There was very little conversation. Kitty had seemed in a state of shock, too tired to dress, content to wear an old grey wrapper provided by Mrs. Hackett. She was looking at her brother with new eyes. Clearly she thought that he should be punished. *Mashed.*

And yet, Mrs. Hackett thought, how could a man be more mashed, more thoroughly laid low than Hackett had been on the foredeck, flat on his stomach, clutching the base of the mast with both hands, his white hair aloft in the wind. It was a telling sight. It would be one of the lasting memories of her life.

After they had reached the dock he had spent some time on the boat, tidying up the lines and the sailbags, then walked wearily up to the house and stayed endlessly in the shower. Finally he came down, damp and subdued, like his sister too exhausted even to dress, wearing his dark-blue robe with a gold H on the pocket.

"Well," Mrs. Hackett said toward the end of the meal, "I think all in all it was a lot of fun. Strenuous but a lot of fun. And I think that under the circumstances our nice little boat performed beautifully."

Hackett and Kitty, brother and sister, looked at her as if she were an object in a display case.

Too exhausted to demur, Kitty had retired early and the Hacketts soon followed, he with hardly a word, a man stunned, as he had been stunned ever since they reached the dock, or indeed much earlier—ever since the spinnaker turned the boat into a disaster area.

Yet Mrs. Hackett knew she could not afford to become overconfident. She had heard his remark to Harry when Harry had boarded them like a cowboy springing from his horse to the backs of a runaway team. She remembered what he'd said about how she'd had a "bone in her teeth" and how they'd "really had 'er walkin'."

Once more she found it wise to remind herself that never in all their married life had he made a decision that he did not think was straight out of his own head, and the more she opposed it the greater the certainty that he would make it.

Presently she heard his car enter the driveway and the tires come slowly to a stop on the gravel. She greeted him as he came sagging dispiritedly into the circle of lawn chairs.

"Was there a lot of traffic?" she asked sympathetically.

He shook his head. "All going the other way . . . "

She wondered if there could be any significance in the fact that he wore no vestige of boating attire, none of the new togs associated with the boating period of his life. He wore a dark-blue sports shirt and the nice white flannels with the pin stripe that she last remembered seeing at a farewell company picnic in Rahway.

"Is anything wrong?" she asked.

He shook his head, saying nothing.

"Would you like some coffee? Some iced tea?"

"No thanks." A tone of elegy.

"Would you like to go to the cocktail party at Roberta's?"

"Why would I? I didn't win anything."

She looked at him for a moment. "Walters, what is it? Is it the boat? Is it the boat, Walters?"

He did not reply. He was slumped in a director's chair of blue canvas and in his eyes there was an expression she could not interpret.

Her fears suddenly broke loose and ran free. She began to imagine what had happened. On the drive back from Annapolis he had figured out a way to continue racing. He had bucked himself up, given himself a pep talk. He would scout around for a crew and would find no one available. No one but herself. And the next thing she knew they'd be doing spinnaker drill.

Mrs. Hackett took a deep breath. "Walters, dear," she said. "I don't think you should be so down on the boat. It's a dear boat, it really is."

He was still looking toward the dock, and his expression now seemed one of grim determination. In his eyes there was a steely glint.

"It's such a wonderful challenge for you," she said. "Such a—wonderful outlet for your energies."

It was as if he had not heard her. He was lost within himself.

"And for your very first race you did beautifully. You have no reason to feel inferior. I think that under the circumstances the boat did beautifully—and so did you." She paused, glanced at his face and went on. "I *love* the boat. So sturdy and solid. Maybe you should think twice about selling it."

"Too late for that," he said.

"*What?*" Mrs. Hackett's every sense was alert. "What do you mean? Surely you don't mean you've—already *sold* it?"

"No, but I put a notice on the yacht club bulletin board."

"You mean—a For Sale notice?"

"Yes."

"Just now?"

"No."

"When?"

"As I was leaving town with Kitty."

"You mean—four *hours* ago?"

He looked at her curiously. "Yes."

"Oh, dear. How much?"

"I said make offer."

"That's all? 'Make offer'?"

"Make offer. Sacrifice."

"Oh dear." She sat back with an expression of deep concern, waiting for the telephone to ring.

It rang five minutes later.

He went in to answer it and when he returned he had the decisive look of a man in command of his life. "It's gone," he said.

"Oh dear . . . well . . . I guess that's that . . . "

She sat there, head hanging. Presently he got up from the director's chair and came to her side, put his arm around her shoulder. Still looking across the lawn, she reached up and took his hand, pressed it. He pressed hers in return. "Look, Mag," he said, "you're being unrealistic. You know damned well—listen, for one thing we're both too old for it. We came to it too late in life, that's the plain, simple truth of it. I think it's something you should face and not be so —so unrealistic."

She was still looking across the lawn, her features composed in an expression of regret.

"I can't believe you care all that much," he said.

"I get too easily attached to things, I guess," she said. "It was such a doughty little boat. I grew to love it. And what an exciting trip we had down the bay . . . "

He let go of her hand, walked back to his director's chair, plopped down and glared at her. "You're crazy as hell, Margaret. It was a *lousy* trip down the bay." His voice rose. "It was torture. We did lousy. We got blown off course, we couldn't control the boat and we made *fools of ourselves! It was a goddamn fiasco!*" His face was red. "Why in the hell don't you have the good sense to admit it?"

He was on his feet again, turning away and turning angrily back. "Boating stinks! I *hate* boating! You either get heat prostration from no wind or else you're getting knocked around in some goddamn hurricane. Now stop being foolish! I'm glad to be rid of it."

He took a deep breath and sat down again in his director's chair. His voice softened. "I'm sorry. It certainly wasn't your fault."

She spread her hands.

"Listen," he said, "you've still got your bridge club. Your yoga lessons, your flower beds—all the normal ordinary pleasures of retirement. The things you like so much. You should be content with those."

"Of course." She looked pensively across the lawn. "And what will you do, Walters?"

"I don't know." He shrugged and in his face now there was something very forlorn. "I just wish to hell I'd taken it up when I was younger. I might have been pretty good at it. Boy! We really had 'er walkin' out there in the Choptank, didn't we, Mag?" He looked down. His voice had broken.

"Oh, Walters . . . " She moved to his side and there were tears in her eyes as she put her arms gently about his neck.

Twenty-seven

LATE THAT AFTERNOON trophies were presented to the successful skippers. The presentation took place at a cocktail party on Roberta Lodge's freshly mowed rear lawn, a beautiful rectangle of deep green shaded by old trees and running all the way back to the river. Down the lawn, dividing it approximately in half, ran a brick walkway bordered at uniform intervals with plantings of young English boxwood. Spotted among the boxwood were carefully tended rosebushes, each surrounded by peat moss and dripping with huge yellow roses. On one side of the walkway, a deep-red crepe myrtle was just coming into bud. On the other side stood a large magnolia tree with shiny green leaves and large white blossoms. Here and there through the trees a sail could be seen on the sparkling blue river.

The focal point of the occasion was a table perhaps twenty feet long and covered with a white cloth. One end of the table served as a bar. The other end held an array of trophies—pewter bowls, tumblers, shot-glasses, bud vases, in all enough to take care of first-, second-, and third-place finishers in eleven different classes.

It was a dressy affair, much dressier than the dance held the previous evening at the yacht club. Women in long dresses, bronzed men in blazers, strolled through the grounds, stood in clusters drinking and talking, waiting for the trophies to be presented. Some lived locally; but for most, the long boat trip back up the bay still lay ahead.

Anthony Korbut, in a bright-green jacket, lingered over the trophy table. He was picking up the trophies, scrutinizing the inscriptions and then carefully arranging them according to class. The presentations would be made by Roberta and it would be his job to hand her the right trophy.

Into this affair, Mel Fontaine and Elaine Fowler made a late entrance, very much as they had done on Friday evening at the yacht club in Annapolis. Once again their arrival created a stir. What people saw was what had been on view in Annapolis, an older man and a younger women doing a grand walk through a crowd. The man was even wearing the same outfit, featuring a blue denim jacket and a red bandanna.

Regatta

On this Sunday afternoon, instead of the expensive jeans she had worn in Annapolis, Elaine was wearing a white dress. Spaghetti straps cut into her smoothly tanned shoulders. Beneath its long waist the dress was a mass of billowing white material, as soft and light as gauze, ending just below the knee.

Once again the waters seemed to part as the couple moved slowly down the walkway. Once again all eyes were upon them and once again there were diffident greetings. Yet there were differences. In the case of Fontaine, all the gestures were there, the smile, the jaunty wave, but something was missing, a fine edge of confidence perhaps.

And so too with his girl, who two evenings earlier in Annapolis had seemed in such control, so self-contained. Now like Fontaine she seemed subdued.

Standing beneath a maple tree, Harry watched them arrive. He wore his jeans and an old blue seersucker jacket that he kept on the boat. In his hand was a glass of ginger ale. With him were some of his old cronies from the surrounding area, the men he had grown up with. These included Clem Vale, who had by now escaped from his experience in Baltimore and returned in time for the presentation ceremony. Badly hung over, Clem, of all those present, was making no attempt to hide what he felt about Fontaine. "Son of a bitch bought Royce and me a drink but I still don't like the son of a bitch." His friend Royce told him not to talk so loud.

As Fontaine and Elaine neared the long table, Roberta Lodge, in a dress of crisp white linen, moved forward to welcome them, then directed them to the right-hand end of the table, where the drinks were being served.

To the left, at the trophy end, seated all in a row, were the three elderly women for whom she had provided chairs. All three were drinking straight bourbon and ice.

After seeing to them for a moment, Roberta returned to the table and tapped on a glass with a spoon. "Keep drinking," she called with a smile. "Keep eating and drinking and you can even keep on walking around if you like. But I think that out of consideration for those who still have to sail back to Annapolis we should begin our little presentation ceremony . . . "

Thereupon she set about it—consulting a list, calling a name and then handing over the trophy that was passed to her by Korbut, who stood just to her left.

" . . . third place, Delta Two . . . Willis Poindexter, Annapolis Yacht Club . . . Willis? Is Willis here? Oh, here he comes. Congratulations, Willis."

Most of the award winners were present, although a few were not. Their trophies were accepted in their behalf by friends.

One trophy was unclaimed.

" . . . Cal-25s . . . first place, *Pottagold*, Gus Whitney, Arundel Sailing Association . . . Gus?" Roberta looked around. "Is Gus here? Gus Whitney?"

"He's sailing back to Annapolis," somebody called. "I saw him leave about an hour ago."

"Did he appoint a surrogate?" Roberta raised a pewter tumbler. "No?"

"I'll take it to him," somebody said finally.

As the presentations continued, people kept moving and mingling. Some of the winners made short speeches of acceptance, which few paid any attention to. One reason perhaps was the distraction offered by Fontaine, who was making himself eminently approachable, full of noblesse oblige, much as he had been two nights earlier in Annapolis, the VIP in constant search of the modest, self-effacing phrase.

Even more of a distraction was his girl. People watched her from close up and from a distance. Those at a distance talked of her, particularly the women among them. Like Ava Gardner when she was young, somebody said. A starlet he's grooming for television . . . Like a Gibson girl, somebody said . . . Like a Eurasian princess . . . Like a high-class whore.

As Fontaine held court, the girl in question stepped

away and moved alone across the yard to one of the rose-bushes, bending to bury her face in one of the huge yellow roses. She then continued down the walkway toward the river.

Roberta was looking toward Fontaine. "Class A," she said. "First place, *Iceman,* Mel Fontaine, Royal Ocean Racing Club . . . Mel . . . "

Fontaine, with a sedate smile, walked slowly to the table, accepted his trophy, shook hands with Roberta and turned. "Thank you, Mrs. Lodge," he said. "Let me say first of all what a privilege it is to be in such a uniquely beautiful town. I assure you this will not be my last visit." He turned to Roberta. "Next I'd like to thank you, Mrs. Lodge, and the members of your committee for putting on such an expertly managed regatta. And finally . . . my thanks to my fellow yachtsmen for giving me and my guys all the competition we could handle!"

Clem Vale's whiskey voice rose in the silence. "All you could handle and a little bit more, *I'd* say!"

"Shut up, Clem," Harry muttered.

"Hey, Cap'n Fontaine," Clem shouted. "Wouldn't you agree with me, Cap'n?"

Fontaine waved. "Your boy is some sailor, believe me," he said and turned away. As he headed back to his place he seemed to be having trouble smiling.

Elaine had reached the foot of the yard and stood looking out over the river. Now she turned and headed back up the walkway.

"The final award of the afternoon," Roberta said, "is one that gives me great pleasure to present. First-in-fleet—*Sundance!* Harry Crowder!"

Halfway up the brick walk, Elaine had paused to watch.

While Clem and his other cronies yelled and raised hell, Harry walked slowly across the lawn to the table. Handing him the bowl, Roberta grasped his hand. Harry smiled. "Thanks a lot, Roberta," he said.

Elaine was looking at him from the walkway. Their eyes

met for a moment before he moved away and returned to the noisy group beneath the maple tree.

Once more Roberta tapped the glass for attention. "That takes care of the trophies," she said. "And now I'd like to say a final word or two. As you all know, I've been a part of the regatta this weekend, a passive part, a non-sailing part, true, but even so I've been doing some thinking and something has occurred to me."

Harry caught Fontaine looking in his direction. He was no longer smiling. His face was a mask.

"To a group of seasoned sailors . . . to a group of knowledgeable *men* . . . " Behind the black-framed glasses, Roberta's eyes began to sparkle. " . . . it may sound naive even to mention it, but I must say I think it's rather remarkable. All of you out there on the bay, out there on the rivers, working and sweating. Out there in the horse latitudes, waiting for a breeze . . . "

Removing her glasses, she placed them on the table. "It's not like a lot of things. There's no money in it. No reward except the satisfaction and maybe a hunk of pewter to put on a shelf—and for most of you not even that. It's all quite refreshing and I hardly know how to account for it—*well!* Thanks for coming. Let's do it again next year, and now—drink up and stay just as long as you possibly can!"

Roberta reached for her glasses again and as she did so they fell to the ground. She stooped to retrieve them and Tony Korbut stooped at the same moment.

Korbut reached them first. He picked them up and handed them to her. Looking at her closely, he began to smile. She smiled with him. Eyes dancing, she pressed his hand. "Thank you, Tony," she said.

"Thank *you*," he said, smiling.

Many by now had begun to make their farewells. Some were already turning away and heading back up the brick pathway to the street.

Fontaine was shaking Roberta's hand, then turning

from the table and shaking hands all around. Shaking many hands but not with pleasure. His mind didn't seem to be on what he was doing.

Elaine by now had rejoined him and stood by, waiting for him to be done.

As she waited she looked again in Harry's direction. Harry smiled and after a moment she started walking toward him. He moved forward to meet her. She offered her hand.

Fontaine, even as he held court, was watching them.

"Congratulations," she said.

"Thanks," Harry said.

"I think I'm going to New York or someplace," she said. "Maybe we could get together some time."

"I'd like to," Harry said.

"Harry . . . "

"Yep?"

"I hope things work out for you." She paused. "I hope you don't lose your son. Don't let them take him away from you. For God's sake, don't."

"I'm not going to," he said.

Again Fontaine was looking in their direction.

"I wish you luck, Harry," she said. "I really do."

She was looking at him, half smiling. Her eyes were heavily made up with mascara and blue shadow. "That's a terrible-looking coat," she said.

Harry looked down the front of his seersucker jacket and shrugged.

"It's really ugly . . . " Her voice caught and she turned away.

In another few minutes she and Fontaine were leaving and this time it was no promenade. Standing beneath the maple with his cronies, Harry watched them move rapidly up the brick walk to the street and turn left, headed for their boat.

There was a lot of laughing and joking about Clem's trip to Baltimore but Harry found he wasn't listening, and after fifteen minutes or so he thanked Roberta and left.

Laura, the little towheaded girl, was still running her tender service, although by now most of the boats in the anchorage were gone.

As he approached the dock, she was just pulling in. "Still at it, huh, Laura?"

"I'm getting tired though." She looked at his trophies. "Wow!" she said softly.

"Can you take me out to my boat one more time?" he asked.

"Sure, hop in."

"Thanks."

"Hardly any boats left," she said as they circled away from the dock.

"Has *Iceman* gone?"

"It just went," she said. "See?" She pointed down the river. "See? There it is."

"I see it," Harry said.

When they reached *Sundance* he handed her another dollar and kissed the top of her head. She giggled. He pulled himself aboard. "Thanks, Laura."

"Okay." Moving away, she glanced over her shoulder once and waved. Harry waved back. After a moment he tossed his trophies through the hatch. They landed on the cushions.

Starting the motor and letting it idle, he moved up to the foredeck and hauled up the anchor; then, returning to the cockpit, he eased the boat into gear and headed for the channel.

He could see *Iceman* far down the river now, moving under bare spars.

Behind him the river was almost empty. It had a lonely look, the way it always looked after a regatta.

The ferryboat was far over toward the Bellevue shore, a small white oval with a single stack.

Downstream, the mast of *Iceman* glinted in the late afternoon sun.

Harry advanced the throttle. Only a few hours earlier, at midnight, he had taken the same route in the dark at speeds up to thirty knots. Now, even though he was riding an outgoing tide, five would be the best he could do.

The moderate breeze was out of the southwest. The northwest wind had abated and moved down to the southwest overnight, a common pattern in summer.

Harry looked ahead and then over his shoulder, lining up his course. The falling sun was lighting up the Oxford shore.

Far ahead now, *Iceman* was rounding the black stake protecting the sandbar at the mouth of the river, the sandbar the Hacketts had bumped across so ingloriously.

As it cleared the stake, *Iceman* slowed down and pointed into the breeze, ready to put up its sails. Harry saw the huge mainsail going up and then one of its big racing jibs. As he watched, the sails filled and *Iceman* bore away on a starboard tack, headed down to the south shore of the Choptank so as to get upwind as far as possible before making its next tack.

Harry checked his knot-meter. It read almost four. Abruptly he jammed it forward as far as it would go. Almost six. Running at full throttle, the boat vibrated and the vibration set off a steady, rapid, metronomic clink, the sound of a glass hitting against a bottle down in the cabin.

Iceman was beginning to fly and he could not help but admire the spectacle it made, close-hauled, cutting through the deep blue water, the tall mainsail all but obscured by the strapped-down jib, sails sparkling white and shimmering in the afternoon sunlight.

On Harry's right, the black stake was coming up. Rounding it, he set a course straight for the mouth of the Choptank . . . straight for the bay . . . straight for the falling sun.

Down against the south shore of the Choptank, the big black boat was going about now and bearing away on its new tack. Harry could see that its slant was good. The new tack was almost a direct line to the mouth of the river, and again he was forced to admire the sight the boat made as it cut through the water.

Twenty minutes passed. The breeze was holding up well, blowing against the ebbing tide and producing a slight chop. *Sundance* dipped its nose into a wave and the spray flew high, sailing back to the cockpit and dousing Harry's face. He was following the line of mid-channel buoys followed by the oceangoing ships on their way back out to the bay from Cambridge. Ahead on the right, a buoy bobbed in the chop. Against the sun it was only a black dot but he knew from his years on this river that it was red flasher 12-A. As it fell astern and the sunlight fell on it, he turned and looked at its faded red paint and its white 12-A.

Standing well out from the south shore now, *Iceman* was still moving on the same tack, the slant that probably would carry it all the way to the mouth of the river and thence out into the bay. It might be possible to intercept it somewhere along this line, yet if the breeze should pick up, *Iceman* would be traveling faster under sail than he could move under power.

To the right, Broad Creek was on the beam now. The rays of the sun flashed on the windowpanes of distant houses.

Another ten minutes passed. The breeze had not moderated; it was if anything a little stronger, and he could estimate now that when *Iceman* crossed his path it would be a good two hundred yards ahead of him.

Another red flasher danced by.

The binoculars lay on the seat. Holding the tiller between his legs, Harry slung the strap about his neck and raised the binoculars. They were powerful enough for him to make out every detail in *Iceman*'s cockpit. There was no one on deck but a young helmsman and another crew member seated on the rail.

Placing the binoculars back on the seat, Harry reached inside the cabin and grabbed the air horn which he had last used thirty-six hours earlier to get through the Severn River drawbridge. Pointing the horn at *Iceman*, he pressed the trigger three times. Three long blasts sounded over the river. The boy at the wheel looked over his shoulder, faced forward and then looked back again. The other crewman stuck his face into the hatch and a few moments later Fontaine emerged.

He stood in the stern, looking back over the water. Harry waved and blasted the horn again. He saw Fontaine reach for the mainsheet. He was slacking the mainsail and now the crewman was slacking the jib.

Its sails no longer drawing, *Iceman* lost speed and as *Sundance* steadily narrowed the gap Fontaine stood frowning on the cockpit seat, one hand grasping the backstay.

A hundred feet from the big boat's stern, Harry cut the throttle. He could hear *Iceman*'s sails luffing and snapping in the breeze. More crewmen had come up from below.

Fontaine still stood in the stern. "What now?" he called as *Sundance* drifted closer.

"I'd like to see Elaine," Harry called back.

"She's taking a nap. What do you want?"

"I'd like to talk to her."

Sundance was now less than twenty feet from *Iceman*'s stern. Harry put his engine in neutral and let the boat drift. As he did so, Elaine appeared in the hatchway. She moved aft and stood next to Fontaine in the stern. Fontaine had changed his party clothes but she had not changed hers. She still wore the white dress with the thin straps and the gauzy skirt.

"Would you like to come with me?" Harry called.

She looked at him with disbelief. *"What?"*

Members of the crew were standing on top of the cabin now and all over the deck.

"I said, would you like to come with me," Harry called.

She was still looking at him with disbelief, but beginning to smile. "Are you serious?"

"Come on, I'll take you aboard."

She glanced quickly at Fontaine.

From somewhere among the crew there was a subdued cheer.

When Elaine had emerged from below, Fontaine had stepped back from the transom. Now he moved close again. "Harry, old boy," he called in tones of reason. "Why don't you go get lost? You're making a nuisance of yourself."

Harry ignored him. "Elaine . . . " His voice drifted across the water.

Fontaine said something over his shoulder and all in an instant his sails were coming down. Two of his crewmen were on the foredeck, taking care of the jib, and three were furling the mainsail.

Elaine and Fontaine were talking. Fontaine was shaking his head. Looking back at Harry, he shouted: "She's not coming."

Elaine grabbed his arm. Pushing her away, he crouched and reached for the ignition. The motor roared into action.

"Mel, you *bastard!*" She was pounding on his back with her fists.

The boat was already moving, headed due west.

Turning on his engine, Harry followed but *Iceman* was quickly picking up speed, engine roaring, hull slicing the water, sending out stiff ridges of wake.

Harry's throttle was already wide open but the gap between them continued to widen.

The big boat was perhaps a hundred yards ahead when Harry saw the flash of white, and then a splash.

He set his course directly for the splash but it seemed a very long while before he saw her head come to the surface. She was treading water and as he roared toward her he saw *Iceman* begin to move in a wide arc. In another few moments it was headed back and he could see Fontaine all the way up in the bow, leaning over the bow pulpit, pointing ahead at the water.

With the tiller between his legs, Harry raised the lid of the cockpit seat and grabbed a life ring and a coil of line, and then his boarding ladder. Still holding the tiller with his

knees, he tied one end of the line to a cleat and the other end
to the life ring. Letting the tiller go for a second, he quickly
hooked the ladder over the transom and grabbed the tiller
again.

She was less than fifty feet ahead now and they were
bearing down on her, the two boats from opposite directions. Twenty feet away, Harry cut his speed, shifted into
reverse, and then again gave it all the throttle it would take.

She was just off the beam now, treading water, the white
dress billowing out all around, her face and hair streaming.

When his momentum was broken, he cut the engine,
tossed the life ring overboard and dived after it.

He came up to see her swimming for the life ring; now
reaching it, grabbing it. He shook the water from his eyes.
"Are you okay?" he called.

"Yes." She was holding the life ring with one hand,
brushing the water from her eyes with the other.

He swam for the life ring and as he reached it he heard
her say, "My God!" He looked up. *Iceman* was bearing down
on them, still headed straight for the life ring until, at the
last second, it veered to port and backed down its engine
with a mighty roar. Now it lay broadside and Fontaine was
back in the cockpit again, staring down at them, saying
nothing. The members of his crew were lined up on deck,
watching in somber silence.

Elaine was holding the life ring with both hands. Harry
rested one hand on the ring and with the other he slowly
treaded water. Against the low idling sound of *Iceman*'s
motor there was only silence—and now a faint splash as a
seagull landed. From the boat the chop had seemed insig-
nificant but now, low in the water, Harry could not even
see the rim of the land. He saw the seagull ride up the slope
of a wave and stare down at him.

"Hang on," he said. "I'm gonna pull us in."

As he gripped the line and started pulling, he saw Fontaine at the rail, looking down. Harry kept pulling. When
they were close to the boat he put his hand under her seat

and gave a shove, hoisting her up the ladder.

A moment later they stood in the cockpit.

Fontaine said something over his shoulder and *Iceman* began to move. With one of the young men at the helm, it began describing a circle around them, barely moving.

Panting, they stood side by side in the cockpit, Elaine's hair hanging in wet strands, the white dress clinging to her body.

Slowly the big boat continued to circle. For a few moments longer Fontaine stood there, his face impassive, looking fixedly at Elaine, as if seeking an answer, looking for confirmation of something he didn't want to believe.

She returned his gaze.

Fontaine's face was brick red. Harry stood with his hand at Elaine's elbow, waiting for his next move. Finally Fontaine turned his back. He gave a curt signal to the crew a moment later *Iceman* was cutting away in a swirling half-circle. Quickly it picked up speed, heading once more for the bay. Fontaine disappeared below.

Elaine seemed to sag. She turned and let her body fall against Harry. She clung to him. "Thank you," she said. He held her close. Although the air was warm and the water had been warm, her teeth were chattering. Her face was against his chest and her body was trembling. "I'd better get these things off," she said. "Do you have an old shirt or something?"

"You'll need more than a shirt," he said. "There's a blanket in the foreberth. Wrap it around yourself until you get warm."

When she went below he pulled the life ring back aboard and then the ladder, all the while keeping his eye on *Iceman.* Would Fontaine keep going, or would he be unable to accept what had happened and return? How much was the bastard capable of?

Harry kept watching. Gradually he could believe that Fontaine was not coming back. Still under power, the big boat was far away by now, angling off to the left against the

falling sun, on a course that would take Fontaine southward, down the bay, down the coast, down to the play-
grounds of the Caribbean; to the next woman, and the next.
Until he lost his powers, Fontaine would know no other life
and Harry sensed that he would not regret it. He prided
himself on a sort of existentialist sophistication. Such a lost
man, for all his success; a masked man, keeping his cool to
the end.

Still soaking wet, Harry sprawled on the cockpit seat.
He heard Elaine moving about below and called down to
her. "Are you okay?"

"Yes, thanks."

"Did you find the blanket?"

"Yes."

"Have you stopped shivering?"

"Almost."

"I'll heat some water . . ."

"No, I'll be okay. I'm warmer now."

He liked knowing she was down there, liked knowing
that she was on the boat. Why? Why had he changed his
mind and followed her? Because he felt sorry for her? Because he hated for her to be in Fontaine's clutches? Because
she was beautiful? Because he had wanted to show up Fontaine again? Or was it more complicated? Did it have something to do with Marcia and Roger and the fact that he had
telephoned Massachusetts that morning and broken an
eight-year trance? They were gone. Without his ever fully
accepting it, they had been gone a long long time.

Bending to the ignition switch, he started the motor and
let it idle. *Iceman* by now was a speck against the setting sun.
He sat on the rail and watched it disappear, thinking once
more of Elaine. Maybe it had something to do with second
chances. He kept thinking of her as a beautiful little girl in
a gingham dress and black stockings and high black shoes,
digging in the dirt in front of the trailer . . . before the fates
would lead her to Marioso and Fontaine, by way of her
father.

She was coming up the ladder, wearing his khaki shirt, the old yellow blanket draped over her shoulders, rubbing her hair with a paper towel, smiling at him. "Are you okay?" he asked.

"Fine." She sat next to him. All the makeup was gone from her eyes. They were bloodshot from the water. Her face became somber. "But I don't want you to feel any responsibility for me, Harry. I'm grateful for what you've done, but—no obligation. Okay?"

He smiled. The engine still idled. The boat was drifting slowly with the tide. "Don't worry about it," he said.

"I've lived through a lot," she said. "I'm still young. After all I've seen I'm still only twenty-three, just imagine. I've got a lot of years left. I can still pull something out for myself. You're not responsible for me." She shook her head. "Nobody is."

He put his arm around her shoulder and then, twisting on the seat, he pulled the blanket tight around her body and kept pulling it tighter, up under her chin. He sniffed. "This thing smells like mildew."

Her eyes smiled. "Yes. It stinks—but I'll take it."

He sat back again and looked off across the water, smiling faintly. "It's gotta mean something," he said.

"What does?"

"I chased you all the way down the Choptank River and then jumped overboard to pull you out. That's gotta mean *something.*"

He put his arm around her shoulder again, still holding the blanket tight under her chin. She let her head rest against his chest and they sat that way for a while, saying nothing.

Presently Harry reached out with his foot and kicked the boat into gear. He took the end of the tiller in his fingertips and *Sundance* moved on down the river on a slant that would carry it between the gas bell and the tilted silhouette of Sharps Island Light, taking the race course in reverse, headed back to Annapolis.

Regatta

The breeze had died and twilight was falling. With the
departure of the sun, the shadows had disappeared from the
creeks and coves, to be replaced by reflections in smooth
dark pools of quiet water. A duck glided along, dragging a
straight silver line of wake behind it. A gull flew over and
in the water its grey and white reflection moved swiftly
through the reflection of a cloud, past a crescent of shore
where the mud was exposed, seamed and cracked and ooz-
ing. On a grassy bank stood a heron, a slim vertical line, a
bird with all the supple slimness of a snake standing motionless on its tail. Near the heron loomed half-dead trees
with huge limbs lost to lightning and blight, torn trees
casting reflections at their own gnarled feet, repeating
themselves in the dark water.

Out over the river the sky had turned purple and green.
Gulls were diving and wheeling, and lights were coming on
along the shore.

As far as the eye could see the river was empty. The regatta was over, a game played on a summer's day. The boats
had scattered and the people had gone back to the land.